# PENAL CODE
## Section 487(d)(1)
# GRAND THEFT AUTO

Billie Dureyea Shell

# ACKNOWLEDGEMENT

What's up y'all first and foremost I want to thank all my readers for buying the books that I've been putting out and supporting this journey that I'm going on writing. You guys have really made this writing shit something that I love to do the more you read it the more I write it without y'all putting these books out wouldn't even be worth it so I thank y'all and I love you all 2022 is here so let's get it......... To my Lord and Savior Jesus Christ thank you for blessing me with this talent and these skills I love you more than words could ever say you died on the cross for me and I know I wasn't worthy of it, so every day I'm going to try to prove to you that it wasn't in vain. To my mother, Mom I love you more than words could ever say we've been through the storm in the rain and we still here he was the first woman to ever have my back and I will always love you for that you know there's nothing that I won't do for you. And there's not enough money in the world to pay you back for all the shit I sent you through but I hope it was the things I am doing for you now I'm showing you how much you will appreciate it you always be my number one girl I love you Mama. To my little sister Glenda I miss you and I love you, you know I got your back no matter what and no matter what we go through I got to never change. To my beautiful wife and the love of my life Shatoya I never thought and I could find somebody that I would love just as much as I love myself yet a lot more everything that I have is yours and my heart belongs to you you always tell me that I'm the best part of you or little do you know you're the best part of me you get on my nerves and sometime I wonder is that your job. I love you for now forever and for always 1437. Call my kids and it's a lot of y'all so let's start in age order:

Jazmine, Ant'Juan, Devon, David, little Dureyea, Dillon, Alura, Avi, Cameron, Premiere, Shanice, and Anthony I love all of y'all you guys are the reason I smile. To my grandchildren Jordan, little Devon, and little Roman I love each one of y'all to Uncle Woody thank you for all you done in helping me to become a man you will always be my favorite uncle and a person I turned to for advice when this world get too hectic for me. To my cousin Zane R.I.P nigga I miss you more than words could ever express but just know that I'm down here holding it down and taking care of business and I promise you you'll never be forgotten. Call my nieces and nephews I love you all. To my big brother Lawrence thank you for all that you've done for me and showing me how to get it to my even older brother Fred you maybe you crazy but I still love you to my little cousin Cella you know I got you when you need me and I love you we are the fuck we got and we all fuck we need. To My uncle Woody only son R.I.P you messed and we love you and you won't be forgotten. To everybody else I didn't mention it ain't that I forgot you you just you just wasn't worth mentioning to all my dark side niggas you already know what it is keep doing what you're doing. Oh yeah a few shots cuz I don't want these people to think I'm saying fuck them Margo love you little sister Sade Love You Selena love you Shay Shay love you little Brandon and Lil Brian love y'all auntie Chris love you shit I think that's about it now enough of all this mushy stuff let's get to this book I hope you all enjoy reading as much as I enjoyed writing Happy New Year it's 2022 stay safe keep your mess on and let's get this money .....

**Author Billie Dureyea Shell**

*Chapter 1*

# THE SPOKESMAN

The Spokesman woke up on this beautiful morning not feeling any sympathy or the slightest regret for what he's about to handle. The work must be done. The only thing he had swimming in his mind. The work must be done. No matter the consequences. He got up from his king size bed and stretched. He walked over to the window and opened the curtains. What a wonderful day it is, he thought. Finally, I will get what's mine. He took a quick shower and sang love songs the entire time. He got out of the shower and continued to give himself the nicest shaven face you will ever see. Got to look good for the big day. He went into his closet and picked out his street gear. He put on a tee-shirt, jeans, Air Force 1's and an Atlanta fitted cap. He took one look in the mirror. Damn, I look good. He shut the closet door before going into the kitchen. He made himself a nice peanut butter and jelly sandwich. He sat at the dining room table and flipped through his contact list while he ate. "Here we go." He muttered with a mouth full. He removed a card and stared at it to make sure it was the correct one. Absolutely, it was the one. He read the words across the card to himself. "Private Investigator, Lenny Daverson." He hated Lenny with every ounce of blood he possessed in his body. But today, today he needed him. Today was the day he would love him. Today, if he paid close attention and did his job the way detectives are supposed to. Lenny would make him the happiest man in the entire world. He took the final bite of his sandwich and flipped the card into his pocket. No more delays, he must act now before he would miss this perfect opportunity. The work must be done. He grabbed his car keys and headed for the door. He locked up the house and got into his car. He sang along with Usher while he drove to the other side of town. Out of sight, out of mind. He thought about this situation numerous times before. This was definitely the best way to handle it. He found a busy gas station. Good mixed crowd. Nobody on this side of town would notice him. He parked his car at pump eight. He went inside and paid for some gas. He walked pass his vehicle without bothering to set the system up. He thought if someone was to notice him. They would approach him while he's standing at the car pumping gas or on the pay phone. His mind decided to handle that instantly. The pay phone was at the far end of the gas station. He walked over nonchalant, not wanting anybody to notice him. He retrieved the card from his pocket. He lifted the phone and dialed the private investigator's number. The phone rang three times and a woman answered. "Hold please." One minute later detective Lenny answered. "This is Inspector Daverson." The Spokesman smiled. "Let's get to the point. You're looking for Twenty, right?" Lenny felt his spine quiver. "Who is this?" "Does it matter? All you need to understand is that I know the time and place Twenty's next lift will be. Get your pen and pad."

*Chapter 2*

# BLIND MAN

Twenty stepped out onto his room balcony. "Damn it feels good outside." Today is payday for him. Later tonight, he is going to lift the last car on the list for a buyer name, Money. The car is a 1969 Boss 302. Money, a notorious drug dealer on the other side of town who loves old school cars. He created a list of his fifteen most wanted cars and hired the best car thief around to handle the job. Each car was valued over $100,000. The job is for one million dollars and the man who is known to be the best, is Twenty. He has been lifting vehicles for anybody who had money since he was seventeen. This is the way he survives. He even has his own crew called, The Lifters. Three years of lifting vehicles professionally and this one is going to be his biggest payout. He has already received half the money up front and the other half he would get when the job is completed. His team of lifters included his best friend,

10

Jeff. He has known Jeff since the first grade. The second member of his team is Paula. They met Paula when they were thirteen years old. They lifted their first car in a grocery store parking lot. They saw a 96' Chevy Impala on 26-inch rims left running. They thought the car was beautiful and Twenty wanted it. It's funny how your best friend gets dragged into tough situations. Although, Jeff wasn't about to let Twenty steal the car all by himself. The coast was clear. At least, they thought the coast was clear. Twenty rushed over to the vehicle with Jeff close behind. Twenty hopped in the driver seat and Jeff hopped in the passenger's. Twenty put the car in drive and floored the pedal burning out of the parking lot. They got halfway down the block before hearing a voice in the back seat. It was Paula waking up from her nap. "What are you doing in my dad's car?" She asked sheepishly. Twenty was super excited about lifting his first car that he didn't notice the girl in the back seat. "What the hell!" He swerved the car because he was a little nervous that there was someone in the car with them. "A girl is in the back seat!" Jeff yelled hysterically. "What's going on?" Paula climbed over the front seat. "What are you doing little girl?" Twenty asked. He swerved the car back on track. "I'm twelve going on thirteen. In one month I'll be a teenager for your information. I'm not little." Paula answered with attitude.

"Twenty!" Jeff yelled. "We got to get out of this car for the police come. I don't want to go to jail man. I'm only thirteen." "Shut up you big baby." Paula hissed without knowing what was going on. "Why would the police come?" Twenty turned to her attention. Suddenly, he was struck by her beauty. This was the prettiest girl he has ever seen in his life. She had caramel skin, brown hair, and hazel eyes. He was lost for words while staring at her. How was he to answer? "Twenty!" Jeff yelled hysterically. Twenty focused back on the road. He had swerved into oncoming traffic. "Shit!" A car was coming right at them. He maneuvered the Chevy back into the proper lane. The Impala kept swerving out of control and they hit a fire hydrant. The boys got out and ran for it. Jeff took off first and Twenty was right behind him, but he stopped. He ran back to the car. "Hey… hey! You ok!" Paula didn't move. He pulled her from the car. She hit her head pretty good on the dashboard. Too late to run. The police showed. They took Twenty away and he got put on probation until he was eighteen. Paula would never forget what he did by coming back for her. The next time they had met was their tenth-grade year. Ever since she turned bad girl, she's been a part of The Lifters. Twenty loved her bravery. The last member of the team was a computer geek named Tony, but Twenty called him Tech. They met in computer class. Twenty noticed how good he was with solving problems with engines. Twenty came to him one day and flat out asked him did he want to be a part of the team. Tech being the smartest guy in school without any friends, agreed. From zero friends too three friends is how he looked at it. There were people who cared about him, real friends not computer friends, but real friends at school. Twenty used Tech to fix all the cars they had lifted. If something happened to one of the vehicles while they were on the move. Tech would fix the problem at the garage before the vehicle was delivered to the buyer. Tech was the best and he had the best friends. Twenty went back into the bedroom. He picked his phone up from the nightstand and dialed his best friend's number. Jeff answered in two rings. "Twenty," "Jeff," Twenty took the sheets off a fine exotic redbone. Twenty was addicted to the fast life. Money, cars, clothes, drinking, and his biggest addiction were women. He loved being with a different woman. That's why Paula never hooked up with him except for two times, one being prom night. Paula had turned down every boy at school except for Twenty. He took her that night and they had the best time. Paula knew he was a player and she gave him some anyway. That was her first time. After prom, they decided to go back to their ways. Their friendship was more important. The other time happened two months ago when Paula had her twentieth birthday. They had got drunk and ended up in bed together. Another slip. It felt more like love to Paula, but decided against it. She knew better than that so she bottled it up and kept it to herself. "What's going on man? You ready to get this money?" "You know it," Jeff replied. "Are you?" The girl woke from the chill of not having any covers over her naked body. She looked at Twenty puzzled. Twenty tossed her clothes at her. "Time for you to leave." He pointed to the door coolly. She frantically grabbed her clothes cursing him out the entire time she put them on. She slammed the door with great force as she left that it shook every picture on the wall. "Whoa, crazy." He muttered. Jeff knew exactly what was taking place. He knew about Twenty being the player he was. He was doing the usual, putting another one out after a long night of hot sex. "Redbone from the club last night? "Yeah man, I didn't know she was going to be that damn emotional. I just met her and she knows she doesn't live here." Twenty joked while sitting on the edge of the bed and falling back. Jeff laughed through the phone. "Well, maybe she thought she did. You need to start being more careful." "Why is that?" "These women are crazy. Once they met the guy they really want to be with. He uses her and then she goes five years without dating. Finally, she meets a guy like you all tattooed up, nice teeth and muscles, 6'3, 220lbs, cornrows and great conversation. She figures in her mind, she's met the right guy. Soon as you dump her like trash the next night. All hell breaks loose. Now she's trying to kill you and every corner you turn man. She's there.""Damn," Twenty said. "You described me well. Have we dated?" He joked. Jeff laughed. "You think that shit is funny but I'm telling you man. Watch out. Females are emotional creatures, my man." "Thanks for being my counselor of love. I can handle myself, buddy. I've been doing it for twenty years now. I pretty much got a good grip. Anyway," he got up. He was pissed because he was comfortable. "You talk to Tech?" "He said he'll be at the garage waiting for us." "What about Paula?" Twenty asked. "With this being the last car. I didn't think you wanted me to tell her. The three of us don't need to lift one car, do we?" Twenty thought about that. Hell, he's right. The three of us don't need to lift one car. Really, it would only take the two of them to do it. Jeff would drop him off at the Antique Cars of Atlanta tonight. He would lift a 69' Boss 302 with no problem. The older cars were always the easiest cars to lift. He would race the car back to the garage. Tech would look it over. First thing in the morning Money would be there to pick up the fifteen cars Twenty had stored for him. Pay him the $500,000 owed and it would be simple as that. A piece of cake. Paula could pick her portion up tomorrow when the money arrives. Her job was finished until the next order. "You're right about that. Meet me at the garage so we can go over the final plan and inspect all of the cars again. Tomorrow's the day and we don't need any problems." "Cool, give me an hour and I'll be there." "See ya," Twenty hung up the phone. Out of this deal, he was making $400,000. Everyone else was making $200,000 for the job. That's good money with a team of four. Twenty entered the garage and greeted Tech. He was already inspecting the cars. Jeff came ten minutes later. They spent the rest of the afternoon going over the plan. It started to get late and Antique Cars of Atlanta closed two hours ago. Jeff drove Twenty to the dealer. Twenty saw the beautiful Boss 302 through the glass of the building. "Look at it. That's money right there." "Twenty, man I don't know." Jeff was hesitant. "I got a bad feeling about this one." "Jeff every car we lifted, you had a bad feeling." Twenty got out and shut the door. "Stop worrying. This is the last one and we get paid. We'll chill for a while after this, cool?" "Cool." He gave Twenty some dap. "Be safe, bruh." "No doubt," Twenty vanished into the night.

*Chapter 3*

# THE CHASE

Twenty crept along the building of Antique Cars of Atlanta. He surveyed his surroundings carefully. When he was certain no security was in proximity of him. He made his move further around the building while staying close to the wall. He came to the back door. He retrieved his lock pick tool from his pocket. "Piece of cake." He muttered to himself. The back door wouldn't be any challenge to him. He picked harder doors before. He stuck the lock picking tool in the keyhole and listened carefully as he turned to pick it. He listened for all the correct clicks. He mastered the lock and on the last turn the door popped like magic. "Yeah baby, that's it." He muttered. Before he walked in he did what he normally does before walking through a door without knowing who's on the other side. Maybe security, maybe not. He didn't think security would be lurking around inside of a dark building waiting for him to come but what the hell. Better safe than sorry. He knocked on the door three solid times and ducked off. He patiently waited. Nobody was home. After two minutes he crept back to the door and opened it quietly as possible. He peeked his head in. Look at all these sweet cars just waiting for me to pick one, he thought. He crept in. "Anybody home. I just wanna borrow some sugar or a 69' Boss 302." He joked to himself. He cautiously searched for the area that would have the alarm pad. Tech told him he would have two minutes to disarm it after stepping foot in the building. If he didn't want the police all over his ass, he better get to it. He kept a cool demeanor as he scanned the room. "There we go, baby." He found the alarm pad on the center wall under an oil painting of an old Ford GT500. One minute to go. He hurried over. He flipped the alarm case down, revealing the number pad. "Ok Tech, you fucking better be right or I'm fucked. What were the numbers, 3, 4, 0, 2?" He knew if he got the numbers wrong he would have one more chance. One more chance was something he wanted to avoid altogether. Tech told him if he got the code wrong the first time the pad would beep. Signaling to him he was wrong. The second time it would turn red and the police would be on him before he had the chance to whip his ass. What he needs is for the numbers to light up green, signaling that the alarm was disarmed.

Tech broke into the dealer's computer system and retrieved the code. That's how they were successful at entering dealerships that had cars on the list. Tech is a genius. Without him, it would be a brick through the window and a swift wiring of the vehicle then a fast getaway or prison. He was grateful to have Tech on the team. It gave him more leverage and with the extra needed time. There was no need to wire the vehicles anymore. He'll just find the keys instead. He punched the numbers on the pad. "3, 4, 0, 2." He mumbled pressing each button. The pad made a loud beep. "Fuck." He muttered. One more chance. Get it right or break for it, he thought. "Ok," he raised his hand, thinking about the code Tech told him over and over. "3, 4, 0, 3." He almost broke a sweat. Thinking he was going to have to break for it. The pad turned green after a long second. "Hell yeah." He found the key room without any problem. He found the mini safe with the key to the Boss. He began to pick it. The safe was already unlocked. "Dayum, somebody is going to get fired." He thought it was odd but brushed it off. Time is money. He hurried to the garage to lift it so he could drive the Boss out without any damages. Suddenly, the dealer's lights cut on. He heard freeze! "Fuck!" He rushed to the Boss and hopped in and fired up the engine. Police swarmed the car lot. "Get out of the car!" Daverson yelled. "Twenty!

It's over! Police are everywhere, you're cornered!" Twenty began to realize he was set up. They were waiting for him. What to do? He looked at the glass doors. "I can't go to prison." He floored the Boss and busted through the glass doors. The engine growling through the parking lot. He shifted the motor into high gear. "Fuck!" The police were at the front entrance. He shifted to reverse and burnt out backward, leaving a trail of smoke. He couldn't get far. A helicopter lowered close enough to the ground and blocked the car in. The police had weapons ready for business. He watched his young life go. No choice, he surrendered.

*Chapter 4*

# TRIAL

Twenty knew there was nowhere for him to go. They had finally caught up to him. He rested his head on the headrest in the Boss 302. He exhaled deeply waiting for them to apprehend him. Police cars were everywhere. Two helicopters hovered over the car with their lights directed at the vehicle. He thought about what his best friend Jeff said before he left. He didn't feel right. Out of all of the times he has said that, he was right about this one. The last one for a while, Jeff. Then we can chill, he thought. He smirked to himself thinking about the consequences. He knew exactly who voice it was in the building that told him to freeze. It was detective Daverson. Daverson has been after Twenty for the past three years. Ever since Twenty became a professional car thief. The GTA number went up three hundred just in the area. One hundred and seventy-five of those he believes belonged to Twenty. His signature twenty dollar bill was left on the scene. Pay for what you steal is how Twenty looked at it. He could never catch up to Twenty until now. The tip from the Spokesman put him one step ahead. "Twenty, it's over son." Daverson said. "Hold your hands out of the vehicle and come on with me." He had his Glock aimed at Twenty through the driver side window. Emotions ran through his mind as he still couldn't believe he had been caught. He thought about his best friend Jeff. It was now that he realized he actually loved Paula and wanted to spend the rest of his life with her. He wanted to tell her he's sorry for being a no good dog and for how he treated her. Now, that will never happen. Tech, he wanted to tell him that he really was his friend before he asked him to join the team. He thought he was kind of weird, but cool for a computer geek. The Lifters, his family. "Daverson," Twenty answered casually. "You finally got me, huh? Doesn't it feel good?" "Twenty," Daverson spoke over the commotion. His clothes were blowing from the helicopter wind. "You couldn't run from me forever son. I told you I'll catch you. Now come on and step out of the vehicle quietly and come with me. I got a party to go to." Twenty smirked. "What kind of party is that? Am I invited? I promise I won't steal a car." He joked. "A party for busting the best car thief around. Now, bring your funny ass with me son." Twenty smiled and stuck his hands out of the window slowly. The police moved in on him and removed him from the car cautiously. He saw Channel 2, 5, and 11 news vans out. Reporters were swarming the scene for information on Twenty. They cuffed him on the hood of the Boss 302. Daverson lifted him from the hood. He noticed that all of the police officers were smiling and giving each other high fives. They were excited to bring down the greatest car thief in Atlanta's history. Promotions for everyone. Twenty nonchalantly kept a cool smile watching the SWAT team and the FBI party for his arrest. Daverson shoved him forward. "Chill playa, this shirt is worth more than that promotion you're about to get." Daverson shoved him again. "Told you it was going to be a party. After this, I'm going to bust the rest of your friends. Move your ass son." A reporter approached Twenty with a cameraman. "Is there anything you would like to say to the people?" She held her microphone out for him. Daverson spoke arrogantly. "Yeah, he wants to say he's retired." "We want to know if the man they call Twenty have any comments?" The reporter was struggling with her hair blowing from the helicopter wind. She held the microphone up to Twenty. "Is that any way to speak for a famous person Lenny?" Twenty taunted Daverson. "Yes, there is something I would like to say." He knew by now that everybody in Georgia was watching this or soon will be. There was only one person he wanted to talk to. "I frequently don't do this, but I want to tell Paula I'm sorry. Sorry for everything I ever did. I want to tell you that I love you, Paula. Jeff, you will always be my best friend. Take care of her for me. She deserves a guy like you. Both of you would make a great couple. Tech, you always have been my friend since computer class and you always will, man. Take care, I'm fuckin' out. Holla." They got him booked in and later he made his one phone call to Jeff. He told him the court date. A week later, every one of the Lifters showed up to support Twenty. He faced the judge for the final decision.

# Chapter 5

# PRISON

Life without the chance of parole. Twenty knew it was coming. He sacrificed his own life to save his friends. They threaten to put every one of them behind bars for fifty years. No one would have a life to live. He cared too much about Paula and the rest of the Lifters. He wouldn't let something evil as that, happen. He manned up and took the one hundred and seven six felonies. One for each vehicle he lifted. He held his head high and sucked his teeth at the judge before turning to his team. They had no idea he just saved them from fifty or more years in prison. He already told Jeff where his savings were hidden. He had a little over 1.2 million from all of the past lifts. Take the money and get out of the game with Paula. That's what he told him. That was his new plan. For Twenty, it was officially over. The rest of his young life would be life behind bars. He noticed Jeff had his arm around Paula soothing her as she grieved on his shoulder. Jeff looked extremely sad while Tech had his head down in his hands. The scene was emotional as he watched the pain over their heads. Jeff turned his attention to him. He smiled at his best friend and nodded. He knew Twenty wanted him to be strong for the team. They would need his care more than ever now that he was gone. The courtroom police escorted Twenty out to the hall. That's where the other inmates waited chained together. Three officers chained Twenty back up and went back into the courtroom. Twenty put his head against the back wall. He heard chatter all around him from the other inmates, but he blanked them out from his mind. All he could think about was his friends and life in prison. "Life." He muttered to himself. The guards came after all the inmates were finished and took them back to the bus. The longest bus ride of his life and it was back to confinement. What a waste of twenty years of living. The sad part was his twenty-first birthday is in two days. His cracked out mom told him he wouldn't make it to twenty-one. Guess the pipe head was right, he thought. She was hooked so bad it was amazing how she is still alive at 46 years old. She kicked him out when he turned 14 years old and haven't seen him since. He knew she was alive for sure. Paula visited her a time or two. He arrived back at the jail. They informed him he was scheduled to leave with the next prison shipment. The judge wanted him shipped immediately. A menace to society is how the judge and the DA label him. Twenty's bus ride to prison arrived one week later. The deputy chained him to a white guy, huge and heavily tattooed. He resembled a biker. Twenty guessed right. The guy he is chained to is a part of a biker gang called, White Shield. They are known for moving ice and prostituting women and young girls. They respected nothing but their kind. The whites. Twenty settled in his seat. He was chained inside, so he took the window seat. He heard the biker snorting. Obviously, he could sense the biker didn't like him. He could care less. He wasn't afraid to hook with nobody. If it came to that, he already had planned out in his mind how he would take the guy. He had a plan for every occasion and every situation. He always did. He sucked his teeth and faced out the window. All he wanted to do was ride in peace to his next destination. He didn't want any problems with nobody. Not even the bus driver. The biker snorted again. He was breathing over Twenty. "You suckin' your teeth at me, nigger?" He was sounding real tough. "I said you suckin' your-" That's as far as he got before Twenty elbowed him without looking. He caught the biker off guard. Blood shot from the biker's mouth all over him. He shattered his front teeth. Pandemonium broke out on the bus as the guards tried to rush to the back. The prisoners were standing in the aisle, making it difficult. The biker groaned. He was feeling light headed. "Ah!" He tried to reach for Twenty. Twenty had immediately followed with another elbow and the biker blacked out. Two swift shots to the face violently. The biker fell forward and his head rested on the front seat. Twenty nonchalantly faced the window until the guards arrived. They were shocked. "What's going on here," One of the guards roared. "He's thinking about prison." Twenty answered the guard coolly while still looking out of the window. The guard looked at Twenty. Twenty stayed facing the window while ignoring him. Minding his own damn business, he thought. The biker was sleep and heavily snoring with his body leaned forward and his head resting on the front seat. Blood was pouring from his nose like a water fountain. The guard hadn't noticed it until a large puddle of blood formed around his feet. Only five minutes into their long trip to Jackson County Prison and the bus had to stop. The guards finally got all of the prisoners to settle back down. Their guns and Tasers came in handy with cruel threats. "Wake him up." One of the guards told another. The guard that was standing in the puddle of blood tried to wake him. He was trying his best, but the huge biker remained asleep, out cold. "Sir," he cried. "He's not waking up."

"Unchain him and move him to the front of the bus. We need to stop the bleeding." He ordered another guard to help him move the biker to the front of the bus. The two guards took ten minutes to move the guy. Dripping much-needed blood from the biker's nose and mouth the entire way. They propped the biker up in the front seat and begun to operate on his wounds while he was still asleep. The bus got back on its course headed to the prison. The head officer spoke to Twenty arrogantly. "If I have any more problems out of you." He was close enough to kiss Twenty on the cheek while he had his index finger pressed against the temple of his head. "Your ass is going to the hole for one month immediately. You'll be pissing and shitting in a bucket and wiping your ass with your hand. I'll make sure of that, believe me." He was sweating ferociously over Twenty. Twenty didn't want to show any signs of weakness to these guards or anybody else at the prison. If he's going to be there for life, they were going to respect him no matter what he has to go through. He moved his head away from the guard's finger and mushed his head away as he spoke. "Man, back your sweaty ass off me. Your breath smells like shit." He said nonchalantly. Then he faced the window. The head officer was furious. He whipped out his Taser and zapped Twenty until he passed out. "Looks like we got ourselves a smart-ass, boys." He laughed and walked back to the front. Twenty stayed sleep the rest of the trip. It seemed like only five minutes. The bus came to a harsh stop waking him up. His vision came back into sight as he looked out of the window. He was looking at his new home. "Fuckin' bullshit." He muttered to himself. He still felt shocks from the Taser. The cage door up front opened and two guards hurried to the back. "You're coming with us." One officer lifted him from the seat. Both of the guards dragged him harshly off the bus. He was faced backward as they dragged him. When he got to where the biker was seated in the front. He violently kicked him in the face busting his nose and mouth back open. The biker was in too much pain to try an attack. He vowed to kill him on the prison yard. The guards threw Twenty off the bus cuffed. He hit the ground and dust covered his face. The guards came off and gave him a good whooping with their batons. Afterward, they immediately dragged him all the way to the hole. He heard one say. "Two months tough guy!" Then slammed the door. "Fuck you!" Twenty yelled. He picked himself up and brushed off. Prison was already hell. This is how he had to spend the rest of his life, in hell. He sat back against the wall and closed his eyes. He thought about what had gone wrong at the Antique Cars of Atlanta. The safe for the Boss 302 key was open. His instincts told him something was wrong then. They were waiting on him. Waiting for him to make a move to catch him red handed. What a setup. He smiled. Nothing to do about it now. Two months in the hole were hell. It was time for him to leave the shit and piss smelling room. The guards came to get him. The fresh air hit his nose and cleared up his breathing. They hauled him out of the hole and dropped him off at his cell after a shower and his medical shots. He entered his cell and the guards removed the cuffs. "Remember boy." One guard growled. "We run this prison." He slammed the door. Twenty sucked his teeth. "Please, we'll see." He muttered. He turned around and a Chinese man was doing pull ups. The Chinese man stopped and stared at him. "John Kim." He held his hand out. "Twenty." He shook his hand.

*Chapter 6*

# THE BIKERS CLUB

Twenty made his bed and then he laid down. Just lying on a bunk made him feel ten times better. The floor in the hole wasn't exactly the best place to sleep. John sat at the table in the room. "So what are you here for?" "Lifting." Twenty muttered. He put his head back and closed his eyes. "Lifting," John asked? "What kind of charge is that? Shoplifting?" "Exotic, antique, luxury," Twenty was exhausted. "Any kind of vehicle you want." He exhaled. He really wasn't in the mood to be getting to know his roommate. He was tired and happy he had a place to lay his head. "Oh, you steal vehicles for people." John leaned back in the seat. "Good money?" Twenty shrugged. "Make a decent living." "What they give you?" Couldn't be much, John thought. "Life without chance of parole." Twenty sat up in his bed. Since John wanted to know so damn much. He might as well find out about him. He's in the same room with the guy. Bastard could be insane. "Damn," John was shocked by that. "They gave you life for GTA?" "Yep, fucking life." "You must've been one bad motherfucker to get life." "One hundred and seventy-six felonies." Twenty assured him. "One for each vehicle." "Wow, how they know?" "They knew. The entire three years they knew. They just couldn't catch me. I actually lifted over 250 cars. I just started leaving my signature twenty dollar bill on the last one seventy-five. Too many people tried to take credit for my work so I began leaving a twenty at the scene of my lifts. Pay for what you steal." Twenty stood and walked over to the cell bars. John thought that he heard about a guy stealing cars and leaving behind a twenty dollar bill. They talked about him getting shipped to the prison two months ago. He never showed. "They caught you at the Antique Cars of Atlanta right, 69' Boss 302?" "That's me." He said looking out to the prison. "You must watch the news?" "Nah, I heard the guards talking. News gets around in no time here. You'll soon learn that. I thought you were supposed to arrive two months ago?" Twenty exhaled. "I did. I ran into some trouble with a biker and some bus guards. I spent the last two months in the hole." "You're the guy who whooped the biker and then mush the lieutenant in the face." John sounded excited. "News does fly around here." "The bikers have been talking about taking you out for two months," John assured him. "The guy who harmed one of their brothers. White Shield have good numbers here. They want your ass bad. You better be careful man." "Not worried about a bunch of bikers." Twenty spoke calm and casual. "I have life, nothing they can do better than that. Not even kill me." The guards did the prison count and release the prisoners for free time. Twenty stayed in his cell and slept except the last ten minutes. He needed to take a shower. He followed John. John joked with him telling him not to drop the soap. Twenty actually thought John was alright. He could tell he's a smart man. They got in the showers. Twenty and John washed side by side. "I've been waitin' on your nigger ass!" A harsh voice roared. Twenty turned around and saw four huge bikers standing in front of him. He quickly sized them up. The one with the busted nose and missing front teeth is the one he beat down on the bus. He had a handmade shank in his hand. The others were his biker brothers. White Shield presumably. There's no way he can take them all, but he'll die trying. His plan registered in his mind the moment he turned around. Only chance, take the shank and fight for your life. The biker swung the shank trying to cut Twenty in the face. He ducked and gave him a brutal jab to the lower gut. The biker bent from the blow and he followed up with a knee to the face. The biker slumped to the ground and dropped the shank. The other bikers roared and jumped on Twenty. He tried to defend himself. Taking multiple harsh blows were a toll on him. Suddenly, one biker went flying backward and then another. Twenty noticed John Kim karate the shit out of two bikers. Twenty handled the other biker with a fierce combination to the head and finished with a knockout blow. The first biker retrieved his shank and went at Twenty again. Twenty blocked it. The biker's force combined with the wet floor caused both of them to fall. The biker landed on top of him. Twenty back ached from the 300-pound man. His body seemed lifeless laying on him. The biker wasn't moving. Twenty muscled the biker off of him. The biker rolled off the top of him and slumped to the ground. He stood to his feet. John had the bikers at a standoff. They were too scared to pursue a battle with the Kung' Fu master. The third biker was out cold with the shower raining all over his body. Twenty looked down at the biker who attacked him. Blood running from the lifeless biker stomach turned the shower waters red like a plague. The shank had inserted into his stomach with a death blow from the fall killing him instantly. Both biker's eyes grew wide when they had noticed. They both grabbed their biker brother who was lifeless under the shower water and swiftly shouldered him away. That was the last time he ever had to deal with them. He caught his first body. The bikers didn't want any more of their brothers killed and they sure as hell feared John Kim and his skilled fighting. They were no match. They retreated for good. Twenty and John Kim made it back to their cell in a hurry without any problems. They heard the prison alarm sound and the voice over the intercom telling all of the prisoners to get in their cells immediately. Twenty closed the cell bars before he turned to John. "I think it's about time to tell me why you're here?" "Murder," John muttered. He looked at Twenty. He remained silent. John continued. "Five guys broke into my house one day when I wasn't home. I came home and noticed the door had been kicked in. I heard my wife screaming from the bedroom. I hurried up the steps to the room where I found my wife being raped while the other men held her down. She was beautiful and innocent. She never did any wrong to anybody. I attacked them all. I blacked out and when I could finally think straight. I was in handcuffs. Five murders, all from broken necks. I didn't find that out until a week later. The Judge gave me some sympathy and sentenced me to 25 years. I have ten more to go. Then my wife and I can be together again." "Touching story." Twenty sat on his bed. "All broken necks huh. I don't have any problem with being in the same cell with you. You handled your business back there with the bikers. You didn't have to help me out, but you did. I don't appreciate that." John looked at him confused. "You not telling me you knew karate. You deadly muthafucka." Twenty smiled. "You could've torn off in my ass up in here. You know how long I've wanted to learn that shit." John stood up and smiled back at him. "That means I have ten years to teach you." John held his hand out. "Long as I know how to break five necks in one room. I won't waste your time." Twenty smiled and shook hands with John. His new friend. The next morning guards came to the cell. They grabbed John and hauled him out of the room cuffed and then gave Twenty the exact treatment. The guards dropped him off in a room by himself. Ten minutes later a man in a suit came into the room and sat across from Twenty. He had a file in his hand and a cup of hot coffee. He crossed his legs and stared him down for five minutes without speaking. Then he fired up a cigarette. "Smoke?" He offered Twenty. Twenty had met his stare the entire time not breaking one drop of sweat. "Never have. It'll kill you." He smirked arrogantly. "That's exactly what I'm here to talk about." He blew smoke in his face nonchalantly trying to piss him off. "What happened in the shower?" The smoke didn't bother him. "Don't know what you're talking about." "Don't fuck around with me. The biker who was killed in the showers?" "Oh yeah, him. Somebody told me he dropped the soap. When he bent over somebody stuck a dick in him. It killed him. A guy ran out of the shower passed me. If I was a good guesser. I would say that guy physically resembled you in the face." The officer immediately punched Twenty in the mouth. Twenty ate the violent punch. "That would be for keeping me from telling on your punk ass, huh?" He spat blood in his face. The officer rushed him again and Twenty caught him with a headbutt. The other guards rushed in and they punished him while he was still chained to the table. Another two months in the hole. He found out John caught two months for not snitching. They returned to their cell two months later and began Twenty's training.

*Chapter 7*

# 10YRS. LATER EL' NINO

The limousine of the biggest cartel in Georgia pulled up to a Mexican restaurant on Jimmy Carter off highway 85. The driver got out of the limo and surveyed the scene. He then came around to open the door for the massive bodyguard named Nacho. Nacho is the hugest Mexican killing machine around. He won the job for guarding El' Nino with his life by killing an alligator with his bare hands in a pit fight. Nacho stepped out the limo and surveyed the area himself. He scanned every little detail around. Not even a fly was allowed to land on El' Nino without dying. Nacho adjusted his suit jacket where his 9mm was holstered. He waved the driver off. "It's clear boss." He stood next to the vehicle while El' Nino emerged from the limo. El' Nino stepped from his limo. His $5,000 tailored suit made him look like a celebrity. He flipped his suit jacket closed before fastening the middle button.

"Good job Nacho." He led the way in his restaurant. They entered the restaurant and the host immediately recognized El' Nino and greeted him. Completely stopping whatever he was doing to respect his presence. Nacho knew everyone in the restaurant recognized El' Nino. Everyone wanted to speak and greet him. There were too many faces for him. Nacho paved to way to the back office. El' Nino settled in his office. His private waitress brought him a Cuban cigar and a rare glass of Henri IV Dudognon Heritage Cognac. "Nacho, how are we looking with the list?"The waitress cut the end of the cigar for him and lit it. He blew out a puff of smoke. Nacho stood by the desk. "The list is complete. The buyers have picked the vehicles they desired and are ready for delivery."The waitress offered him a drink and he waved her off. Drinking on the job was not an option. He had to be ready at all times. El' Nino took a sip of cognac. "We have somebody to handle the job for us?" "Nobody yet," Nacho closed his suit jacket. "Nobody we've interviewed has been qualified." El' Nino blew out smoke thinking about the job he had to get completed. He had less than three weeks to get the job done. He needed to dig deep into his resources. He needed the best. The best person money could buy. The best car thief known to man. That's how El' Nino rolled. Always desiring the best at whatever needed to be done. "What about this guy I heard about, Twenty. Why isn't he available for my services?" he blew smoke from the very tasteful Cuban cigar. "No one has heard from that guy in ten years Boss." Nacho elaborated. "They say ten years ago, he was set up. He was the best around. They thought this guy Twenty couldn't be caught. The day the Feds brought him down. It was all over the news. They caught the guy at an antique dealership in Atlanta. Pure setup." "That's interesting." El' Nino took another sip. "Why would The Spokesman suggest his name? If the guy is in the system what good is he to me?" "Don't know Boss." Nacho replied." If The Spokesman suggested him, he must be the best. Maybe he is getting out soon? The Spokesman never lets us down when it comes to valuable information. Maybe this is the only guy suitable for the job?" "There must be someone else who is suitable?" Nacho took the cigar from his mouth. "I don't have any time to wait for anyone man in the system. My goal is to get these vehicles soon as possible for my buyers without any mistakes. There's too much money on the line here. We surely wasted too much time already. We must act now. Get me The Spokesman on the phone immediately." "Yes, Boss." Nacho began rolling through the contact list on the desk. El' Nino turned his office chair around to face out his large window. He pushed the button on his office remote control. Large curtains in the room separated slowly revealing the city. Every time something was on his mind. This was the best way for him to think. He blew smoke in ring puffs. Thinking about why would The Spokesman suggest a man for an exclusive job as this one? Who is no longer accessible? Who is in the system? El' Nino recalled the day the news broadcasted Twenty's arrest. That was the same day he killed his boss and took over. "Boss, he's on the line."

*Chapter 8*

# DEPARTED

Twenty and John Kim made their way through the prison lunch line. Real soon John would be leaving the prison. His 25-year sentence was up. John has been Twenty's inspiration and mentor for the past ten years. All of the looking out for each other and the training made them build a tight bond with each other. You would say it's a miracle how well John Kim trained Twenty in the art of Kung' Fu. Ten straight years of mastering the art made Twenty a skilled beast. His training has made him a more disciplined self-human being. They proceeded through the line and grabbed their usual seat together. The two were well known for their fighting skills because every chance they got they would train. Especially on the yard. Others would watch and gawk at their training sessions. Sometimes inmates would imitate their movements trying to teach themselves. Twenty swallowed a bite of chicken. He was thinking about John Kim leaving. He didn't want him to go but inside he knew it was right. John was his only true friend at the prison. Unfortunately, not one of the Lifters wrote, sent money or came to visit him in the prison. For the entire ten years, nothing. Just training with John was all he knew. Sometimes at night when he settled in for bed, he thought about what the Lifters were doing. If they were retired or still lifting without him. If they were carrying on with their lives together or separately. Whatever the case might be, no one contacted him. Not once reached out to inform him what was going on with what he thought was his only family. What was his best friend Jeff doing? Is he running the Lifters or not? Is Paula ok? Is she married with kids and living happily ever after? Maybe she was still lifting? Is Tech still the smartest guy around? Had he finally decided to go to college and get a master's degree? He was fragile about his friends. John Kim trained him well in mind, body and soul. One thing was for sure, he prayed they had changed their lives around for the better because he changed his life totally around. The prison wouldn't get the best of him. John Kim snapped his fingers. "Yo Twenty, what are you thinking about? You look spaced out." Twenty took another bite of his sweet chicken. He wanted to avoid mentioning he was going to be hurt because John was leaving. How selfish would he be? "You're going to be leaving any day now. Training by myself for the rest of my life is going to be hell. Then there's the problem with receiving a new roommate. How tough is that going to be? I don't want to get to know anybody else. I'm thirty years old now with no damn friends. That's a damn shame." John Kim sipped his water. He thought about where Twenty was coming from. Some time ago, he thought about this very conversation. As the years drew near he realized he would be leaving soon and Twenty had become his best friend. The only problem was, he is finally going to be free and going back to his lovely wife. Twenty was not, he was going to be here for the rest of his life and left without anyone. "Twenty," John spoke with seriousness in his voice. "I'm always going to be your friend no matter what. You changed my life around also. Whenever you need me, I'm just a phone call away. Always keep in contact with me. You're my best friend. We spent ten years in the same room together. I'll come visit you every chance I get. That you can count on." He held his fist out. Twenty smiled and dapped him up. "My brotha." Twenty felt that they were even closer to one another than he was with Jeff. Ten years straight, reading the bible, working out and training. He became one with one's self and for that, he loved John Kim as a brother for teaching him willingly. Later that night, they said their goodbyes. Twenty was emotional as John. They released John that morning. Eleven hours later, he got a new roommate. Younger dude, white, blonde hair and looked around twenty-one years old. Twenty stopped doing his pull-ups and turned around. "Twenty." "David, bro." They shook hands.

# Chapter 9

# THE TOUGH GUYS

El' Nino took the phone from Nacho. "Thanks, Nacho." El' Nino put the phone to his ear. Nacho nodded and stood next to the desk. "My favorite guy to speak with. How are you doing today my friend?" El' Nino puffed on his Cuban cigar. The Spokesman seated himself at his home office chair, not before he shut the door for privacy. "My friend, what service can I provide for you today?" The Spokesman was the info guy around Atlanta. If there was anything anyone needed to know. The Spokesman would charge them a small fee for his knowledge. He is like the underworld government of information. El' Nino is his top customer. "My good friend," Nino spoke looking out to the city. "I pay you well for your services. Is that correct?" The Spokesman already knew where the conversation was headed. He prepared himself wisely for this very moment. Of course, this was also a part of his own plan.

"Yes, you do. You pay me very well. You are my best customer. Top dollar for all the information I've ever provided you with. My family is well taken care of. We have no worries." He wanted to make El' Nino feel like a king. That's the way he expects to be treated at all times. In El' Nino eyes, he is a king. Anybody treated him differently. Nacho would surely pay them a home visit. "If this is so." El' Nino puffed out a ring of smoke. "Why did you provide me with information that is not valuable to me in the slightest form?" "Please forgive me El' Nino." The Spokesman knew the best way to defuse the situation, ask for forgiveness. "But what piece of information have I provided for you that isn't any us to you in the slightest? Please tell me and I will seek the answer that you're looking for." The Spokesman kicked his feet up on the desk. He loved being in control. Knowing what people wanted before they asked for it. This is his territory, his way of perceiving their mind. He was a vicious player at this game and he dared himself to venture with El' Nino. "The one they call Twenty." El' Nino took a long sip of his 2 million dollar cognac. "You recommended him for the job that I'm in immediate need for. Why is this? A man who is in prison? Why do I feel like you test my patients? Are you trying to test my patience, my friend? Is this a way of saying fuck that Mexican El' Nino? The money I gave you for the information about a man who is in prison. I want to know the best man for the job my friend. Not the best prisoner for the job. Must I remind you," He spoke sternly. He wanted his point across without losing his demeanor. If that was to happen and he totally lost it, he would go out to the restaurant and openly free pick a person to murder. Murder is how El' Nino calmed his nerves by periodically killing someone at least two times a month at random. "I see where you are coming from my friend. Please let me elaborate the situation." The Spokesman smiled. This is what he gets paid to do. Give information and get paid more money to solve the problem. If there is one to ever occur. "Sorry for the misinterpreting the first time. With the business conditions we have here. The man they call Twenty is the best person for the job. This is true, he is serving a life sentence behind bars. It's awkward enough because I put him there behind my own concerns. Do not underestimate the power of your own hand. What I tell you, will put you in a position to win. Your hand is strong enough to reach the Mayor. The Mayor's hand is strong enough to reach the Warden. The Warden can have the judge give him a retrial. Let the study show that the evidence against Twenty wasn't enough to somehow imprison him for life. I'm sure they can think of something. Within a week, your guy will be released.

For the favor, he will be in your debt. Twenty is the man you seek." El' Nino puffed on his cigar. He did have the power to reach out to the Mayor by force. He strong armed plenty prominent figures before. "This I agree. You will receive your money once Twenty is free." They hung up. "Nacho, get the soldiers ready. We have to visit the Mayor."

*Chapter 10*

# MY BRO'S

Twenty went back to doing his pull-ups while David settled into his new home. Twenty thought while he worked out about his new roommate David being so young and in prison. His life was wasted just like his. He thought it was crazy how they come in so young. He would've never known himself if he wasn't arrested. He prayed every day for a second chance. He understands why people say that now. If I had a chance to do it all over again, I'll do it better the next time around. A second chance. If I had a second chance I'll cherish the hell out of my life, he thought. David interrupted him from his thinking about the outside world and his fierce workout. "Twenty right?" He asked while unpacking. He heard the name Twenty before. He just couldn't place it. He didn't want to come at Twenty wrong on his first day. The name was intoxicating his mind and he wanted to ask what he was

51

in here for? Twenty stopped his intense workout. His shirt was off, showing all his bulging muscles. Every single cut in his muscle line was intimidating to David. His tattoos made it worse because he looked like a gang member. Twenty exhaled deeply through his nose. "That's right." He continued to inhale and exhale trying to catch his heart rate. He went over to the sink and splashed water on his face. David finished unpacking and seated himself on his new unwanted bed. He wished he could be back at the house on his queen size. Twenty, he thought. Where in the hell do I know that name from? I know that name from somewhere. He watched Twenty splash water on his face. He read the word tattooed shoulder to shoulder on his heavily inked back. "Lifters." He muttered to himself reading the words. That's where he remembers the name Twenty. My boy Bobby. "Lifters, that's like a gang of car thieves' right?" David didn't want to come at Twenty like that and he hoped he didn't decide to come over and pummel his face. He heard stories about crazy men in prisons. They react to any and everything. The prison fights, the rapes, oh the rapes. He prayed a million and one times before he entered the prison that no one would take his booty. He would probably commit suicide. Being taken from behind reluctantly was something he wouldn't be able to live with. He hopes Twenty not a butt chaser. Twenty turned the water off. He looked in the mirror at his freshly shaven face. He heard David mention car thieves and it brought an extraordinary amount of memories and emotions. Now he was staring the demon in the eyes again. He turned around. David looked like he was about to run for his life. His eyes said he just took a shit on himself. Twenty understands that David is scared of him. He probably fears being in prison with a man all by himself at night. Not knowing what would happen to him. He's good at reading people. John Kim trained him well in that art. "Not a gang, was a family. We didn't steal cars. That sounds petty. But yes, we lifted vehicles. You must've watched the news?" "My friend Bobby told me about you guys." "Bobby?" Twenty thought about the name. "Don't know any Bobby." "Oh, I know you don't know him. He's a… I guess a lifter too. Well, he steals vehicles. He always talks about being the best. Better than Twenty he would say. He knows all about you. He said he wished he and his brother Jimmy Neutron could join your Lifters crew. He was motivated to get into it from you. He's the best in the area. If you ever get out, he hangs at the Scores Bar and Grill. Look him up. He'll be good for your team." Twenty smiled. "Listen, I'm done with lifting. I'm sure your friend Bobby and his brother um… Jimmy Neutron are great guys. That's life, I'm done with. I'm here for life." David looked to the floor concerned and worried to death. He thought he had offended Twenty. "Sorry." Twenty smirked. "I don't like boys."

*Chapter 11*

# STRONG ARM

A blacked out limo pulled up to one of the most marvelous house in Atlanta. A black Mercedes Benz SLS AMG with two Mexican soldiers pulled up behind it. They were waiting for orders from the limo to go handle the type of business they both loved to do. It was 2:30 in the morning. Nobody was awake in the nice size brick house. All of the lights were off in the house. El' Nino cracked the window for some fresh air. His personal bodyguard Nacho and The Spokesman were seated with him. The Spokesman came just for the thrill of it all. He was with El' Nino two other times they strong armed prominent men in the city. While they were doing their thing. He would secretly roam around for qualified information. It was convenient since El' Nino basically did the hard part. There was no better way to get information on somebody than at their home. He loved it. El' Nino grabbed a plate off the table in the center of the limo. He picked up a nicely rolled one hundred dollar bill. He lowered his head down to the plate. He put the rolled bill in his nose and snorted from his mountain of cocaine. The coke rushed through the bill into his nostril entering his system. He sat the bill back on the plate and passed it to The Spokesman. He was feeling much better and he took a sip of the cognac to add to the rush. The Spokesman took an even longer drag of the cocaine. He tried to pass the plate to Nacho. Nacho turned him away and The Spokesman took another long drag. He felt like the coke was clearing his mind for what he was about to witness. He was feeling like he could fly right through the limousine's sunroof. He started giggling to himself. The cocaine had him geeked out of his mind. "Nacho." El' Nino turned his attention to the powerful man. "Send the call to the soldiers." He was ready for action after the bump of coke and cognac. Nacho nodded. He emerged from the limo and signaled to the men in the Benz that the time was now. They exited the vehicle and followed Nacho to the front door with their pistols in hand. Nacho approached the door and without thinking about it. His massive foot successfully went through it. He stepped in and stood by the door. The two soldiers rushed upstairs to the bedroom. One opened the door to the master bedroom letting his weapon lead the way. The Mayor had woken up and was one number away from calling the police. The soldier had made it just in time. He stuck his pistol to the Mayor's head and the other soldier grabbed his screaming wife. He backhanded her across the face, silencing her completely. The soldier made the Mayor hang up the phone. They brought him and his wife downstairs to Nacho. Nacho appearance horrified them to death. He made them have a seat on the couch. They both held each other trembling with fear. Nacho walked back to the limo and informed El' Nino the job was complete. El' Nino emerged from the limo followed by The Spokesman who was high out of his mind. They followed Nacho back into the beautiful home. When El' Nino entered the house he immediately noticed the Mayor and his wife in fear for their lives. He waved the gunmen off. "Put the guns away." He ordered them. "You're scaring our Mayor and his wife to death." The soldiers put their guns away. He saw The Spokesman giggling to himself. He was already searching the house in his own world for valuable information. He turned his attention to Nacho. "Nacho, show the Mayor's wife how much I care about them." Nacho nodded and approached the Mayor's wife. The massive man stood over them. They held each other tight. Nacho pulled them apart and grabbed the Mayor's wife by the throat and lifted her from the couch. The Mayor jumped and Nacho kicked him in the stomach. He held his chest while his wife's feet dangled in the air. Nacho tightened his grip. She was losing air. Nacho punched her in the stomach and blood instantly shot from her mouth. The Mayor cried for his wife. He laid on the floor in a fetal position. She passed out in Nacho's massive bear grip. El' Nino smiled. "Mayor, your wife doesn't have much time. If you cooperate, she'll live. If not, you'll be planning a close casket funeral for her tomorrow. Now, I need a man released from prison. They call him Twenty."

*Chapter 12*

# WHAT I PRAYED FOR

Twenty came back from the showers and laid out on his bed. He worked out long and hard. It's been a week since his friend John Kim left the prison. David was cool in his own way. He had good conversation. Especially, being young as he was. He talked mainly about females and the nightlife. Things that were really no concern to him anymore, but David was funny. And hearing about all the things he used to do. David loved females just like he once had. He had a different girl for every day of the week. They traded stories about their different women. Twenty had a lot more than David ever dreamed of. Twenty dated so many different women it was hard for him to remember them all. It didn't matter, though. He no longer saw himself has a player. He realized over the years that he only needed one woman. That woman was Paula. When he talked about Paula, David could tell that he was more than in love with the woman. The only thing Twenty didn't bother to talk about were the times he lifted vehicles. Under the circumstances, he did tell him about the first one he ever lifted. Only because that's how he met Paula. David never bothered to ask him about any of the lifts. He understood that Twenty changed his life around. If he wanted to share them, he'll do it willingly. Twenty closed his eyes and began dreaming about the second time he ever met Paula their tenth grade year.

***

Twenty was walking down the school hall not paying any attention to what was in front of him. He was chatting away with Jeff while they were about to be late to class as usual. Hell, they had skipping next period on their mind any way to go lift the Principal's new Jaguar. Twenty stole the key right under her nose when he had a discipline visit. They strutted down the hallway like tough guys. Suddenly, Twenty bumped into a girl who was rushing to class and all of her books fell from her hands. "Damn, I'm sorry." He apologized without looking at her. He bent down to pick up the books just when the tardy bell rang. He gathered the books. "It's ok, I've been late to all of my classes. I'm kind of new here." She said warmly. Twenty handed her the books and when his eyes met hers, he was shocked. Jeff watched both of them confused. Twenty's mouth dropped to the ground. He noticed her long hair, beautiful skin tone, them hazel eyes that screamed out at him. He knew exactly who he was staring at and being stared by. It was the girl that was sleeping in the back seat of the first car he ever lifted. The only difference was, she's older now and has a bangin' body. "Do I know you from somewhere?" She asked. "I don't think you do." Twenty wanted to get away before she found out he was the one who lifted her dad's car. "Come on Jeff, we got something to do, remember?" He pulled Jeff by the arm and tried to get away. She stepped in front of him to prevent him from passing by. "You're in a rush to steal another car?" Twenty eyes got wide. "I know who you are. How could I ever forget? You and this crybaby tried to steal my father's car when I was sleeping in the back and you wrecked it like idiots." She reminded them. "I'm not a crybaby." Jeff insisted. They both ignored him staring each other down. Twenty was hot that this girl called him an idiot. He hated to be called names. He thanked his cracked out mother for that. Where ever she was. "That's right and don't forget I would've got away if you hadn't been there. If you had never distracted me. I would not have wrecked the car. Not to mention, I came back to make sure you were ok and if you want to know goody two shoes. We are about to steal another car, the Principals.

Now run along to class. You're already late." "Oh shit," Jeff muttered to himself. He noticed the two were at a standoff. Paula has never been talked to that way in her life. For some reason, she liked Twenty and wanted to show him she wasn't a goody two shoes. "I'm coming with you or… I'll tell." Jeff was lightly shaking his head no. Twenty smirked. "Damn right you are." That was why he told her in the first place.

***

Twenty, Twenty. Hey bro, wake up. You got some mail. Twenty heard David calling him in his sleep. He slowly sat up in the bed. He wished he could've slept a second longer. When he saw his friends in his dreams that was the only contact he had with them. Dreaming kept him from being in the prison. "Mail?" He asked curiously. Damn, I got some mail, he thought. It's been ten years since I got some mail. "Yeah bro," David assured him. "You got some mail, two letters." David handed him the mail. "Who did I get some mail from?" He muttered to himself and taking the two envelopes. "I didn't read anything but your name on the front bro. I didn't want to get all up in your business." David took a seat on the table and watched him. He thought to himself, he must never get mail. Twenty tore into the first envelope without bothering to read who the second one was from. He was excited that his friend John Kim had written him. "It's my boy John." He began to read the letter. Twenty, What's going on man? How have you been? Hopefully good. My wife and I are picking up where we left off. I told her about you and how we trained every day. We plan on renewing our wedding vows. We're taking a trip to China. When I get back, I'm going to come pay you a visit. Twenty continued reading the rest of the letter. David noticed that the other envelope had fallen from his lap. Twenty was far into the letter to pay any mind. David thought it would be a nice thing to do if he picked it up for him. David retrieved the envelope from the ground. He couldn't help but notice the gold letters across the front. It was from the Supreme Court of Atlanta. He already knew Twenty was serving a life sentence. Why would the Supreme Court send him a letter after ten years? He held the envelope up. "Twenty, bro." He said efficiently. "I think you want to crack this one open. It's from the Supreme Court of Atlanta." David handed him the envelope. Twenty sat the letter from John Kim to the side. He was already reading it a second time while thinking about what he would write back to his buddy. He was too caught up in the letter that he completely forgot about the second envelope. "The Supreme Court of Atlanta." He read the gold words across the top. He began to open the letter. Why would they send me a letter after ten years? Maybe they decided to give me the death penalty or something? These crackers won't leave me alone. Don't they know I got life? Isn't that good enough? He began to read the letter. As he read the letter his heart began to race. Blood drained from his head. He couldn't believe what he was reading. The situation was hard for him to comprehend. His eyes became three sizes bigger. He felt like yelling at the top of his lungs. Life rushed back into his mind full speed. This new excitement was taking over his body. A second chance. David noticed the expression on Twenty's face. He looked extremely excited about something. He couldn't wait to hear. He couldn't hold back any longer. The big smile across Twenty's face made it impossible for him to resist asking. "Twenty, what is it bro? I'm dying over here to know." Twenty held the letter down. He brought his attention to David still smiling. "They're giving me an immediate retrial." "A retrial!" David said excitedly. "Man, that's fuckin' awesome bro!" "I can't believe it myself. They said the evidence against me wasn't clear. There wasn't enough to convict me of one hundred and seventy-six crimes. They're giving me a retrial in a week. I'm free! Yeah!" He couldn't hold it any longer. He was too damn excited. There was a chance he could be free. A second chance. Every night he prayed for a second chance and now he was about to get one. "Man, you're going home bro." David gave Twenty some dap. "This is the chance I've been waiting for. Ten years in here and now I might get the chance to go home. How about that." "God works in mysterious ways bro." "Yes, he does." They talked for the rest of the night and drank coffee like crazy. Thinking of freedom made it hard to sleep.

*Chapter 13*

# RETRIAL

The guards came to pick Twenty up from his cell two days later. He was headed back to Gwinnett County Jail. Back to where it all begun. They shoved him onto the bus. He took a seat in the very front. There were no other prisoners on the bus, just him, two guards and the bus driver. He settled down in his seat thinking to himself in two more days he'll be free. There was no other way in his mind this trial would go. He thought about his friends and if they knew he was given a retrial. If they were happy about him having a chance to come home after all these years. Would they be there watching or not? There were questions that couldn't be answered. There were no hard feelings about them not contacting him. Although, there was some in the beginning. After he got into the Bible with John Kim. He knew that God forgives and he wanted to forgive them. He would question them about it. There has to be a reason behind not contacting me. He vowed if they released him. This would be his last prison experience. The bus pulled up to the jail. The guards lifted him from his seat. Twenty swung his arm away. "I got it, you don't have to put your hands on me." He said sternly. The word had got around that Twenty had been training with John Kim for the past ten years. The guards knew too and they wouldn't dare try him. Not even in handcuffs. John Kim hands were registered as deadly weapons and his were just as deadly. John taught him all his secrets. Twenty got himself off the bus. Smelling the country air was refreshing to him. He inhaled and exhaled deeply. "Ah." He knew he was home and soon he felt that he would be free. They led him into the building. They searched him again and placed him inside a holding cell by himself. After he was in, they took off his handcuffs. One guard stopped at the door. He turned around. "Hope it goes well." He smirked. "And not for you, asshole." He shut the cell door and locked it. Twenty sucked his teeth and leaned his head against the wall. "Cracker." He muttered. One hour later a guard unlocked the door. A unit worker entered and handed him a peanut butter sandwich and an orange juice. "Here you go my guy." The unit worker handed him an extra sandwich secretly. "Twenty, right?" "Yeah, that's me." Twenty slipped the sandwich inside his jumpsuit without the guard noticing. "Beat them crackers at trial for us." He whispered. "No doubt." Twenty pounded him up. "C'mon." The guard ordered. "Don't fucking talk to the inmate. You want me to fucking lock your ass down with him?" "Fuckin' cracker." The inmate worker muttered to Twenty. "Stay up, dawg." The unit worker vanished with the guard. Twenty sat down and worked on his first sandwich. He demolished it and then killed the orange juice. He figured he would save the other sandwich for later. He tossed the trash by the door. He stretched out on the bench. It was colder than a bitch in the cell. He put his arms inside his jumpsuit and closed his eyes. He thought about what the unit worker said. The word must've got around that he was getting a retrial. He was considered the greatest car thief in Atlanta's history. The guards came to get him from the cold holding cell and the bus ride over was just as cold. He entered the courtroom. Something he thought was impossible to see again. He met his lawyer there. Twenty scanned the courtroom when it was his turn. Every news channel were once again on hand to see the verdict. Not one of his friends showed. After an hour of trial that magically favored his side. The Judge ordered that 175 of his previous charges had a twenty dollar bill left behind and the one they caught him in did not. There wasn't any evidence to link him to the others. The Judge ordered time served for one GTA. Twenty broke down and began to cry for joy. He was a free man. Twenty stood up in the courtroom. His lawyer hugged him and shook his hand. He couldn't believe he was a free man. He finally got a second chance. He would use the opportunity to change his life around for the better. He went from having a life sentence, to going home as a free man. He was truly a blessed. Reporters swarmed around him like a bee hive. There were too many of them with too many questions coming at once. He couldn't hear what was said with all of the commotion going on. His lawyer led him through the heavily crowded courtroom. Two police officers were on their side helping lead the way. It was mayhem. Twenty was dragged along and at the same time, he tried his best to continue to scan the courtroom thoroughly for just one of his long term friends. Still, there was no one in sight. Why wouldn't they show at a time like this? They could wish me off, but they couldn't welcome me from the damn place? What type of shit is that? He was happy to be home. His feeling hurt deeply because his friends never wrote him or came to a trial. He emerged from the courtroom. The outside air, followed by the sunray immediately let him know he was a free man. Especially since this is the first time in ten years he's been outside without any handcuffs on. There were double the amount of reporters and people taking pictures of him on the outside. His lawyer had stopped at the top of the stairs and so did he. He began to answer some of the questions. Twenty just sat back amazed that there were so many people. The news channels are probably going crazy right now for me. Famous for lifting automobiles. That's fuckin' crazy. I'm a famous man for stealing vehicles and these people love that shit. I definitely have to change my life around. All of this is not the way I want to be known. What the hell would my kids say when a teacher asks them what their dad does for a living? Would they lie and make something up or would they tell the truth? Oh yeah, my dad stole your dad's vehicle. He's famous for stealing cars you know. I can't wait to be just like him. A reporter shoved her microphone in Twenty's face. "How do you feel after spending ten years in prison to getting a retrial and finally be free?" Twenty stared at the woman like she was stupid and that was a stupid question to ask. "What you mean how I feel? How would you feel if you were facing life behind bars and you were set free? I feel fuckin' great. Ask a better question next time or find yourself a better job." He turned his attention away from the reporter. Someone had caught his eye. The person looked a lot different after ten years. He knew exactly who is standing next to the truck with his legs crossed nonchalantly. It was his best friend Jeff. At least he thought Jeff still considered him a friend. Twenty blocked out all of the other reporters from asking questions and made his way down to Jeff. He pushed passed all of the people until he stood face to face with him. After ten seconds of staring his old friend down, he spoke. "Why?" Jeff knew beforehand Twenty would ask that question. Why didn't he try to stay in contact with him? "Twenty, first I like to say welcome home. I understand what you are asking me. The DEA, FBI and everyone else was out to get us. They told us if we were to have any contact with you. They would slam us. Just like they did you, man. You know Tech is not built for life behind bars. Paula was pregnant at the time. Couldn't have a prison baby you know." "Wait, Paula has a child?" Nothing else concerned him anymore. "Yes." Jeff held his head down. "Paula and I have a ten-year-old daughter name, Janet." Twenty was hurt to hear that and he thought Jeff and Paula deserved each other. "That's great." He muttered. "You did the right thing." Jeff smiled and he gave him some dap. "We're family, man." At that moment, a black limo pulled up......

# Chapter 14

# THE BAD GUY

Twenty and Jeff didn't notice the all black limo at first. They were too busy reuniting. The limo parked in front of Jeff's truck. A huge Mexican man emerged from the limo. Twenty noticed him immediately. Jeff was facing toward him still explaining the situation about how the law came at him and the crew ten years ago. He never seemed to notice the Mexican beast in the tailored suit and dark shades. Twenty watched the Mexican approach them and Jeff speech came to a stop. Twenty looked the guy over and he didn't recognize the man. For some reason, he felt like the massive Mexican knew who he was. Hopefully, somewhere back down the line there wasn't beef with a job that went bad because of his imprisonment. Nobody took a loss did they? Maybe come to straighten it out? He couldn't recall any bad blood. This guy appeared to be about real business. Twenty spoke as the Mexican approached him. "Do we know you?" Nacho smirked at Twenty. He kept his focus on him and paid Jeff no mind. His business was with the man they called Twenty. "I need you to come with me, my friend." He came closer towering over him. Nacho was close to 7'2 and Twenty was just over 6 feet. Nacho is 400 lbs. of solid muscle. By the way the Mexican man spoke to him. Twenty anticipated this man to be violent and very dangerous. "There isn't any reason to come with you. I'm good right here talking to my friend." He stared the Mexican down. Not showing any fear in his heart. Nacho slowly opened his suit jacket. He revealed his large pistol holstered inside. "I think otherwise my friend." He spoke arrogantly. "Twenty," Jeff spoke. "Maybe you should go with him. You don't want all these reporters making this situation out to be wrong. The last thing you want is for this guy to start shooting on your first day out. They might put you back in prison for good this time. I'm sure this whole thing with this guy is a big mistake. Let's go with him and work this out like men." He cried. Twenty sucked his teeth and thought about what his friend Jeff was asking. He didn't wish any controversy outside the courthouse on his first day out. Although, on the other hand Jeff was unaware he had been training in the art of Kung Fu for the past ten years. There would be no problem laying this big guy on his back before he drew his weapon. Twenty thought about all of the innocent people around them. He didn't want anyone to catch a bullet on his behalf. That would send the media into a frenzy and raise questions like why was he released in the first place? "The limo right?" Nacho closed his suit jacket. "I'm coming too," Jeff was trying to follow. Nacho turned around and his huge hand pressed against Jeff's chest. "Just him." "Twenty," Jeff spoke being blocked off by the huge Mexican. "I'll be right behind you in the truck." Nacho and Twenty were greeted by that Mexican they call El' Nino in the back seat. He looked like he was worth millions and he was. "And who you supposed to be?" Twenty asked nonchalantly. "El' Nino, the man who freed you from that hell hole." He cracked the window and puffed on his cigar. The limo pulled off. "Freed me from that hell hole?" Twenty asked confused. "Don't worry about it. I pulled a lot of strings to have you freed, my friend. Take it as a favor. Your life is restored. I gave you your life back. I could easily take it away. In return, I need a necessary favor from you." El' Nino crossed his legs casually. Twenty was shocked. Had this man really pulled the necessary strings to set me free? And what is his favor? Twenty relaxed in the most comfortable seat he has ever sat in. He exhaled thinking about the situation that was unfolding in front of him. Whatever was going on he could sense that he wished no part of it.

He could tell this man El' Nino was a boss by the way he carried himself with his expensive tailored suit, the nonchalant attitude, the enormous bodyguard and the expensive limousine. This wasn't what he expected on his first day out. You have to be on your shit to make something like this happen. Plus, owing a favor. Even though, you freed me from a life sentence. This guy is probably not to be fucked with. He already has that summed up in his mind. Twenty eyed El' Nino while he was puffing on his Cuban cigar. "What do you want from a man that's been confined for the past ten years? What can I possibly offer? I have no connections, no business and no money." El' Nino smirked and so did the enormous Mexican monster Nacho. He studied Twenty for a moment before he spoke while puffing on his two hundred dollar cigar. "Friend, does it look like I need your connections, your business or your money? I have plenty of those things. What I need from you is your service, my friend." "A man who is well connected as you I suppose, need my service? That's why you went through the trouble to free me, for my service?" Twenty didn't like the way the conversation was going. He knew what type of service El' Nino was asking him and it wasn't cooking dope. "That's what I'm asking you for." El' Nino elaborated the situation for him. "You are the best at what you do my friend. That's how I roll. I only get the best. I have 2 weeks to deliver 30 vehicles. My buyers will seek a new dealer at the end of the deadline. One thing El' Nino hate is bad business. I have the list of vehicles that need to be gathered for me. I have a secret garage you can hide all of the vehicles in for me until delivery. At the end of the mission, I will have three million dollars for your service. Everybody needs something. El' Nino is not greedy my friend. Under one condition, the vehicles can't be damaged in any way, shape or form. I'm sure you can handle that. Nacho will provide you with the list." Twenty's mind trailed off. What El' Nino was asking him to do was what he was against. He changed his life around. He vowed to never lift another vehicle again. Even though El' Nino gave him his freedom and offered him three million. The deal was no doubt sweet. Ten years ago, he probably would've had a great partnership with El' Nino. Times change, this was his second chance at life. There was nothing El' Nino could offer him. There's no way he could accept the deal. He gave El' Nino a sharp stare. "You should've left me in prison." The Mexican boss smirked. He blew smoke out casually. "Are you saying fuck that Mexican motherfucker El' Nino my friend?" "Not as mean," Twenty answered coolly. "Thanks for getting me out, though. I think this ride is over." El' Nino felt punked. "Nacho!" Nacho immediately went for his gun. Twenty already saw the situation unfolding and was ready for action. Nacho drew his gun and aimed it at Twenty. Twenty chopped him at the wrist and bent it while taking the weapon. He had turned it on Nacho and El' Nino. Nacho was shocked and his wrist was in a terrible pain. "Stop the fuckin' limo!" Twenty ordered the driver. "Right fuckin' now! The limo stopped. El' Nino began to laugh. "You have no option but to take the job for me. I will find you wherever you might be. I'll kill your friends and everyone else in your family. Including the kids. This is your last offer." "Fuck you," Twenty began to cautiously exit the limo. "I'll be at the Mexican restaurant on Jimmy Carter when you change your mind. You'll see the limo parked out front." El' Nino faced the window like Twenty was no threat and continued to puff on his cigar. "Find someone else!" Twenty vanished. El' Nino smirked. Why, when you'll do it for me.

*Chapter 15*

# BACK HOME

Twenty hopped in the truck with Jeff. "Let's get out of here." He ordered Jeff. Jeff saw the look on Twenty's face and that it couldn't look more serious. "What's going on?" He asked concerned. He noticed the gun in Twenty's hand. "You got a gun?" "Jeff," Twenty said frantically. "Just get us the fuck out of here and I'll explain." Jeff hit the gas on the new Ford F-250 pulling away from the limousine. Twenty was relieved Jeff finally cooperated. He turned his attention back to the weapon he took from Nacho. He popped the clip out and began to wipe the weapon clean. "They wanted me to go back to my old ways. There was another Mexican man in the limo. He called himself El' Nino. Have you ever heard of him?" Jeff turned his attention away from the road just a little. "Never heard of an El' Nino. He must be a new guy in town. Ever since Janet came along I've been focusing on a new life." Twenty continued to clean the weapon. "This guy El' Nino wants me to lift thirty vehicles for him. He looked at it as a kind of a favor for getting me out of prison." "He got you out of prison?" "That's what he said and he definitely sounded serious about it." Twenty assured him. "This guy El' Nino must have some major connections to release a man from life in prison. How did that come about?" Jeff turned right at the stoplight heading toward his house. "He really didn't say." Twenty explained. "He just assured me I was the best at what I did. That's the reason he wanted me out the prison. He also said that at the end of the mission there would be three million dollars for me. I tried to tell him that I changed my life around for the better. I couldn't do it. He wasn't happy about that. He sicced his guard dog on me, the huge Mexican that met us outside the courthouse. He points this fuckin' gun in my face. I managed to take the weapon from him and turn it against them. El' Nino paid me no mind and ordered that I did the job for him anyway. He said he would kill the kids in my family. He has to be a cruel muthafucka to kill kids." "This is some serious shit to get into on your first day out. This El' Nino guy means business. What you want to do?" Jeff pulled into his neighborhood. "What you mean what I want to do?" Twenty asked sarcastically. "Nothing is what I'm going to do. That's not the life I want to involve myself in anymore. I finally get a second chance after serving ten harsh years of my life locked away from everyone I cared about. You can't possibly imagine how I feel right now." Jeff couldn't understand how Twenty felt and he knew that. He did feel where his friend was coming from although. "I can agree with you on that. What if he tries to make a war out of this entire misunderstanding? He said he'll kill the kid's man. A guy who thinks like that has to be fuckin' insane." "I'll do what I have to do then." He muttered. "I'm not about to get pushed around on some bullshit. El' Nino seems like the type that doesn't take no for an answer. I'll have to really watch my back" Jeff parked the truck in front of his house. "Whatever it might be I got your back. I won't let you fight this one alone. You left me once and I won't let that happen again." "Thanks, but you have a family to look after now." Twenty reminded him. "Twenty, my man." Jeff shut the motor off and turned to him. "Paula would kill me if I didn't. You know we consider you a part of our family. Hell, we are a family, aren't we?" Twenty thought about the others, Paula, Tech and now the new one, Janet. "Fuckin' right, we're family." Jeff smiled and shook Twenty's hand. Twenty slipped the clip back into the nice chrome pistol. "Nice 9 huh?" The 9mm was all chrome with an exclusive black marble handle. "That's a nice piece. C'mon lets go inside." Jeff exited the vehicle. Twenty tucked the beautiful 9 in his waistband under his shirt. It would be a good idea to keep the weapon on him. He never had to carry one. With El' Nino threatening him, although. He felt the need to. Welcome home, he thought. Twenty followed Jeff into the house. Suddenly, he was surprised by Tech, Paula and her daughter Janet. He was astonished by the warm welcome. There was nothing that could feel better right now. He was home with his family. The first person he noticed was Paula. She was still beautiful. Ten years of not seeing her. She was twenty then, now she's thirty and looks more like a woman. To him, the most beautiful woman. Tech came to greet him first. "Twenty, welcome home man." Tech held his hand out not aware if Twenty was upset with him or not. He hasn't tried to contact him in ten years. He wanted to more than anything, but the law prevented him. In his mind, Twenty was the first real friend he ever had. Twenty look at Tech. He noticed he had a worried look on his face. What was done, was done now. He knew it wasn't Tech's fault for not keeping in touch with him. Twenty was happy the computer geek was standing in front of him. Twenty grabbed him by the hand and forced Tech into a huge. "Come here my man!" He patted Tech on the back while they embraced. "Twenty," Tech squeezed out. "You're killin' me." Twenty release the stronghold he had locked on him. "I see you still got the strongest grip around." Tech was the skinniest guy in the world. He was only 5'8 and 130lbs. Twenty smiled. "What I keep telling your skinny ass, man." He joked. "That I need to eat and have a lot more sex to get my weight up." "That's right," Twenty patted him on the shoulder. Paula walked over to them. "Glad you're back," she sounded unconcerned he was back and immediately vanished into the back room. Not giving him any chance to respond. Twenty watched her disappear into the back room dumbfounded. It was hard for him to comprehend what was going on. What had he done to upset her? He wanted to go after her. Tech stopped him. "Twenty," Tech spoke seriously. "Leave it alone man. Give her some time. She's still pissed off that you left us. Well, her to be exact." "What the hell are you talking about Tech?" Twenty didn't know what the hell she possibly could be upset about. He just basically did ten years for her. Jeff walked up to them. "The day you left to lift the last car. You never told her you were going. You always told her about every lift except that one. She felt left out man. Maybe she thought things would have gone differently if she would've known. She'll be alright, though. She just needs to be left alone for a while." Twenty thought back ten years. He remembered when he planned on calling her. He decided against it to keep her safe. Ten years of being upset with me, he thought.

She must hate my fuckin' guts. I have to explain to her that it wasn't my idea, it was Jeff's. Then again, I can't do that. They're together now. I don't want to ruin anything else. I already caused her enough pain. She's better off being mad with me. Hopefully, she'll learn to let it go. Twenty heard a light overwhelming voice. "My name is Janet," the little girl held her hand out. Twenty looked down at the small girl. Absolutely struck, she resembled her mother in every way. She looked just like a little Paula. Jeff was a lucky man to have such a beautiful family. He thought for a minute, if only. Then blocked that thought out immediately. He was supposed to be serving life. "You're my uncle Twenty right?" Janet asked. "This is my uncle, right Jeff?" "It's Dad," Jeff corrected her. "How many times have I told you? Yes, this is your uncle Twenty. Now go make sure your mother is ok." "Alright Jeff," Janet ran out of the room before her father could respond. "It's Dad!" Jeff called after her. He turned to Twenty. "She never calls me dad. Kids these days. Too much TV." Uncle Twenty. That's pretty cool. Never thought I would've been an uncle being the only child. "Cute kid." Jeff shook his head. "And takes after her mother."

*Chapter 16*

# THE OLD HOME

Twenty, Jeff and Tech stepped outside on the front porch for some fresh air. Twenty wanted to ease the tense situation. He was already having a hell of a time. He wondered if he would've been better off staying in prison. He smirked at the stupid thought, hell nah. Anything is better than that place. He had a Mexican boss threatening his life for a reluctant job he vowed not to ever do. He almost got his head blown clean-fucking-off. Even worse, Paula has been upset with him for the past ten years. His first day out isn't going as he planned. Jeff noticed the smirk on Twenty's face. "What's going through your head?" He asked him casually. "I know that look. Something is rattling your brain." "Yeah," Tech followed. "What's going on up there in that head of yours? This is supposed to be a good day. Your home man, lighten up." Twenty didn't want to necessarily tell them what he was thinking about. Tech

84

was right. This is his first day out and he was going to enjoy himself. Although, there was one thing in particular he wanted to let them know. "I'm cool, I was just thinking about where I'm going to stay." "That's what you're worried about?" Jeff spoke up. "My home is your home. Don't ever think you don't have a place to stay. You helped me out in the beginning, right?" Twenty didn't have to think long about that one. "Nah man, I can't do that. You have your family here. I can't invade on that." "Trust me," Jeff assured him. "Why you think houses come with guest rooms? Shit, I've been waiting to use mines. I rather get bothered by you than anyone else in the world." Twenty slowly shook his head. There was no way he could live in the same house as Paula. Jeff wouldn't understand how that would make him feel. He needed to free his mind of her totally. Being in the same house, under the same roof was not the type of rehab he wished for. Far away as possible, that's his best bet. Tech noticed what Twenty had on his mind. The problem was, Twenty was in love with Paula now. Jeff didn't understand that, but Tech understood the situation quite well. He noticed how he looked at Paula and reacted to her being upset with him. Tech wasn't the best with women, but he was smart enough to make it out if he saw it. He spoke up before Twenty could respond to Jeff's offer. "He could stay at the garage. It's all decked out now." The garage, Twenty thought. That's a great idea. The garage was their old spot where they would bring the cars they lifted. It had two office type rooms and was big enough for ten vehicles at a time. "That's what I'll do, I'll stay at the garage." "Cool," Tech said. "You'll love it. I spent time changing the rooms around. I laid new carpet in the entire place. I turned one into a bedroom already, bed, table and a TV. Everything you'll need. I even got a mini refrigerator." "Yeah, Tech really laid that place out." Jeff praised him. "I'll live there, it's that clean now." "That's great." Twenty spoke. "I can't believe you guys still fuckin' have the place." He thought for a moment. Are they… Nah, couldn't be. "Y'all… not… still lifting are you?" he asked skeptically. Jeff smiled. "Hell, nah. I told you. We're done with that. We were being watched too hard to continue. Tech just bought the place and decided he wanted to fix it up." "It was all I had left to remember us by. I couldn't let them tear it down." Tech muttered. "Cool," Twenty said in relief. "That's good you kept us alive Tech. You're the man." "C'mon." Jeff walked towards the truck. "Let's go check your new spot out. You won't believe what he did to the place. They all loaded up in Jeff's F250 and headed over to the garage. Twenty couldn't believe his eyes when he stepped into the place. Tech had the place laid out just like he had mentioned. It resembled the inside of a five-star hotel lobby. "Yeah, you did your thang Tech." Twenty surveyed the place. Tech came over with a beer. "Welcome to your new home."

***

El' Nino pulled up to the front of his Mexican restaurant. Twenty wasn't cooperating the way he intended. There was only one way to handle the problem. For one, he didn't wish to kill him. That was considerable. Twenty is his only resort and he would make him cooperate. He had to weigh his options and use his strong arm once again. The first thing he needed to do was get in contact with The Spokesman. This was his guy. To El' Nino, The Spokesman had no other option. Help him solve the problem or die. If he didn't cooperate and El' Nino lose his buyers. Everyone had to die for it. That's just the way El' Nino is going to resolve the problem. Everyone is going to fucking die. That's the way that Mexican they call El' Nino rolled. Kill every fuckin' thing. Nacho emerged from the limo first. His hand was in excruciating pain. The monster ignored the harsh amount of pain because he didn't want to show El' Nino he was weak. Twenty had got the best of him once. Next time, he would be more than ready or El' Nino would surely make him pay with his life. "Clear Boss." Nacho surveyed the scene and led the way for El' Nino.

El' Nino stepped from the limo with an extreme amount of anger simmering. His face wouldn't show his expression. Something he was taught to do before his mother killed his father. He was only seven when that happened back in Mexico. His mother told him if he cried at the funeral. She would kill him too. She had no patience for a weak child. She was the boss of the family. She only needed his father to get pregnant. When it was time to train El' Nino to be the next boss. That was the first lesson. Never show signs of weakness. El' Nino walked passed Nacho with one thing on his mind, easing his anger. He opened the door for himself and stepped into the restaurant area. Everyone stopped and their attention focused on him. He made his way through the crowd of people. One man tried to get his attention. "Hey El' Nino, how are you d- That was as far as the man got. El' Nino pulled his desert eagle from its holster. He blew the man's head clean off his shoulders. Blood covered the entire area. The man's body was still standing without his head. El' Nino nonchalantly pushed the body out of the way as he spoke. "Don't feel like talking my friend." The wife and eleven-year-old daughter were at the table. They were screaming at the top of their lungs. El' Nino turned the .50 cal. on the wife. He pulled the trigger three times, finishing her for good. Blood from the wife shot all over her daughter. The girl was completely covered in her mother's blood. She grabbed her dead mother. She held her while begging for her to still be alive. Her mother and father slaughtered like wild animals in front of her. Nacho caught up to El' Nino and stood by his side surveying the scene. There wasn't a sound in the restaurant except the little girl. Everyone feared El' Nino and wouldn't dare tell a soul. Their families would meet the same fate if someone would dare to be brave enough. El' Nino turned to Nacho. "Have the men clean the bodies up and order me three tacos and a large fruit punch. I'll be in my office." Like it never happened, the people in the restaurant turned continuing their meals and chatting. El' Nino began to walk off. Nacho listened to the girl scream. "Boss, what about the girl?" El' Nino turned around and couldn't look even more serious. "Clean her up and sell her to the prostitution ring. Young white girls are fetching good numbers right now." And that's the way it went. El' Nino could destroy your family in a heartbeat. The crime ring, loved and protected him. There were billions made every year through him, long as the money flowed. Everyone was happy. El' Nino settled in his office chair and called The Spokesman.

*Chapter 17*

# POWER MOVE

Twenty, Jeff and Tech all sat around the 60inch flat screen TV. They were talking about the past ten years. Tech went to the mini frig and got them some more beers. Twenty told them all about his experience with the White Shield biker. They were shocked to find out he tried to attack him and ended up killing himself. He told them how John Kim became his close friend after the incident and how they trained every day. "So you know Kung Fu'?" Tech asked karate chopping the air. "I know enough to kill someone, that's for sure." Twenty drank some of his beer. He never thought for a second in his life. That he would be home free enjoying a beer with his friends. He pinched himself a couple times to make sure his new life wasn't a dream. He probably would kill himself if it is a dream and he woke up. "Man, I want to learn some of that shit." Tech said. "The girls love that Kung Fu' shit. I did my first girl to a Bruce Lee movie." "Tech," Jeff replied nonchalantly. "C'mon, you know you didn't get none." He gulped some of his beer. "Well, I stuck my finger in there at least." He spoke with assurance. "That's close enough for me and that's for damn sure. Tell him, Twenty." They all began to laugh. Tech was thirty years old and still haven't got any. He isn't gay. He is scared out of his mind to speak to women, though. Every time he actually got a girl and sex came up. His confidence shot down to zero. Twenty is his mentor, he always gave him advice and fixed him up with different women. "He's right." Twenty spoke while still grinning. "He was in there and after the girl stormed from the house. He put his finger to my nose. It smelt like shit and it was some on his finger." Jeff started cracking up. "You stuck your finger in her ass goofball?" "Well…" Tech felt embarrassed. "One the first date," Twenty grinned. "And stuck the shit to my nose like he was the man or something. Like he really did his damn thing." "You weren't supposed to tell him about the ass part," Tech muttered. "I can't believe you guys never told me about that," Jeff spoke. "That was funny as hell." Jeff sipped on his beer. His phone began to ring. He was laughing with the guys as he checked the caller ID. "Oh man," he told them. "Paula's calling me. I better get home. Janet's probably driving her crazy. I'll talk to you guys later." He dapped them up and went to the door. "A'ight, call me later." He told them. He picked his phone up while exiting. "Paula is probably fine now," Tech spoke while walking over to the computer. "Janet be driving her crazy sometimes. Come check this out, though." Twenty walked over to the computer. "What do you have going on over here?" "Check it out for yourself." Tech clicked the mouse and pointed to the screen. Twenty focused in on the computer screen. "Dayum, that's a sweet engine." He said. "Got to cost a fortune?" "It will when I finish designing it," Tech spoke proudly. "That's you?" Twenty pointed to the screen. "All me," Tech replied. "Been working on it for the past year. I'm making custom parts for it. I've almost got the cutting done. Then I'm going to start the assembly process." "What's the numbers looking like?" Twenty sipped his beer. "Close to 1800 horsepower." "1800 HP," Twenty repeated with wide eyes. "That's a fuckin' monster. Are you going to sell it when you're finished?" "I really don't know. I started the engine for fun at first. I have never thought about selling it. I might pass it along to my kid if I ever have one. Maybe he would keep it and pass it on or sell it. It will be worth more money then." Tech suggested. "Maybe it will, maybe it won't." Twenty said. "Somebody might come along and make a better one. Get it while you can and go down in history. I feel the kid thing too. Well, I'm going to head upstairs and check the room out. Call me if you need me."

***

Nacho looked at the house from the black Benz. There were two soldiers with him for their next mission. Nacho was speaking to El' Nino on the phone making sure he was at the correct location. He already had one fuck up for the day. Everything had to go just as El' Nino ordered. After seeing El' Nino vaporized the innocent because of his anger issues. This had to go right. There wasn't any telling what his mind would do. Nacho hung up the phone with that Mexican they call El' Nino. "This is the house." He informed the two soldiers. The soldier in the driver seat cut the engine. "All we need is the girl right?" he pulled his pistol out ready to carry out another sin. The soldier in the passenger seat held his weapon at the ready. "Just the girl?" he was looking up to the house. Nacho wanted to let them understand their assignment one more time for assurance. "We go in and take only the little girl. No one is to harm the female. She's the key. If she dies, El' Nino will kill all of us. Before that, I will kill you first. Remember, we need her to convince Twenty for the job. Do I make myself clear on what is to be done?" Nacho went over what was to only take place. "Just the girl, don't harm the woman."The driver spoke. "Easy enough for me to follow." The passenger assured Nacho. The Spokesman had given El' Nino the directions to the only person in the world that could convince Twenty for the job, Paula. She had a ten-year-old daughter name, Janet. They were to kidnap the girl without harming Paula. Tell her if she ever wants to see her daughter again. She'll convince Twenty to do the job for El' Nino and she'll get her daughter back at the end of the job. How great it was. The Spokesman always kept a trick up his sleeve. Money is the ruler of all evil. "Let's get this over quiet and quick." Nacho emerged from the Benz follow by the two soldiers in the same motion. He closed his tailor suit jacket and snap one button. He casually approached the door and he knocked twice. The soldiers stood on each side of him. Nacho heard a small girl's voice approaching the door. He smirked hearing her voice walking right into his trap. "Someone's at the door mom!" Janet called out. "Who is it!" she opened the door without her mother's permission. "Don't open the door without looking first honey!" Paula called to her. Janet was frozen looking up to the largest man she has ever seen in her life. She wasn't half his size and he frightened her to death. "Honey," Paula called walking to the door. "Who-" she was shocked by the enormous Nacho. She couldn't get the words out. She sensed something bad was about to happen. She was right. She heard one of the soldiers against the house. "Run honey!" Paula yelled and tried to slam the door in their face. Nacho massive hand caught the door and easily forced it open. He noticed Janet had taken off like a track meet. "Go around back." He ordered the soldiers. Nacho grabbed Paula while the soldiers went after Janet. Janet ran out of the back door and climbed up to her tree house. Just like her mother taught her. She opened her secret box and waited. One soldier went climbing after her. The other waited at the bottom. Suddenly, several shots were fired. The soldier's body fell from the tree house and crashed onto his comrade. Janet aimed her 9mm at the other soldier and emptied the clip. "What the fuck!" the soldier shielded himself with his fallen comrade. Hoping a ten-year-old wouldn't end his life. He heard her gun click. Empty, he thought. He pushed the body off and hurried up the tree. He saw her reloading the clip like a pro and this was something she did on the regular. Shit! He knew he was a second away from getting his head blown the fuck off. This little girl was dangerous. He amazingly beat her to the punch. He pointed his gun at her face. He captured her and struggled to get her back to Nacho. Not only did she know how to work a 9mm. She's strong as hell to be ten. Fuck it, he thought. He stopped and placed his gun on her temple. "If you keep putting up a fight I'm going to blow your fucking brains all over the place you little bitch!" the soldier was furious and almost forgot what Nacho said. I'll kill you if you harm the girl or the mother. "You're a pussy for messing with a little girl." Janet didn't fear the man even though there was a gun to her head. "You little oh bitch." She started laughing. "Yeah, that's what you are. A little oh bitch." The soldier was pissed off. His finger vibrated on the trigger. "Go ahead and do it." She teased him. The soldier gritted his teeth to the point where his gums started to bleed. He wanted to kill Janet so bad that he didn't mind facing Nacho but El' Nino was the problem. He's too powerful and would find him where ever he went in the world and would surely slaughter his entire family back in Mexico. "Just move!" he shoved Janet forward as hard as he could and it caused her to fall to the ground. "Get up!" he saw the opportunity and kicked Janet in her chest. The powerful kick flipped her over on her backside. "Ugh." Janet was in an extreme amount of pain from the soldier's brutal kick. "You're… still… a little bitch." She coughed out. She began to laugh through the pain. It made the soldier feel good until she started laughing to piss him off some more. He picked her up by the foot and dragged her through the rough conditions to Nacho. Nacho spoke. "You didn't kill her did you?" he then noticed the girl. "No… she killed Louis."

# Chapter 18

# NO OPTION

ech was keying away at the computer. Twenty must've taken a nap because it's been thirty minutes and he still hasn't returned. It's been ten years since he felt a bed comfortable as that, he thought. No wonder why he's stuck up there. He figured he would let him catch up on some rest. He had some new ideas for the engine. He needs to do some configuring first. He punched the numbers into the computer. His mind was going one hundred miles per hour. The phone next to him rung ten times before he noticed it. He keyed in the last number and then answered the phone. "Tech's garage." He held the phone with his shoulder while he worked. He heard the panic in a women's voice. "Tech!" Paula said frantically. "Get Twenty immediately!" she cried. "They took my daughter, I can't believe they took my daughter!" Tech was confused for a moment. Then he noticed the voice on the other end of the receiver was

Paula's. She was crying frantically. "Paula," he responded. "Where's Jeff?" "They took my daughter," she repeated over and over. She was beginning to lose control of her mind thinking about it. "They took Janet?" Tech asked concerned. He didn't quite comprehend what was going on yet. Did someone take Janet? Paula wasn't getting what she wanted and she snapped from losing patience. "Just get me Twenty on the phone damn it!" she roared through the receiver. Tech ears popped and he had to remove the phone from his ear. Something had happened to Janet. He never heard Paula sound like this before. She was emotional and pissed all the way off. He remembered her only being this mad and emotional was when Twenty had been sentenced to life without parole. Tech sat the phone down and hurried up the stairs of his two-story garage. He opened the door to the room Twenty was in. He was passed out on the king-sized bed like he had thought. "Twenty!" Tech yelled busting through the door. Twenty jumped up and aimed his chrome 9 at Tech. He was having a bad dream that he was back in prison and Nacho and that Mexican they call El' Nino were his new roommates. He woke up in a cold sweat. He was breathing heavily because of the nightmare. "Twenty." Tech cried hysterically. "Don't kill me, man." He held his hands up. His heart fell to the floor. It probably was still down there beating because he was still alive. He never had a gun pulled out on him before and he never had any pussy. He prayed Twenty didn't accidently pull the trigger before he had a chance to get some. Twenty lowered the weapon. "What's going on with you busting in here? You know I just got out. I could've accidently blown your fuckin' head off. You're lucky it was on safety because I swear to you. I pulled the trigger." Twenty got up from the bed. "Sorry," Tech regained his composure. "Janet man, somebody got Janet." Janet, Twenty thought. Who's Janet? He didn't recognize the name, but he soon remembered. "What are you talking about?" he tucked the 9 in his waistband. "I don't know. Paula's on the phone and I heard her say it when she told me to get you. I know something is wrong because she was crying like she was dying." he informed him. "What," Twenty said confuse. "Where's the phone?" "C'mon." Tech led the way. Twenty followed Tech downstairs to the computer. Tech handed him the phone. Twenty answered and Paula told him what had happened. He didn't let her get the chance to explain the part about Nacho telling her to convince him to do the job. He immediately told Paula he was on the way and hung up not wanting to waste any time. Tech saw the heated look on his face. "What happened?" he sounded concerned. "Someone kidnapped Janet!" Twenty and Tech rushed over to Paula and Jeff's house. Tech floored his Mitsubishi Lancer Evolution SE the entire way. He had fast and the furious road rage. Tech skidded the Lancer up to the house almost popping the curve. Twenty got out and bolted to the front door. He left Tech behind, getting to Paula was the only thing on his mind. What Paula told him over the phone ripped a piece of his heart away. Somebody had kidnapped Janet. He opened their front door frantically inviting himself in. Thinking this was the worst day in his life when it was supposed to be the best day in his life. He spotted Paula on the couch crying her eyes out. He rushed over to comfort her. Paula immediately embraced him. She held him close while crying in his arms. "They took my daughter Twenty, my baby. They took her from me." Twenty held her by the head while noticing Tech coming through the door. "Paula," he muttered. He thought for a moment not really knowing what to say. He didn't want to fill her with hopes and dreams of her daughter's safety. There were a million guys in prison. He knew how those animals acted. Most of the time the outcomes were bad. Rape and murdered, only 10% of the girls or women were left unharmed. He hoped Janet was a part of that percentage. "We're going to find her. We're going to get her back." Tech noticed that Jeff's truck wasn't parked out front. He wondered where his friend could be at a time like this. "Where's Jeff?" Tech walked over to them. "I thought he was coming home." Paula didn't respond. Twenty lifted her head a little. Her eyes were puffy and red, tears were streaming down her face. Twenty's love for her made him angry that this had happened. Someone had hurt the only woman he has ever truly loved. This was something he would go back to prison for. "Paula," he whispered. Paula looked into his eyes. Tears rolling down her cheeks. "Where's Jeff, was he here when this happened?" "No, he… he came after… " she stammered. She tried to gather herself. "When they had left. He had just pulled up. I… I told him what had happened and he rushed out of the house after them." She began to cry all over again. "He went after them?" Twenty asked. "How long has he been gone?" Paula sniffed and Twenty wiped her tears away before she spoke. "About," she thought for a quick second. "About ten minutes before y'all got here. Maybe, sooner." "Paula." Twenty spoke seriously. "Have you called the police?" he notice the police hadn't shown. Maybe Paula was traumatized and forgot to phone them. They should've been here by now. "There's no reason to." She looked up at him with teary eyes. "That's what I was trying to tell you before you hung up the phone. They said my daughter would be dead if I called. They were here for you, Twenty. A big Mexican man. He told me to deliver the message that his boss name

El' Nino, is waiting to make a deal for her. There's a job for you to do that requires your service and you know what it is. He said you got to the end of the day to answer him or my daughter will be sold for prostitution. He said he'll be at the restaurant." Paula broke down in tears and placed her head in his chest. Twenty held her head thinking about everything Paula just laid on him. This was his fault. He had no choice but to fix it. He would never forgive himself if he didn't. El' Nino had Janet and he vowed to himself to bring her back to Paula safely. He wouldn't be able to look himself in the mirror without killing the image looking back at him. "Paula, I'm going to bring her back to you safely. I promise." He got up from the couch. Paula held her head in her hands. "Please, you're the only hope for my daughter's safety." She cried. Twenty walked over to the Bible that was resting on a tall stand in the living room. He put his hand on it and closed his eyes. "God forgive me for I am about to sin." He opened his eyes. He pulled his 9 from his waistband and cocked it before he left.

Chapter 19

# WE'RE HIRING

**T**wenty and Tech pulled up to the Mexican restaurant that belongs to that Mexican they call El' Nino. Twenty noticed the limousine parked outside. He gripped his chrome 9. "This the spot." He told Tech. Tech had never seen Twenty's face look so violent. However, this situation went. He had Twenty's back until the end. He would ride for him even though he wasn't the violent type. Hopefully, he wouldn't do anything stupid, like kill somebody. "Let's be smart when we go in here. Who knows what type of monsters are in there?" Tech being Tech, always looking for reasoning. "Right," Twenty said sarcastically exiting the Lancer. He heard what Tech said in one ear but it exited out the other that wasn't listening. He didn't give a fuck what went down. He never feared anyone and wasn't about to start. He had one thing on his mind and that was getting Janet back to Paula even if he had to kill someone. Twenty held the 9mm in his right hand hurrying to the front door. He heard Tech scrambling to keep up with him. He forced the door open to the Mexican restaurant. He resembled a beast standing in the doorway. Every eye in the place was on him. He stepped in scanning for the huge Mexican or El' Nino. He was immediately greeted by the host speaking in Spanish. Twenty had his right fist balled tight and he struck the host nose with his backhand quicker than a snake striking its prey. The host dropped to the ground. It happened too fast for anyone to actually know what had happened. Blood gushed between the host hands uncontrollably. Forgetting John Kim had trained him to be a deadly weapon wasn't useful. He scanned the room listening to the people mumble amongst themselves. "I'm looking for El' Nino!" he yelled angrily. Tech had entered the Mexican restaurant. He noticed the host laid out by the door and was being cared for by a co-worker. Blood was all over his uniform. He looked like he was about to die. Both of his eyes were black and his nose seems to have a piece of bone showing. At first, he thought Twenty had shot the guy in the face. It was confusing because he didn't hear any gunshots. Broken nose, he thought. He heard Twenty yelling for that Mexican they call El' Nino. He stepped over a puddle of blood. El' Nino emerged from his office. He noticed

Twenty standing front center with a weapon. "You're looking for me?" he said nonchalantly. One thing you don't do. Try a man on his own turf. About fifty guns clicked. Everyone in the restaurant had a gun pointed at Twenty. Even though they are guest just eating in his restaurant. They're loyal crime lords as well. Tech watched the entire scene play out. "Oh shit," he muttered at all the armed guest with their weapons pointed at Twenty. He slowly walked up to his best friend. He tapped him on the shoulder. "Hey man, we got a problem." Twenty didn't care if he had a million guns aimed at him. His mission was to get Janet back. "Where's the girl," he asked El' Nino sternly. El' Nino began to laugh. "Are you that crazy my friend? What would you get from killing me? Look around you. You kill me, you not only get yourself killed but your friend behind you. Don't forget about him. He'll die and the girl would die too, your call. I'm ready to die anyway, are you? I'm going in my office. Hopefully, you will make the right decision." El' Nino turned around not afraid to die and entered his office. Twenty thought about what he said. He lowered the gun and followed him into the office with Tech trailing behind. El' Nino took a seat behind his office desk. Nacho closed the door behind them for privacy. He walked over to his boss and stood by the desk. His private waitress brought him a cigar, she clipped and lit it for him. He puffed on the Cuban cigar. "Have a seat." He offered them. They both took a seat at the front desk. Twenty spoke up. "Where's the girl?" he asked. "Just give me the girl and I'll handle the business you need me to do." El' Nino smirked puffing on his cigar. Thinking, he must think that fuckin' Mexican they call El' Nino is stupid? "My friend, if I give the girl back and you don't do the job for me. Do you know what I will do to every single person around you? That's serious, what you just asked me to do for you. I tried to reason with you before all of this my friend, but you know what you said to me. You said, fuck that Mexican El' Nino. Then you spit, not in my face but on my fucking thousand dollar loafers, alligators too. You disrespected me, my friend. I get you out of a life sentence. I offer you a simple job and to make you a rich man. How simple is that, no violence involved. You pushed me, my friend. Now you ask me for another favor. Release the girl. C'mon, you haven't done anything for me and I'm steady doing for you. Nacho, what do you think?" He asked his bodyguard. Nacho stood next to the desk like an enormous statue. "He needs to work. Then get the girl." "All I want is to make sure she is safe." Twenty pleaded. "I'll do the job. You have my word. The girl has nothing to do with this. She's innocent." Tech sat in the chair soaking up the two going back and forth. He was scared to death. He was ready to go. Nacho was looking at him like he wanted to practice wrestling moves on him. El' Nino wasn't going to give the girl back. Tech knew that. Twenty needed to agree to do the job and hopefully, get the girl back. He saw it as Paula's only option to get Janet back. He feared if he disagreed. Twenty, Janet and himself were all going to die today. El' Nino might go for as killing Jeff and Paula. Just to rid us all. He kept repeating in his head, just agree, just agree, just agree… El' Nino puffed his cigar eyeing Twenty. After a moment, he let him know exactly how he felt about what he said. "I'm thinking more like if I keep the girl. You will do the job. It adds pressure to the whole thing. If I give you the girl, I see problems ahead. I don't like problems, my friend. This is my last offer for you. Do the job or don't walk out of here alive. I'm going to be serious with you. I hate to play cat and mouse my friend. How do you black guys say it? You-feel-me-shawdy." El' Nino joked. Nacho had a smirk on his face. Listening to El' Nino sound black with a strong Spanish accent. "Did I get it right that time Nacho?" El' Nino asked. Nacho nodded. "Good, I try to keep up with the kids these days." He turned his attention on Twenty. "What's it going to be?" Twenty was thinking about pulling the gun out and blowing El' Nino's head off. He put him in a situation that he never wanted to be in, lifting cars. He promised God that he would never do another job again. On the other hand, he promised Paula that he would do whatever to get Janet back. God would have to understand. He turned to Tech. Tech had a look on his face like he wasn't ready to die. Everyone, would die on is count. He looked at El' Nino with all the hate in the world. "I'm hired." He spoke through clenched teeth. El' Nino smiled. He had his man. "Nacho, provide him with the list." Nacho pulled the list from his pocket and handed it to Twenty. Twenty stood and put the list in his pocket without looking it over. It didn't matter what is on the list. He was going the get the job done, he had to, for Janet. "How long?" "One week, you finish. You get one million and the girl back. You don't… everyone is dead."

*Chapter 20*

# THE HIT LIST

Twenty and Tech mad it out of the restaurant safely. Twenty ask Tech for his cell phone as he settled in the passenger seat. Tech closed his door and handed him the phone. He took the phone and scan the contacts list for Jeff's name. He pushed the send button. The phone rang three times before he answered. "Twenty," Jeff spoke frantically. "Where are you guys?" "We paid El' Nino a visit. We're on the way to the garage now." Twenty signaled for Tech to start heading that way. "What happened, were you able to get my daughter back?" Jeff sounded emotional. "Please, tell me you got my little girl back?" Twenty heard Paula in the background asking the same question while crying her heart out. He felt bad. The words were hard to form. How could he tell them that he didn't get her back? That would crush them. They were a family, he knew it was his fault. "No," he muttered. He was hurt and saying the words felt like a sharp sword slowly piecing his heart. "I'm sorry, I had no choice but to take the job. When the job is complete, he assured me that he would hand your daughter over safely with a million dollars. I have a week to finish the job or everyone is dead. I promise Jeff, I'm going to get your daughter back safely." Jeff was silent for a moment. "I'm going to help you." "Jeff, you know what you're asking?" Twenty spoke. "You could go to prison." "Twenty, I'm coming to the garage," Jeff told him. "This is my daughter we are talking about. I would die for her. I'm going to help." Twenty heard Paula in the background. "I'm going to help." Twenty thought for a moment. He was going to need help. El' Nino said there were thirty vehicles on the list. He knew how tough it would be by himself. If he didn't get their help, he was asking for a family funeral. They all would die. Tech overheard them arguing to help. If Twenty were going to need someone's help. It was him, he is the brain. His job would go a lot smoother and lower the chance of getting caught. "I'm helping too." He informed him while driving. "You'll need me." Twenty was getting hit from every angle. Jeff, Paula and Tech demanded their assistance. He felt something creep back up on him. Something he thought would never be again. His team was back, The Lifters. And they had a job to do. "OK," he gave in. "You and Paula meet us at the garage so we can get started. I have the list." "We're already on the way," Jeff told him. They hung up. Tech got them to the garage in ten minutes. Jeff and Paula arrived at the same time. They all entered the garage. They sat around the computer screen. Twenty took the list from his pocket. He read the name of each vehicle. "A Ferrari 430 Scuderia, BMW 650i convertible, Mercedes S63 AMG, Mercedes AMG, Mercedes CLS 63 AMG, Nissan GT-R, Hennessey CTS V700, Bentley Mulsanne, McLaren MP4-12C, Chevrolet Corvette C7, Porsche 991, 2012 Dodge Viper, Aston Martin V-12 Vantage, Porsche 911 Turbo, Porsche 918, Lamborghini Aventador LP700-4, Lexus LFA, Mosler Photon, Maserati MC-12, Ferrari FF, Chevrolet Camaro HP ZL1, Mustang Shelby GT500, 2012 Mustang Boss 302, Lotus Esprit, Ferrari 458 Italia, Lamborghini Gallardo, Ferrari 599 Replacement, Jaguar C-x75, Nissan-Renault DeZir, Bugatti Veyron 16.4 super sport." He was confused by the last vehicle on the list. "And the President of the United States Land Rover." What the hell, he thought. The President's Land Rover? He read the passage next to the vehicle. "The President will be arriving in Atlanta on Saturday. It is the only type of Land Rover available in the world. There is something special I need inside." "What!" Jeff jumped from the seat. "That's insane, the President's Land Rover?" Tech was at the computer typing in every vehicle Twenty mentioned. He finished. "Twenty, I have the cars entered. There are close to ten cars on the list that are not available." Twenty examined the list. "I know, I have VIN numbers and locations right here. They're concept vehicles." "What about the President's Land Rover? How are we supposed to lift that?" Paula asked. A knock at the door interrupted Twenty from answering. Who could be knocking at the door, he thought. Did El' Nino have someone follow us? He tucked the list into his pocket. "Tech, kill the computer." he didn't want anybody to know what they were planning. "Already on it chief." Tech saved the list on a spreadsheet before shutting down the computer. Jeff and Paula walked over to the bar and acted like they had been chatting the entire time. Twenty turned the TV to the sports channel and sat down. "Tech, go ahead and get the door." Tech walked over to the door and looked through the peephole. "Shit," he muttered to himself. He couldn't believe who was standing on the other side. Twenty noticed Tech reaction. "Tech," he whispered and threw his hands up. "Who is it?" Tech looked at Twenty nervously. "It's detective Daverson." He whispered and pointed to the door. "Fuck," Twenty muttered to himself. "What the hell is he doing here?" Daverson continued to knock on the garage door. He knows we're in here. Tech and Jeff vehicles were parked outside. He hasn't done anything wrong, at least not yet. "Let him in, he might get suspicious." Tech opened the door and tried to act surprised. "Oh, it's detective Daverson everyone." Daverson pushed past him. He was being followed by his new partner, Matt Gains. Daverson was 55yrs. old now and is going to retire soon. Matt is going to be his replacement at the private investigator's office. "Shut up you skinny punk. Where is Twenty? I can smell him a mile away. I know he's here, son. Don't lie to me." Twenty stood up. Not wanting to hide from the arrogant detective. "I'm right here old school." He called to him. "What's up, what are you here for? Don't tell me you wanted to welcome me home? You're getting soft on me gray hair?" Daverson stormed over to him. "Look here son." Daverson was nose to nose with Twenty. "I know you're up to something. I know you can't resist but to fuck up and when you do. I'm going to be there to bust your ass, son. Send you back to where you came from. In my opinion, they should've left you in prison. The city was better off without you. I see, you already got the team back together. Don't tell me it's a coincidence that you, Jeff, Paula and Tech are here together." Twenty backed away from Daverson. "It's a coincidence, now get the fuck out." Twenty was heated. It was hard for him to hold his temper. The old man was pushing the right buttons. Daverson smiled. "Believe me son, this time around. You won't be able to save them. All of you will have a nice bunk in prison for the rest of your lives. Let one car get stolen. I promise son. I'll be all over your ass like flies on shit." Jeff walked over and stood next to Twenty. "If you're not here to arrest anyone," he spoke to Daverson. "I think it's time for you to leave." "Jeff," Daverson turned his attention to him. "The woman stealer." Daverson knew that Twenty cared for Paula from the interview the reporter gave him ten years ago. Jeff went at Daverson. "You sonofvabitch!" Twenty caught Jeff by the arm. "That's what he wants, Jeff." He said restraining him. "Let it go, man." Daverson smiled in Jeff's face. "C'mon tough guy, hit me." he taunted Jeff. "That's what I thought. I'm going to keep my eyes on all of you. One of you even thinks about stealing a vehicle." He warned them backing up. "I'll be there. C'mon Matt, let's leave these criminals alone to think about what I said." Twenty stepped in front of Jeff. "If I do steal a car, it's going to be your mother's. Believe that." Daverson smiled. He was backing out of the door and held his two fingers to his eyes before pointing at Twenty. He signaled to him that he was watching. Then he vanished. Tech finally took a breath. "Fuck, I can't stand that guy." He muttered locking the door and looking through the peephole. "Just what we need," Twenty spoke sarcastically. "I need time to think things through before coming up with a plan. Lifting the President's vehicle is going to be hell. Meet back here tomorrow morning and we'll sort things out. I'm going to get some rest."

*Chapter 21*

# MEXICAN PROPERTY

They said their goodbyes. Jeff and Paula went home. Tech decided to stay at the garage with Twenty. He wanted to get right to work on the list. Sorting out the vehicles and how tough they would be to lift. Twenty exhaled and flopped down on the couch, watching the sports channel in front of him. He kicked his shoes off and relaxed. "What a fucking day." He muttered to himself. "Tech, you got any more beer in the frig?" "Yeah," Tech called back. He went to the refrigerator and got two beers. "Twenty." Twenty looked over at him standing across the room. Tech tossed him a beer. "Thanks, you're a good man in my book. I don't care what they say about you." He joked catching the beer. "People say things about me?" Tech asked not getting the joke. "It's a joke," Twenty said casually opening the beer and taking a gulp. Tech laughed like he was the one joking. "Of course, I knew that." There was another knock at the door. Tech walked over to answer it. Thinking Jeff or Paula must've forgotten something because they just left. He opened the door. He was so stunned by the woman's beauty in front of him that he dropped his beer. "Is Twenty here," the woman had a seductive Spanish accent. Twenty looked over to Tech. "Yo Tech, what's going on over there?" he noticed Tech had dropped his beer. Tech looked frozen, he resembled a huge block of ice. "Tech, you hear me? And you know you dropped your beer, Dawg." Tech didn't pay him any mind. He was captivated by the Spanish woman's beauty. He finally pushed out some words. "It's for you, man." Tech dragged out. "Tell them to get at me tomorrow." Twenty turned his attention to the sports channel. "I'm tired." You won't be tired after you see this woman, Tech thought. He sure as hell wouldn't be. "Twenty, you want to come to the door. Trust me," he spoke with seriousness. "Damn Tech," Twenty said frustrated. "Just tell them to come in then." Tech stepped out of the doorway to let the woman through. "Sorry about the beer," he told her as she stepped over the wasted beer. "It's ok," she walked into the garage. Twenty heard a seductive woman's voice and it made him turn around. He almost spilled his own damn beer on himself. His eyes grew wide immediately on sight. He was looking at the most exotic woman he has ever seen in his life. She had long jet black hair that fell to her waist, nice skin, cat eyes and the type of body magazine women would kill for. He didn't know what to say. She could not have asked for him. Tech must have been trippin'. "Twenty," she said seductively walking over to him. Twenty slowly stood up to greet the Spanish woman. Damn, Tech wasn't trippin'. "That's definitely me," he muttered. The woman dropped her bag on the floor and embraced him. She started kissing him on the lips and neck seductively while pulling at his pants and shirt desiring him. Tech watched the scene play out from the door while he cleaned up the beer. "Dayum." Twenty couldn't help it, he embraced the woman. They fell back on the couch. He began to think where he knew this woman from. She knew him by name and he couldn't remember her from anywhere. He pushed her away reluctantly. "Whoa, whoa, whoa. Hold up a minute." The woman was still trying to take him. "Where do we know each other from?" She unbuckled his pants. "Does it matter?" She tried to kiss him again. He held her back. "Yes, it does matter. All types of shit happened to me today. I need to know something." "Ok, ten years ago I saw you on TV. The police had you. That day I fell in love with you. I followed your case. You take what you want. You were an outlaw living free without caring about the law. I have wanted you ever since. I even showed up to your trail and your retrial. Take me

Twenty." She grabbed him by the head. "Say you want me too, Papi?" Twenty stood from the couch. It's been a long time since he had a woman. This woman was exotic and beautiful. She convinced him. She stood with a worried look. He grabbed her chin gently. "The bedroom is upstairs."

***

Twenty and the Mexican woman kissed all the way up the stairs while she tore off his clothes. They got to the room door and he pushed it open with his foot. She entered the room backward and he followed. She took a couple steps back while he stood there watching her. She seductively lifted her skirt over her head and dropped it to the floor. He scanned her amazing physique as she stood there with his soldier standing at attention. She had on nothing but a thong. Her breasts were perfect and her hips were stunning. She slipped out of her thong and kicked them to the side. Her clitoris was nicely shaved and had a tattoo just above the entrance. He read the tattoo. "Mexican Property." He muttered grinning. She signaled for him to come over with her finger. He walked over to her and they embraced. She pulled his wife beater over his head and tossed it to the floor. He dropped his pants. They kissed while backing up to the bed. She fell back onto the bed and backed up to the center. Twenty stood next to the bed. How did I get so damn lucky? This beautiful woman said she is in love with me. She followed my criminal career. She showed up to my trails wanting me for ten years and never thinking of ever having the chance to have me. Did women actually want career criminals like me? Of course, they do. Look at Richard Ramirez. I told myself for ten years Paula was the one for me. I told myself I wasn't a player anymore. I only need one woman. Paula has a family with Jeff now. Am I wrong for wanting this woman? The Mexican woman had her legs bent up and she slowly and seductively spread them apart. Her clitoris poked right out in Twenty's face. "Hell nah, I'm not wrong." He muttered. He got onto the bed. The Mexican woman pulled him closer and grabbed his manhood. She entered him into her. Twenty never thought he would ever feel such a desirable feeling again as he penetrated her. She was super wet. Her juices were flowing. Twenty turned into an animal inside of her. He worked her over fast then slow and fast again while she moaned for more. He lifted up one of her legs for better position. He brought the pain to her clitoris as he growled. Twenty loved hearing the sound of her voice. The Spanish accent turned him on and up. He flipped her over on her stomach and penetrated her from the back laying down on her. She moaned as he went deep down into her. Twenty is a monster and every woman he's ever been with, he has got the best of because he is so large. Every time, they would become addicted to him. They would fiend for him. He knew how to handle a woman in bed the right way. He lifted up and the Mexican woman and propped her up doggy style. She had a voluptuous ass. He grabbed on and pounded ten years strong into her. She moaned loud enough for the entire block to hear. For the next hour, he put her in every position he could think of. He was on his back when he felt that sensational feeling creeping up on him. She was riding him like a wild bull. He held her ass until the very end while she grinded. "Oh Papi, I'm cumming again," she moaned. This was indeed the best sex she has ever had in life. She knew for sure she would be back. She desired him for ten years. There was no way she wasn't coming back. She loved this man and she knew it. "Oh shit," Twenty muttered. "I'm about to bust." He felt his body tense up. His body was starting to get weak. He gripped her ass tighter and at the last second and lifted her up so he could cum. "Dayum," he relaxed. "Um," she moaned relaxing on top of him. "That was the best I ever had." She laid on his chest. Twenty felt like ten years without sex could make a man go insane. What if he finished that life sentence? He thought about this exotic woman wanting him for ten years.

"What's your name, ma?" he whispered. "Rosa." She held on to him. "Rosa," he muttered. "Well Rosa believe it or not, you're the best thing that has happened to me all day. Even better than getting released." Rosa, he thought before he fell asleep.

*Chapter 22*

# MONDAY

El' Nino had his plan in order. If Twenty finished the job. Then El' Nino would make an easy five million dollars. He loved making easy money. El' Nino was a billionaire. Five million dollars was chump change to him. His main goal was to bring more buyers to him through the underground car theft ring. There were million to be made. He wanted to build up to at least one billion dollars a year. Once he has success with this first job. The buyers would be satisfied and bring new buyers to him. He would have to search the world for the best car thieves. Twenty was going to be finished after this job and he knew that. He could force him into more jobs. He thought, why bother? Time is money and that Mexican they call El' Nino patience is short. El' Nino puffed on his Cuban cigar looking out to the city. He had two of the most beautiful women money could buy. They were down on their knees pleasuring him at the same time. Sucking him up like a cold ice cream cone on a hot day. He reached over to his desk and grabbed a small platter of coke. He took a long bump and handed the plate to a redhead Spanish woman in front of him. She stopped pleasuring him and snorted the best cocaine she has ever had. She went back to pleasuring him after she passed the plate to the blond Spanish woman. She was sucking El' Nino like it was her favorite thing in the world to do. She took a good bump of the coke. Both of the Spanish women were famous actresses and supermodels on the Spanish channel. The blonde even had a hit song on the radio. El' Nino threw the biggest Spanish party once a year in Los Angeles. That's how he met the women. Everyone in the Spanish world who is famous would come. El' Nino is the man. He knew everybody and he could plug or unplug your career. These two women loved El' Nino. They were simple women until he turned their lives around. He made money off of their success. El' Nino took another bump of the cocaine and placed the plate back on the desk. He grabbed his cigar from the ashtray and puffed out rings of smoke. He grabbed the back of the redhead and forced her to deep throat him. The sensation was great while the other licked on is balls. Then he forced the blonde to do the same performance while the redhead licked. He got up from his two thousand dollar office chair and made both of the women bend over on his desk. Two voluptuous asses propped up at him. He penetrated the redhead while he fingered the blonde. He pounded the redhead until she collapsed on the desk. Then he entered the blonde and pounded her until she collapsed. The redhead turned over on the desk wanting more of that Mexican they call El' Nino. She took another bump of the coke while he penetrated her deeply. The blonde took a bump of the coke, playing with her clit while she waited. The redhead moaned loud and came all over El' Nino's manhood. He pounded the blonde violently. He was trying to make himself cum, but the cocaine had him wired. Nacho entered the room. "Phone Boss, The Spokesman." El' Nino finally felt himself cumming. He ordered both of the women down on their knees. He jacked in front of their faces. "Yes, yes..." He exploded. El' Nino walked over casually butt naked to Nacho. Nacho's used to seeing his boss naked in ogres. He was hired to protect so it was nothing to him. He handed El' Nino the phone. "My friend." El' Nino answered. "Everything went smooth with Twenty, I see." The Spokesman said. "I'm just calling to say good doing business with you." "Yes," El' Nino puffed on his cigar while looking out of the window. "Kidnapping the girl was a great idea. When Twenty finishes the job, I will give you an extra million to be on my payroll." "Look forward to it Boss."

***

Twenty woke up the next morning. He heard Rosa gathering herself. He looked over at her and noticed she was in a hurry. "What's the rush?" he wanted to hit that again. "Late for work or something?" Rosa slipped her skirt on. "No Twenty, it isn't that." "What, you got kids or something?" "Oh no, no kids yet." She said, "It's more complicated than that." she fixed her long beautiful hair. Walked over and grabbed him by the face. She kissed him passionately. Twenty noticed something he didn't observe before. Rosa had an enormous diamond ring on her finger the same size as a marble. When she released him, he spoke. "You're married?" he asked seriously. Rosa grabbed her purse from the floor and slipped on her high heels. She wanted to avoid answering his question. Yes, she is a married woman. The man she is with she didn't love more than him. How could she explain something like that? She was mad with herself because she forgot to take her ring off. She knew if she would've told Twenty she was married in the beginning that would've lowered her chance of having him. He wouldn't have wanted her no matter how exotic and beautiful she is. She's married. She wanted to cry. "Rosa," Twenty called. "Answer me? You're married?" he asked again while getting out of the bed. He knew he was going to have to follow her because she wasn't answering and was moving. Twenty slipped his pants on swiftly. Rosa clicked her earrings on and got to the door. Twenty caught the door. "Why didn't you just tell me you were married?" Rosa got teary eyed. "Sorry." Twenty repeated. "That's it, sorry?" "How could I tell you?" she cried. "You were going to prison for life. I never dreamed in a million years you would get released. What was I supposed to do? You didn't know about me. I had to move on because I was obsessed with you. I had to find someone in order to stop thinking of you every night. When you got released, it was already done. I've been married seven years and now I'm ready to leave him and be with you forever. Are you ready to be with me?" she asked emotionally. Twenty's facial expression seemed lost to her. He couldn't answer that question. The sad part is… she knew it. "I thought so." She pushed past him and he followed her out. "Rosa," he called to her. "Rosa." He knew she was hurt. The question is, could he be with one woman? The only woman he ever loved was Paula. He knew he couldn't be with her. She has a family. It's still tough for him to stop loving her. What would he do? This woman, Rosa. He has never met or talked to, a day in his life. She knew everything about him and he knew nothing about her. She said she loved him and was willing to prove it by giving up her marriage. How could he let her make a decision like that if there was a chance he would never love her back? With all the shit that took place yesterday. How could he make that decision right at this moment? He had to lift thirty vehicles, avoid dickhead Daverson while doing it and save Janet. Chances were high he could end back up in prison or get killed. How would she feel about that? The situation was rough and he needed time. He caught Rosa at the front door exactly when she opened it. "Rosa, just listen to me." he turned her around. "Listen, I understand where you're coming from. I'm sorry for hurting you. I trust that you do love me. Something inside of me is telling me you are the one for me. Right now I just need time to sort a few things out. If I'm still alive in a week, we'll see." "Well, I waited ten years, a week is nothing." She kissed him passionately. She turned to leave and bumped into a woman standing in the doorway.

*Chapter 23*

# HELP WANTED

Paula stood in the door shocked at everything she heard and seen. Paula never heard Twenty express the way he felt for a woman even though she's with Jeff. She was hurt on the inside because she still loved him. Paula wanted to attack the woman but she couldn't let her emotions show how she felt about the whole situation. Only a day out of prison and he got some hoe over, she thought. The woman was amazingly beautiful, even too Paula. When she overheard Twenty tell the woman, he trusted that he knows she loves him. That made her think how long have they had known each other? Was it before or after prison? Maybe he was trying to run game on her because he wanted some and was back to his old ways? Inside, Paula was emotionally frustrated. Her daughter had been kidnapped and the first man she had ever fallen in love with. He was telling another woman he basically wanted to be with her.

130

What else could she expect from him knowing she was still with Jeff? That, Twenty was going to be single for the rest of his life while she was with his best friend? To her, that wasn't the case. That wasn't the case at all. No one would understand, no one. Tech was being Tech once again. He was at the computer working his ass off. He noticed Twenty when he chased the woman down the stairs. Now he was watching Paula stare her down after a kiss that could've won a Grammy. Tech shook his head slowly. "Oh shit," he muttered to himself. "This can't be good." Twenty notice Paula and couldn't believe she was standing at the door. Dayum. He just spilled his guts to another woman in front of the woman he cares most about. Paula was going through a lot getting her daughter kidnapped. He didn't know exactly how Paula felt about him. He wishes that she could've been somewhere else and not at the door facing Rosa. Especially after saying what he said and kissing her. Man, I wish she was somewhere else right now. "I'm sorry," Rosa apologized for bumping into her. Paula mean mugged the woman hard, letting her know through her mind that she didn't like her. "Whatever." She muttered and pushed passed her. Rosa turned around. She thought that was a rude thing to do. She didn't know this woman at all but she wanted to set her straight. Twenty held Rosa back. "Please," He whispered.

"For me? She's going through it right now. Just call the garage for me later. We'll talk." Rosa restrained herself only because Twenty told her to. "Ok," she kissed him on the lips. "I will." She left. Tech had a beer in his hand and chugged it down. "Woo, this is better than the movies." Tech wondered how Twenty did it. All the women wanted him. He wished he was him. "I don't understand yet how you do it. You're the man bro, you're the man." He muttered to himself. Paula was at the bar. She poured herself a straight double shot of Patron. She threw it back and poured herself another. Twenty felt bad and walked over to the bar. He wanted to explain to her that he loved her. Although, that was something he could not do. That would cause more problems. Especially with his best friend, Jeff. Twenty put his hand on Paula's back to comfort her. "Paula," he whispered. "I-" Paula jerked away from him. She cut him off. "Please, save it for someone who care about your black ass." Paula was emotionally angry and didn't know how to deal with it. She loved Twenty so much it hurt inside. She threw the second shot back. "Ten years you had been gone. Ten damn years!" she slammed the glass on the counter. She couldn't control her emotions anymore. "You left me, you left me by myself. I loved you to death and I still do. Now you show up. My daughter gets kidnapped. Then you're with another woman who says she loves you." Paula began to cry. "Do you love her? Do you!" she cried uncontrollably and hit him on his chest several times. Twenty embraced her into his arms. She had her face in his chest. "They took my daughter. They took my baby." "I know." He whispered. "I know."

***

Someone started knocking on the garage door. Twenty told Paula to fix herself up because no one should see her like this. She agreed and went to the restroom. Tech signaled to Twenty that he got it and walked over to the door. Twenty poured himself a shot of Patron in the glass that Paula had used. Women, he thought. Today was Monday and there is no way in hell he was going to let it be like yesterday. Today is going to go the way he wanted it to. Tech looked through the peephole. He saw who it was and opened the door to welcome his friend. "Jeff." He gave him some dap. "Hey," Jeff said cheerfully greeting Tech. "What's going on?" he stepped in the door. "Nothing much, "Tech wanted to hide what went on between Twenty, Rosa and Paula. Jeff wouldn't understand that. He was sure Twenty and Paula would be happy with his decision to do so. "Been working on the vehicles all morning, you?" Jeff walked to the mini frig. "Working. Well, just got off work. What's going on Twenty my man? Whoa, you drinking early

133

aren't you?" Jeff grabbed himself a beer. "Yes sir," Twenty played it cool. "I see you're joining the club." he held his drink up. Jeff came over and toasted him and gave his best friend some dap. He sat at the bar. "Tech, where's your beer?" Tech stayed facing the computer. He raised up the empty beer bottle with is left hand. Signaling to Jeff he already got started. "Well get another one and drink with us. Twenty's home man!" Tech stayed facing the computer and held up his right hand with a full bottle of beer. Signaling to Jeff he was already on the second. Jeff and Twenty laughed at Tech. One beer could get the computer geek drunk. Jeff noticed Paula wasn't in sight. Her car was outside and she was nowhere to be found. He knew she was going to be here. They were going to come over together. He had to finish up some business at work first. So he told her they would meet here. "Where's Paula?" Jeff asked. He took a gulp of his beer. "The restroom," Twenty replied. "She's been in there a minute?" Jeff asked. "Nah, she just went in right before you came." Twenty took the shot. "Probably girl stuff." Paula came from the restroom. She tried her best to fix herself up. Her eyes were still a little puffy and she still had a little sniff. Jeff walked over to greet her. "Hey honey," he held arms out about to hug her. He noticed something was wrong. "Hey, what's wrong?" he was concerned. Paula didn't want to let him know exactly what was wrong with her. Although she told him what was the biggest reason. "Just thinking about Janet." Jeff embraced her. "It's going to be alright, I promise. We're going to get our little angel back." Jeff wanted to hide his emotions about their daughter being kidnapped. He wanted to be strong for Paula. They all sat at the computer. Tech was telling them how hard it is going to be to lift all the cars in a week. The exotic ones were going to be the toughest. Then, there was the President's Rang Rover. "So you're saying we're going to need some help?" Twenty asked. "Maybe an extra person or two," Jeff muttered. "You sure we need someone?" "Positive," Tech assured him. "Ten years ago we could've lifted thirty vehicles with our eyes closed. That was ten years ago. Times have changed. We're talking cars that are concepts. Blueprints I can't seem to find. Security codes I can't seem to crack. I know I'm a little rusty. It's been a decade. It's going to take me a long time to work and I know it's going to take you longer. One person who's been working the system could definitely put us in there." They all were silent, thinking about the tough situation they just been put in. Twenty thought hard, it's been a decade. Who could he know of? He remembered talking about a bad ass dude with David. "Anybody know where Scores Bar and Grill is?"

*Chapter 24*

# SCORES

Jeff had brought Twenty two weeks' worth of nice shirts and pants. He had nothing when he got out so Jeff made sure he had something on his back. Twenty was more muscular than Jeff so he filled his shirts out. They still fitted him nicely and the pants were perfect. Twenty came downstairs after getting dressed. "How I look?" He asked everyone and holding his arms out. "You look good man," Jeff answered. "Different but nice," Paula replied. She couldn't believe how Twenty changed. She thought he looked amazing in Jeff's clothes. "Still the man." Tech followed behind Paula. "Ok then." Twenty felt better about himself because he was finally able to wear some real clothes. "Who's ready to go get a drink?" They were on their way Scores Bar and Grill. Tech knew where the bar was. He's been there a time or two to catch pay per view fights. They had some fine women there and that made him want to come back again. It took about thirty minutes to get to the bar. The place was jam packed. Twenty hadn't seen a bar so crowded. How were they to find Bobby and his brother Jimmy Neutron in this place? Twenty didn't know what they looked like. He never bothered to ask David that because he never thought he would be lifting cars again. Yet alone, trying to recruit someone for the team. The good thing about it was if he did find him. Bobby would probably want to join the Lifters. The way David put it. Bobby looked up to Twenty as the greatest car thief ever and dreamed of being part of the crew. He hoped Bobby was still dreaming about that because he was about to make it come true. Twenty and Tech got out of the Lancer. Jeff and Paula hopped out the F-250. They went to the front of the bar and there was an enormous line. There was a chance they wouldn't get in the place because the line was so long. Tech wanted to get in badly. There were some fine women in line revealing enough skin for him to get hard. "Wait right here," Jeff told them. Jeff walked to the front of the line. He spoke to the bouncer at the entrance who was letting people in and checking ID's. "Hey," he called the bouncer. "My friends and I are trying to hop the line." He showed the bouncer a hundred dollar bill. "No problem." He took the money. Jeff went back and got everyone. He told them they were VIP and could hop the line. Tech felt like the man for some reason. He was happy they were getting in. Twenty was out and he wanted to prove to him that he wasn't scared to talk to women anymore. He walked to the front of the line with a mean swag. He walked pass some fine looking women. "VIP, baby." He said coolly. The women were smiling at his pimp walk. They thought it was funny but cute because Tech had a geek swag. He didn't know it, but women were starting to dig geeks all over the world. Tech knew he had the female's attention. Good or bad he didn't care. They were watching so he popped his collar. "Boom," he said smoothly while flipping it up. Then he continued into the bar with his friends. They were at the bar and all decided to work it first. They were shooting the name Bobby around to see if anyone knew it. Paula and Jeff worked one end and Twenty and Tech hit the other. Tech bought them drinks. Twenty noticed Tech at the front. "Man, I'm proud of you. You swaged on the females out front." He held his beer up. "Really," Tech was happy he noticed. Tech toasted him. The women out front were in and found Tech immediately. "Call me." One said and kissed him. The other one waited for her friend to turn away. She slipped Tech her number on the low. "Call me." She mouthed and caught up to her friend. "Whoa," Tech responded. "Told you." Twenty spoke. "Two for one." After working the bar and then the floor an hour. Twenty was ready to give up and so was Tech. They found themselves back at the bar. They both had a seat. Twenty was seated next to a long hair blond dude who resembled a surfer. Tech was lucky enough to be seated next to a fine looking female. Twenty was beginning to think Bobby didn't show up tonight. He couldn't come back every night looking for this guy. It would be too late. Janet would be dead by then. He had to get to work immediately. There was no more time to waste. I'm just going to do what I got to do, he thought. The show must continue. There are lives on the line. He signaled for the bartender. After this last drink, he's going to find Paula and Jeff and see what they thought. If they wanted to continue searching for a while, it was straight. If not, he was ready to dip. The bartender came over. Twenty ordered another beer and he noticed that the bartender was different. They must've switched shifts. One more time, he thought. "Hey, I'm looking for a guy name Bobby." He told the bartender and taking the drink. "There're a million guys named Bobby, who comes in here. Sorry homie." He said. "Well, this Bobby is in the car business if you know what I mean." Twenty signed to him. "Oh, that Bobby." He said while wiping a glass. "Who want to know?" "Twenty," he told him. "Well, Twenty." He signed. "It's going to cost you." Twenty was dead broke. He had a lead though and he didn't want to lose it. "How much?" "It doesn't matter how much." Said a harsh voice behind him. "This mu'fucka owes me five hundred thousand and a Boss 302, ya feel me." Twenty recognized the voice and turned around. He was face to face with Money. The dope boy who paid him five hundred thousand for an unfinished job. There was supposed to be another five hundred thousand, but Twenty got arrested on the last vehicle. "Money," Twenty said casually. "I saw you on the news, hot boy." Money spoke coolly. "Lookin' real good in my Boss 302." Twenty noticed Money had about four goons with him. He wanted to avoid any trouble with them. "Yeah. Will, I was set up. It wasn't your color anyway." He noticed Tech was paying attention now. That's two on five. Where's Jeff and Paula? "Yeah," Money spoke with a cold stare. "I heard somethin' like that around the hood potna. I heard you were snitchin' too. You serve ten years on a life sentence. Who you tellin' on mu'fucka?" Money knew the law was after him. They were kicking in his trap houses a lot lately. Then, Twenty shows up. Somebody was snitching and he figured it was him since he knew so much about his past jobs. "Smack this pussy Money!" One of his goons spoke. "This bitch snitchin' bruh!" Twenty knew it was about to go down. He had a beer bottle held by the neck without it being noticed. "I don't want to start anything and I didn't snitch on anybody." Money stared him down. He heard one of his boys yell, hit'em. Money cocked back to bust Twenty in the face. "Bitch nig-" Twenty swiftly jabbed him in his gut. He crashed the beer bottle over the head of the loud mouth goon. Tech jumped on the back of one and put him in a headlock. He couldn't fight so he hung on for his life choking him out. Money got back to his feet and went at Twenty. Twenty caught him trying to spear him. He flipped him up onto the bar. He slid him across into all of the drinks down the line. Twenty was about to get attacked by the last goon. Paula blindsided him with a job in the face. She knocked his lights out. Twenty punch Money in the face five times before he passed out. The bar turned into mayhem.

*Chapter 25*

# NEW MEMBER

Money hung on the edge of the bar. His face was bloody red. Paula signaled to Twenty frantically that it was time for them to go before the police arrived. Everyone in the bar was running wild. Bumping into each other, falling to the ground trying to exit the bar. It was hard for Twenty to hear Paula because of all the yelling and women screaming going on. He finally understood what she was saying. "Where's Jeff!" Twenty yelled over the commotion exiting the bar with Paula and Tech. "He's already outside!" She yelled back while pushing people out the way. "He was looking for you out there!" Twenty and his crew finally got outside of the bar. Everyone was loading up in their vehicles and burning out of the parking lot. Everyone made it out the bar except Money and his crew. When they did, he popped his trunk. Jeff was standing by the truck with a confused look on his face. "What the hell is going on?" He asked as they approached him. "Bar fight," Tech said excitedly. "We were in a real bar fight ad I got two fine females numbers." Tech started punching the air. "What, you guys decided to get into it when I'm not around?" Jeff asked. "I missed the fun? Who was it, you know?" "It was Money from back in the day." Twenty answered. "Money," Jeff asked. "What happened?" "He was upset about that Boss 302 and he said his spots have been getting raided lately. He thinks I snitched, because I got released early." Twenty looked at his bloody knuckles. "Damn," he muttered. "That bastard," Paula said angrily. "How could he believe that it was you?" Twenty shrugged before he heard someone yell out to them over all the commotion. "Bro!" The surfer boy walked up to them. He held his hand out to Twenty. "Who is this?" Jeff asked. "No idea," Tech answered. Twenty shook his hand. "Thanks for helping back there." "No problem bro." The surfer said. "What's your name?" "I'm the one and only white boy with the brochunski swag. I'm Bobby bro and it's my absolute pleasure to finally meet you." "Brochunski swag," Tech muttered to himself. He turned to Paula. "What's the brochunski swag?" Paula whispered to him. "I think it's what the white boys call being cool or something." "Oh," Tech whispered back. "You're Bobby?" Twenty asked. "That's me bro," Bobby assured him. "You were sitting right next to me at the bar. Why didn't you say anything?" "Us brochunski's don't speak unless we know who we're speaking to," Bobby told him. "That's the brochunski way bro. You could've been the feds. When you said your name to the bartender. That's when I recognized who you were bro." "David told me about you," Twenty leaned on the Lancer. Jeff whispered to Tech. "Doesn't Bobby look more like a surfer man than a professional car thief?" Tech whispered back. "That's the brochunski swag. It's a white thing." Paula started giggling with her hand over her mouth. "David, bro!" Bobby said excitedly. "He's a brochunski too. How you know him?" "We were cellmates in prison." Twenty told him. "He told me you were good at what we do. I need a man down on the team. I got a tough job to handle. He said you were the man." "Bro!" Bobby started shaking his hand. "You got yourself a new member!" "Cool," Twenty spoke casually. "Give your number to Tech and I'll call you in the morning." Bobby did what he was told. Police sirens were getting louder. Suddenly, someone started firing shots. "Shit!" Twenty yelled. "Somebody shooting. Ride out!" They loaded up into the vehicles and bolted. There's not an Atlanta party without a shooting. Twenty and Tech raced back to the garage. Jeff and Paula followed them the entire way. Twenty was impressed with Tech driving skills. He couldn't drive at all when they first met. That's why he stayed behind a computer. Tech always beat him at race car games. Maybe all that driving paid off. They got out of the Lancer and headed inside. Jeff and Paula followed. Twenty went to the restroom to clean himself up. Paula turned on some music. Tech got everyone a beer. Jeff jumped behind the bar and started mixing drinks. Tomorrow was going to be the first day of work. They always let loose before they did a job. It was like a ritual. Twenty came out the restroom with his shirt off. He was revealing his decade trained muscles and heavily tattooed arms and chest. Paula noticed and couldn't help to think how sexy he was. Dayum, she thought. She was with Jeff so she couldn't express how she felt. Twenty was making her panties wet. Tech tossed Twenty a beer. "Twin." He said coolly. Twenty caught the beer and popped it open. "Right on." Twenty took a gulp while walking over to Jeff at the bar. "What are you mixing up for me?" "I have my special coming up." Jeff was an expert at creating drinks. Twenty thought he would've been a good bartender if he didn't start lifting cars getting used to that easy money with him. Paula sipped on her beer. She hated the fact Twenty took a seat next to her with his shirt off. She wanted to jump all over him. He was making her more than horny. Paula wanted to get some and not from Jeff. She could feel her heart beating in her clitoris. "Whatever he gets I want one too." "Me three!" Tech said. He was jamming to the radio. He started mumbling to himself. "Geek swag, two girls, geek swag, two girls…" Twenty watched Tech from the bar. "That boy drunk." "He'll be on the couch soon," Paula was watching him. "Here we go. The best drink in town." Jeff slid Twenty and Paula his new creation. Twenty took a sip. "Dayum, this is good." Paula sipped, then took a big gulp. She wanted to get her mind off having sex with Twenty. Hopefully, the liquor would free her mind from the thought. "He's right, it is good. What are you calling it?" Paula finished off her drink. "The Jeff Bomb, baby." Jeff looked at her seductively. Paula wasn't into him right now. She definitely didn't want sex from Jeff. She played along. "Well, give me another Jeff Bomb." So I can get my mind off fucking the shit out of Twenty. "Make it stronger." "Coming up." Jeff started making her drink. "Drinking a lot now?" Twenty asked. He noticed Paula had something going on. Paula shrugged. She couldn't let Twenty know she wanted him. "Clearing my mind." Twenty nodded while he heard the phone ringing. "I got it!" Tech stumbled to the phone. "Yo, this is two girls, geek swag Tech's garaaage." He was drunk as hell. "This is Rosa, can I speak with Twenty." Tech wasn't thinking about it, he just blurted it out. "Twenty, it's fo you. That fine piece you had over last night." He handed him the phone and danced off. "Geek swag, two girls…" Paula got angry inside and left the bar. She had to get away. She went to her secret spot on the roof. Thirty minutes later, Twenty popped up. "What's going on?" He sat next to her on the roof. "You're still coming up here?" "You still know the way?" She asked with attitude. She lit up a blunt. "Paula, what did I tell you about smoking weed? That shit fucks your mind up. He took the blunt from her and threw it off the roof. "Fuck, I'm a big girl now. Go back to the party." "Why," he whispered. "They all passed out from the Jeff Bomb," Paula smiled. "You're still beautiful to me Paula." He said. She couldn't help it. She grabbed him by the head and passionately kissed him. She finally restrained herself. "I can't do this." She left him on the roof by himself.

*Chapter 26*

# TUESDAY

"Twenty, what the hell." Tech got on the roof. "Wake up man." Twenty was on the roof so long he fell asleep. After Paula had left. He started thinking of a plan to lift the vehicles. The morning sun began to shine on him. He slowly woke up to the blinding illumination. He shaded his face as he spoke. "Dayum, I must've fallen asleep." "Dayum right, you did. I've been looking for your ass all morning." Tech told him. "My fault," Twenty apologized. "Jeff and Paula still here?" "They left around two this morning." "Oh," Twenty got up and brushed himself off. "What time is it?" "It's eight in the morning. We need to get started on the list. I already found where most of the privately owned vehicles are located. They are going to be the easiest to lift." "Yeah," Twenty walked towards the window. "I've been thinking about that." Tech followed him through. "What did you come up with?" He asked hopping through. "Well, Daverson is going to be all over me. I have a plan to hide the exotic cars when we lift them instead of driving them all the way to the garage." Twenty went into the restroom to wash the sleep out his eyes while Tech listened at the door. "You still have the automatic lift from the delivery truck?" Twenty asked. He wiped his face clean. "The one we lifted with all the car parts on it?" "Yeah, that one." Twenty exited the bathroom and slipped on a fresh white tee. Tech turned around at the door to face him. "Yeah, I still have it. It's out back. What about it?" he raised his eyebrow. "I was thinking about lifting an eighteen-wheeler." Twenty elaborated while walking downstairs. "We could use the hydraulic pump on it. We could use that to make our own lift on the back doors of the eighteen-wheeler. Something that will open and let down so we could drive the cars into it. That way, if we're getting chased by the law we could easily hide by dodging them and ducking the car off into the eighteen-wheeler. We could transport the cars from our garage to El' Nino's. We'll have to get it done immediately. How long would it take you to build it?" "No time," Tech said following him out back. "That's a great idea. We can hide the cars on the move. Why didn't I think of that?" Twenty spotted the lift. "Good, it's not rusted. What time is Jeff and Paula coming?" "They said around ten or eleven." "That's too late for me,"Twenty muttered. "I need to get an eighteen-wheeler while it's still early." "I can go," Tech suggested. "Nah, you need to be here working on the lift." Twenty thought for a moment. "Call Bobby for me? It's time to test the kid skills."Tech dialed Bobby's number and gave the cell phone to him. "Here you go." The phone rang three times before Bobby answered. "Hello." "Bobby, this Twenty." "Hey, what's going on bro?" "You ready to be a Lifter?" "Born ready." "Where are you now?"Twenty asked. "Dropping the Lil' brochunski off at school. What's up, bro?" "I need you here for a job we need to do.""Give me the directions and I'm on the way."Twenty gave him the directions to the garage. It took Bobby fifteen minutes to get there. They met Bobby out front. "What's up, bros?" Bobby asked. He gave Twenty and Tech some dap. "C'mon in so I can explain what you're getting yourself into." Twenty led the way into the garage. They all had a quick drink while Twenty explained everything to Bobby. He told him about El' Nino and the money they were making from the thirty cars and Janet. "This some serious shit bro," Bobby said. He drank some of his beer. "Yes, it is." Tech added. "What you want to do?"Twenty asked. "You want to be down with the Lifters or what?" Bobby thought about the consequences. He wanted to be a Lifter. "Bro, let's get that eighteen-wheeler."

***

Bobby owned the new Hellcat Dodge Challenger. The vehicle was built with the type of muscle that would get the job done. Bobby and Twenty loaded up into the Hellcat while Tech stayed behind and got started on the lift for the eighteen-wheeler. "Bobby," Twenty spoke seriously. "Glad you're on the team man, for real." "No problem, bro. I always wanted to be a Lifter. It's not about the money you offered me after the job is done. It's about saving that little girl bro." Bobby fired the Hellcat up. The motor sounded like there was a monster under the hood. "Thanks, man." Twenty held his hand. Bobby gave him some dap. "Lifters, bro." "The first white boy to be a Lifter." Twenty joked. "You just made history." "First white boy with the brochunski swag to be a Lifter," Bobby smiled and shifted the car into gear. "Where to?" "Drive a bit from town." Twenty ordered. "Head down south. We don't want to be close. Don't wish to make the area a hot zone." Bobby headed to the highway. Twenty pulled his chrome 9 from his waist. He looked it over. "That's a nice piece." "El' Nino, I took it." Twenty tucked it back in his waistband. "You own a weapon, right? You can't be out here lifting cars without one." "Us brochunski's keep the heat." Bobby signaled to the glove box. Twenty opened it. There was a .50 caliber

Beretta resting inside. "Big weapon." "That's how we roll, bro." Bobby pushed the Hellcat wide open on the highway. They went over a plan to lift the eighteen-wheeler. This job would be simple because they're not looking for supplies. They just need one without designs or wording on the sides. All white would do, less attention when it gets reported stolen. There were millions of all white eighteen-wheelers. When the cops finally find it. It would be destroyed. They only need it 4 days. The plan was to hit a truck stop. Find an eighteen-wheeler good for the job and jack it. Hopefully, the truck driver wouldn't buck. Twenty didn't desire to kill anyone unless he had to. They got to the truck stop after an hour of driving. Bobby pulled the car to the side of the road. They surveyed the truckers from a distance. "Found one." Twenty spoke. He is watching every truck carefully. "He's on the move now." Twenty ducked back into the Hellcat. "When he hits the open road speed up next to him and I'll take it from there." "No problem, bro." Bobby put the car into gear. He waited for the eighteen-wheeler to pull from the truck stop. He waited two minutes for the truck to get a good distance away from the other truckers. "Ready." Twenty signed. Bobby floored the Hellcat. The motor growled the entire way. "There it goes." The truck was fifty yards ahead of them. "Ok, pull up as close as you can." Twenty ordered. "I'm going to jump on the truck. When I do, pull in front and slow it down." Bobby pushed the Hellcat harder and got next to the truck. He maneuvered into the opposite lane when it was clear. Twenty popped out of the sunroof. He held on while Bobby eased closer. "Shit!" Suddenly, another truck was riding down the opposite lane. "Bobby!" He got his attention. Bobby fell back behind the truck then maneuvered back into position. Twenty slowly stood and made the jump. "Fuck!" Bobby swerved the Hellcat off the road just in time to avoid hitting another truck head on. He pushed the car to get ahead of the big truck once more. Twenty hung on to the side of the eighteen-wheeler. The trucker noticed him through the side view mirror and tried to shake him off. Twenty tried to open the door to the truck. It was locked. "Shit." The trucker rolled down his window while maneuvering the big truck lane to lane. The car in front of him was making it difficult for him. He was trying to speed up. The car was making it difficult by slowing him down. The trucker knew exactly what was taking place. He heard about guys on the open road getting jacked by outlaws for their truck supplies. That's why he brought Johnny along. He reached for Johnny while steadying the truck. "I'll show you sons of bitches." He muttered. "You sumbitch's wanna steal my goods!" He yelled sticking Johnny out of the window towards the Hellcat.

"Oh shit." Twenty saw the sawed-off shotgun out appear from the window and aim at Bobby. The trucker fired and the sound echoed in his ears. Twenty had to come up with a plan or the trucker was going to blow Bobby away. "Damn," Bobby said. He whipped the Hellcat. "You want to play hard." He had no choice but to swerve into the next lane out of the trucker's way. Bobby maneuvered back into the lane the trucker was in to continue the plan. "C'mon Twenty, get this fool bro." The trucker fired again. This time, Bobby was ready. He saw the shotgun and he swerved ahead of time. It was still a close call, though. What can I do? Bobby thought while whipping the car in front of the big truck. The trucker was laughing to himself. He was giving the Hellcat hell. He flipped the barrel open and reached in the passenger seat to grab more shells. He loaded two more into Johnny and flipped it shut. "You boys ready to give up!" He started laughing like a crazy man. "Cause I'm not." Just when he was about to stick Johnny out of the window. He noticed the man in the side view trying to make a move on him. He aimed the barrel. "You got this Twenty." He muttered to himself. The trucker stopped swerving and now he could maneuver a little better. He needed to unlock the door. The trucker had a double barrel sawed off shotgun. Between each shot, he was going to have to reload it. When he takes the next shot I'll make my move, he thought. He can't drive, reload and pay attention to me all at the same time. Twenty got as close to the window as he could, trying not to get noticed. Did the trucker run out of shells? He was taking an awful amount of time. Twenty couldn't wait any longer. Holding on to the truck was beginning to make his hands numb. Twenty made his move when the truck slowed down a bit. Bobby was doing a good job now. Maybe the trucker was giving up? Twenty put his hand on the open window. He maneuvered his body into position. He began to peek in the window to get a look at the trucker and the lock. Suddenly, he noticed the trucker and his sawed off shotgun. "Fuck!" Twenty ducked off right before he got his head blown off. He almost fell off the truck. He hanged off the truck with one hand. Bobby noticed what happened through the rear view. "No!" He thought Twenty was going to fall off the truck. Bobby came up with a plan. He gunned the Hellcat far ahead of the eighteen-wheeler until it was out of view. Another truck was heading the opposite direction. "Perfect." He passed the truck and then shifted into neutral performing an 180-degree spin. He shifted back into drive and caught up to the truck riding next to it. The trucker tried to reload. He noticed the car was coming back and was in his lane riding next to another truck shielding both lanes. "You wanna play, boy?" The trucker gunned the big truck toward the car. Everybody was going to die if they collided. They were ten yards away. "Shit!" The trucker became scared of death and swerved off the road at the last minute. He came to an uncontrollable stop. The tailor on the truck fishtailed and was going to flip them if he didn't stop. He smacked his head on the dashboard and blacked out.

# EIGHTEEN WHEELS

**B**obby held on tight to the steering wheel zooming past the truck. He was holding his breath the entire time. He was relieved when the trucker decided to tap out at the last minute. Hitting an eighteen-wheeler head on wouldn't look good at a funeral. He pushed the Hellcat to 180mph the last 100 yards. He would've exploded if he hit the truck. The plan worked and he was excited. He watched the big truck swerve off the road uncontrollably through his rear view. He came to a harsh stop. He put the car in reverse and drove for ten yards before performing another 180-degree spin heading back. He hoped Twenty was alright. Twenty slowly picked himself off the ground. He dusted himself off. His body is in an extreme amount of pain. He felt like he wouldn't survive. When the truck swerved off the road, he got slung off. The big truck trailer almost killed him. It fishtailed while passing over the top of him. The wheels were about to crush him. He rolled out of the way at the last second. He pulled his 9 out and walked toward the truck. He jumped up on the door. The trucker was coming back around. Twenty unlocked the door immediately. He slung the door open. The trucker went for the shotgun. "Don't try it." Twenty aimed the 9 at the trucker's head. The trucker lowered his shotgun. "C'mon and get out." The trucker slowly got out. "This is wrong. This is theft! You sons of bitches can't get real jobs!" He said sternly. Twenty got heated with the trucker. "I got one." Then he slammed the trucker's arm in the door. "Ah." The trucker groaned. He was holding his broken arm. "You sonofva-" Twenty slapped him across the face with his gun. The trucker bent over holding his arm while spitting his teeth out. Twenty brought his elbow down on his back spine. The force of the shot was brutal. You could hear the trucker's back pop. The trucker fell forward to the ground flat. "Watch ya mouth." Bobby skidded the Hellcat to a stop on the side of the road. He hopped out of the car and walked around to the front. He noticed Twenty standing over the trucker. He held his hands up to him. "You good, bro!" Twenty turned to his attention. "Yeah, I'm good!" He hollered back. Bobby jogged over to him. He looked down at the trucker.

"What happened with him bro?" "He got a foul mouth." Twenty tucked the 9 back in his waistband. Bobby smiled. "You know what my mother does to people with foul mouths?" Bobby asked the trucker. "She puts dirt in dirty mouths." Bobby kicked dirt in the trucker's face. "And you're a horrible driver." Twenty smirked. "You're a crazy mufucka Bobby, but I like you. You got some balls to do what you did." "Us brochunski's, bro." Bobby held his hand out for some dap. "Are crazy motherfuckers," Twenty smiled and pounded him up. "C'mon, let's get the hell out of here. If we stay out here any longer." Twenty said. He got in the eighteen-wheeler. "The sun will have you my color." He joked shutting the door. Bobby smiled and turned his attention to the trucker. "Sorry bro, we have to go. Thanks for the truck." Then he jogged back to his car. Twenty sounded the horn to the big truck twice before he pulled off. The trucker watched his truck pull away from the ground. Dust covered him as it got going. Bobby pulled in front of the truck to lead the way back to the garage. Twenty handled the truck well for an hour and a half drive back. They didn't make any stops. Bobby pulled into the garage followed by Twenty. He pulled the truck around back to hide it from public view. It would be much harder to identify and they could work on the doors in private.

Tech saw the enormous truck pull in. He came out and guided Twenty to the back. "Nice truck," Tech hollered as Twenty stuck his head out the window. "Yeah," Twenty hollered. "Got her with a zero down payment."

*Chapter 28*

# JIMMY NEUTRON

Jeff and Paula came from the back of the garage to meet Twenty, Tech and Bobby. Paula noticed Twenty had some cuts and bruises when he jumped down from the truck. She walked up to him. "What happened out there?" She asked concerned. "Where should I start?" Twenty said with sarcasm. "I was hanging from an eighteen-wheeler at full speed. I got my head almost blown off. I just about collided with another eighteen-wheeler head on while hanging on the truck. I got slung from the truck when it spun out of control. Oh, the trailer nearly smashed me to death. I somehow manage to roll to safety while it passed over me." He held the bottom of his chin like it was hard for him to think. "Yeah, that's about it." Everyone was looking at Twenty shocked except Bobby. That's because he was a part of the entire thing. Bobby patted him on the shoulder. "Twenty is tough as nails, bro." Tech thought about all that action that took place and wished he could've been there to witness it. Twenty was amazing to him. Women love daring men. He figured that's why women were so attracted to him. He was a risk taker. "And you're still alive?" Tech asked excitedly. "That's unbelievable. Man, I missed it." "Looks like you still know what you're doing?" Jeff asked. He was looking at the big truck. "Bobby here made it happen," Twenty said. "I would've got killed if it wasn't for him trying to kill everyone." He joked. He walked to the back of the truck. "I wonder what's in this thing. That trucker put up a damn good fight." "Maybe some drugs," Tech caught up to him. "Cartel's love transporting them in big trucks." "He's got a point," Jeff said. He walked behind the truck with them. Twenty unlocked the back doors. He opened them one at a time. They all stood there looking in the back of the trailer. There were a large number of boxes. Twenty hopped in. "Drugs," Tech was looking at all the brown boxes. Twenty looked the boxes over. "I need a knife?" he asked them. "Right here bro." Bobby handed Twenty his pocket knife. Twenty grabbed the knife. "Right on." He began to slice the first box open. He unfolded the flap. He looked inside. "Computers." He slit open another box. "Another computer. This truck was heading from a computer warehouse. Let's unload the truck and see how many we got. Tech, hop up here with me and help pass the boxes off. Build some of those muscles with your skinny ass." He joked. "A man," Tech responded hopping in the truck. "I don't need muscles. I got geek swag." "Here you go with your geek swag." Twenty dropped a heavy box in Tech arms. The box was heavy enough to make him collapse under it. Everyone thought it was funny. "Work them sexy muscles Tech." Paula joked laughing at him. "You got it bro." Bobby cheered him on. "You'll have big muscles in no time," Jeff said helping him with the first box. Twenty worked Tech to death. By the time they were finished. Tech was ready to fall out. It took them an hour to unload the truck. They went through each box as it passed. Paula took a count. There were eighty-five boxes all containing expensive computers and hardware. They had at least $100,000 worth of stuff. They stacked all the boxes in the garage. Tech muscles were pounding. He walked weakly up the stairs. "Hot shower, then an hour worth of sleep. I'll work on the truck after I get up." "What do you want to do with all these computers?" Jeff asked. "I have no idea." Twenty responded. He didn't plan on having the hardware. He just wanted the truck. "We could sell them bro," Bobby suggested. "You know someone?" Paula asked. "Yeah," Bobby replied. "I'll have them gone by tomorrow." They all chilled out for a moment to recuperate. They talked about the upcoming job. Twenty remembered that Bobby had a partner. If Bobby was this good, his partner would be too. "I thought you had a partner or brother that worked with you?" he asked. "Jimmy!" Bobby checked the time. "Yeah, I do. Jimmy's his name. I'm late picking him up. I'll bring him back. He's going to be pissed, bro."

***

Twenty and Jeff were giving Tech a big hand with the truck. They already had the trailer doors off. Tech was building the hydraulic lift on them. He was welding a ramp to the doors that automatically fold out when they opened and then back again when they closed. The unique system is going to be controlled by a button he's going to insert in the front dash. Paula had hot dogs, hamburgers and steaks on the grill while they worked. She thought it was a nice day out for a barbecue. She thought, at the least she could do is feed them while they were hard at work. "The hot dogs are ready." She told them excitedly. Paula was happy everyone was back together again. She wished her daughter was home but was strong and confident that they would get her back. She loved the idea of the Lifters were working again. Even through the harsh time. She rather her life to be exciting then to be a boring housewife. Twenty made her feel strong again. Tech placed the power drill on the ground. "Let me try one." Tech stomach was beginning to growl. He thought he could use a bite to eat. "I'll take two," Jeff said. He put down the welder and flipped up the helmet's shield. Twenty really didn't care for hot dogs. He wanted to work until the steaks were done. They were making good progress with the lift and he didn't want to slow down. The job had to be finished by tonight. The week was counting down on them. "You want one Twenty?" Paula called from the grill. "Nah, I'm good." He said connecting the hydraulic pump to the lift. "I'm waiting on one of your nasty steaks." he joked. Tech laughed with a mouth full. He tried to reach for another hotdog. Paula slapped his hand with a spatula. "Uh." He mumbled. "No more for you since you think it's funny," Paula said while pointing the spatula at him. Tech started rubbing his hand while walking away. Twenty was shaking his head from side to side. He noticed Bobby's car pulling around back. He stood up waiting to greet him and his brother Jimmy Neutron. He tried to look through the windows. Bobby windows were tinted black and it was hard for him to tell what his brother looked like. "He's back," he was looking in Bobby's direction. Jeff turned around in the car's direction. He was having a good time with two hot dogs in his hands. "Bobby," he called coolly. Paula turned her attention away from the grill and stood next to Jeff. She was feeling good about the situation. A new member would make the odds better for them to get the job done. Most of all, help the odds of getting her daughter back. The Lifters were expanding and she loved it. "Hope he is as good as Bobby say he is." She muttered to Jeff. "Don't worry." Jeff said "If he's working with Bobby and if Bobby is the best while Twenty was away. He will be." He stuffed a hot dog in his mouth waiting for Bobby and his brother to emerge from the Hellcat. Tech figured this was the best time to make his move. He crept behind Paula nonchalantly and stole himself one of her delicious hot dogs. He grabbed a bun while muttering to himself. "Little bit of barbecue sauce and I'm good. This black man gotta eat." Bobby emerged from the wet painted Hellcat after parking it backward with an angle of the wheels. "Bro's." he greeted them. He shut the door. The passenger door swung open and a kid emerged. "I want you to meet my little bro, Jimmy Neutron." Twenty looked at the kid. He looked about thirteen. He was confused and he noticed that the others were confused too. Twenty was blown. All that talk David told him about Bobby and his brother Jimmy Neutron. They were supposed to be the best around. This had to be some kind of joke or mistake. Is this high school kid lifting cars? He probably doesn't know what a driver's license is. Bobby and Jimmy Neutron walked over to Twenty. Bobby spoke. "Jimmy, I want you to meet the man. This is Twenty, he's the best, bro."

*Chapter 29*

# WONDER BOY

"Ok," Jeff walked over to greet them. "This is our new partner?" "Yeah, bro." Bobby spoke up. "Twenty don't tell me you are going to allow a kid to lift cars with us?" Jeff asked. "I agree with Jeff," Tech said walking over. "He's just a boy." Paula was shocked and didn't know what to say about the situation. Bobby's partner was a boy. What is going on with this kid, she wondered. She remembered Twenty lifting her dad's car around this age but this kid looked more like a schoolboy, not a Lifter. She shrugged her shoulders. "I've seen it all," she muttered to herself and went back to grilling. Let them figure it out, she thought. "Um… Bobby," Twenty was looking for the right words. "You didn't tell me your partner was a kid. The guys are right. We can't have a boy lifting cars with us. It's way too dangerous." "Bro, I'm going to be in the car," Jimmy told Bobby. "I told you they weren't going to like me," he

168

ran back to the car upset and got in. "Oh man, see bro." Bobby said frustrated. "You guys pissed him off." "Well good, because like Twenty said." Jeff crossed his arms. "It is too dangerous for him to be working with us." "He can hang out for the barbecue," Twenty told Bobby. "But after that. We got business to handle. We still have to finish the lift for the truck and plan the lifts for tomorrow." "Not to mention," Tech added. "I still have to figure out the security codes to the dealerships and the locations for the privately owned vehicles." "Bro," Bobby laughed. They looked at him confused. "That's not going to be a problem. My brother doesn't lift cars. The smartest computer hacker in the world just went to the car pissed." "Your brother is a genius?" Tech sounded like he was interested. Computer hackers did start out young, he did. "Not just a genius." Bobby praised his brother. "The genius of all geniuses. He's a real life wonder boy. How do you think I became the best?" Tech basically took over the conversation with Bobby while Twenty and Jeff listened. "Tell me, what can he do to help us?" "Anything that involves a computer." Bobby elaborated. "Those security codes, every vehicles on the list he can get detail on. Even the concepts you're having trouble with. He can get you a car's tire size five years before the vehicle is assembled. That's how brilliant he is bro. He'll download everything on your computer before it's time for him to go to bed for school tomorrow. That's how fast he is, bro. You're only going to need him one day, that's it." "Genius," Tech muttered. "I'm going to give this kid a chance." He said walking over to the Hellcat. Tech wanted to see what this kid was about. With or without Twenty's approval. If this kid is that good. Janet will be on her way home. Jimmy Neutron could make their jobs easier. Tech tapped on the passenger side window. "Jimmy." "Tech made his mind up," Twenty said watching him. "A wonder boy, huh?" Jeff asked. "Can't wait." "Twenty," Bobby said seriously. "He'll work out bro." "I'm going to give him a chance. We'll see." Twenty said. He turned his attention to the hydraulic pump. "One day won't hurt anybody." Tech convinced Jimmy to get out. They talked for a minute. Tech took him in the garage to get straight to work. He showed him the list and everything they needed. Jimmy went right to work. Tech came back and helped complete the hydrologic lift. They finished around ten at night. "Let's see if this baby works," Twenty said. With the four of them working. The lift got down quicker than he had thought. "Hit the button Tech!" Jeff called from the back of the eighteen-wheeler. "Here we go, baby!" Tech was excited. Twenty watched the doors open automatically and the ramp magically foldout. It was perfect. "It worked." He looked at Tech. Tech hopped out of the eighteen-wheeler and came around to check out the work. "We did it. Test it Bobby. Drive your car up it?" "Yeah, this is sick bro." Bobby fired up the Hellcat and drove up the ramp. Tech hit the button and the ramp folded and the doors closed hiding the car. Good to go. The car vanished. Twenty watched his idea come to life.

***

They finished up the eighteen-wheeler. The job was complete. The idea of hiding the vehicles as they lifted them was a success. They all went back into the garage. Time to plan and check on Jimmy Neutron progress. Jimmy and Paula were laughing and eating hamburgers and French fries. They were sitting on the couch watching a cartoon. Twenty noticed them first. He walked over and stood next to the couch. "Cartoons?" he was confused. "Yep," Paula swallowed a bite of her hamburger, Um. "Jimmy Neutron, it's a good cartoon." Jeff went to the kitchen. He wanted to try one of the hamburgers. Cartoons were not his thing. "I thought the kid was supposed to be working?" he asked anyone who was listening. He put the hamburger on a bun and used BBQ sauce. "I believe he's done everything he needs to do. "Tech answered. He was facing the computer screen. He kept his eye on the downloading bar. "The information is downloading now. Ten more minutes before it is complete." he sat down. He couldn't believe this kid had done what Bobby said he was going to do. He had to admit. If the correct files came back, then Jimmy was the smartest kid he's ever met. Even smarter than him. Bobby sat down on the sofa chair. "Oh, this my favorite one, bro. He gets the cool car in this one." "Wait a minute," Twenty wasn't' a cartoon man. The only cartoon he ever watched was Dragon Ball Z, the GT series and all the DBZ movies. Vegeta's the shit. "You mean to tell me this cartoon is called Jimmy Neutron?" he asked confused. "My favorite one in the whole wide world. Helps me concentrate. I can only work while watching it." Jimmy told him. He still had his attention on the screen. Twenty raised his eyebrows. I see why they call him Jimmy Neutron. He needs the cartoon to help him work. That's the craziest shit I've ever heard. He shrugged. "If it helps, I guess." He went into the kitchen with Jeff. He made himself a plate of food. He had steak, fries, one hamburger and some grape Kool-Aid. He sat at the table with Jeff. He was working on his second hamburger and fries. "What you think about the kid?" Jeff popped a fry in his mouth. "The fact that he's nicknamed after a cartoon or the computer skills?" "The skills, of course." Twenty cut into his steak. "You think he's smarter than Tech?" "Well, Tech couldn't break-in." Jeff reminded him. "If the files are the correct documents after the download." "Then he's smarter than Tech." Twenty finished for him. "I'll say." Jeff sipped his beer. Tech counted down the last minute of the download in his mind. Two seconds, one second. "It's downloaded." He called. Tech looked the files over. Just like Bobby said. Everything was here. "Wow," he muttered. It was more information than he had asked for. Twenty and Jeff stood behind him. They got themselves a personal close up. "The kid is amazing. He even got blueprints for the concept cars. You know what we can do with all this information." he asked them. He started clicking through the files. "Tell me," Twenty wanted to know. "I hate surprises." "It's so much information here," Tech was looking at the blueprint for the McLaren MP4-RC. "We could build the cars ourselves if we had the parts." "Too bad we don't have that kind of time," Jeff said working on his beer. "But we do have time for this." Tech enlarged a particular file. "Check it out." "A key?" Twenty said confused. "How is looking the file over for a key going to help us?" "Think about it," Tech pointed at the screen. "Look, here is the cutout for each vehicle key. I can use these files to duplicate the keys on the cutout machine to create our own keys. Jimmy used the VIN numbers. So these blueprints are exactly for the cars we're lifting." "You can do that?" Twenty asked. "I told you," Tech assured him. "We could build these cars." "How fast could you make the keys?" Jeff asked. "Faster than your local Home Depot," Tech said. "Let's get started," Twenty took a bit of his steak. Delicious.

# MAN OF PEACE

Sayyid was enjoying his plane ride over to Atlanta. He has been traveling for hours. This is his second plane ride of the day. He came all the way from the Middle East. All he wanted to do was to get some sleep. The Americans on the plane were making it hard for him. He overheard them calling him harsh names for what his people had done on 9/11. He had nothing to do with that. Yet, the Americans wanted to call him names for it. One woman said, watch out he might try to take the plane over. He smiled at the thought of single-handedly taking over the plane. These Americans were crazy. With all of the security on hand. There was no way he could've taken over the plane. The thought of something like that wasn't on his mind at all. He wanted to call the woman stupid. Although, he didn't want to cause further trouble with them. They would probably arrest him for threatening her and have him hanged. He closed his eyes and began to pray. He's a Muslim and prayed daily to Muhammad. He felt someone tap him on the leg in the middle of his prayer. He slowly opened his eyes to see who had disturbed him. It was the little girl seated across the aisle. "What are you doing?" the little American girl whispered. She looked about 5yrs old. Sayyid could remember when he and his brother Al Bin Sodd were her age. Those were the harsher times in his life. They were using kids at that age for suicide bombers. They had barely escaped the torture of sacrificing themselves. Their mother and father sacrificed their own lives by becoming suicide bombers. They had to blow up some American soldiers to save their lives. That made them grow up in a war all alone. Sayyid smiled at the little girl and whispered "Praying." She smiled back and whispered. "Praying to whom?" "Muhammad," he whispered. "Who is Mohammed?" she whispered with a curious look on her face. The little girl's mother was lost in a book. She didn't realize her daughter was speaking to the Muslim stranger. The only thing she overheard her daughter say was, who is Muhammad? And that's where she wanted that conversation to end. "He's talking about Muhammad Ali honey. Now turn around and leave that bad man alone." Then she turned to the man. "Please don't speak to my little girl again." She turned around and got back into the book. The little girl looked across the aisle at the man without her mother noticing. She smiled at him again. Suddenly, Sayyid rolled his eyes to the back of his head and put his hand up like an eagle claw. The little girl was scared as shit. The man resembled a demon. She started screaming for her life. Sayyid faced forward leaning his head against the headrest and closing his eyes. The little girl's mother asked her what was wrong with her and she was pointing at the man. She was saying, bad man, over and over again. The mother jumped up from her seat. Her little girl was terrified and all she knew was that this terrorist was the problem. "What is your problem? What have you done to my little girl?" she yelled from across the aisle. "Bad man, bad man." the little girl cried. She took the inside seat. She wanted to get as far away from the man as possible. Sayyid slowly opened his eyes. "Ma'am, I'm sorry." he apologized kindly. "But I haven't done anything at all to your daughter." All of the people on the plane were paying attention to them. They started calling Sayyid names aloud because he frightened the little girl. "Yes, you did. You terrorist sonofvabitch!" She yelled at the top of her lungs while shielding her little girl. "What did you do to her! I want this man arrested!" A flight attended came to see what the commotion was about. "Excuse me, Ma'am." she said. "What's the problem?"

"This terrorist did something to my daughter." She told her. "Is she hurt?" "No, but scared for her life. I want him arrested." She ordered. "Ma'am, I can't have this man arrested if he wasn't any harm. I'll be more than happy to move you and your daughter to first class to resolve the problem." "Ok," she grabbed her daughter and the flight attended grabbed her bags. Sayyid smiled at the little girl looking back at him. He put his claw up and the she quickly turned around. He leaned his head back and smiled.

*Chapter 31*

# WEDNESDAY, LIFT DAY

Twenty looked at himself in the bathroom mirror. Today was the day the real work would begin. The eighteen-wheeler was just a warm up. The challenge up ahead is going to be much tougher. Ten cars a day for the next three days is what they had to accomplish. Ten cars today, ten cars tomorrow and Friday nine cars. Saturday, the President would be arriving in the Land Rover. That's a mission with-in itself. He figured all of the other cars had to be clear by then. He wanted to be completely focused and wanted nothing else to occupy him. They had created a list for each vehicle they would lift. Twenty would lift three a day. Jeff would lift three a day. Bobby would lift two a day. Paula would lift two and Tech will drive the eighteen-wheeler. Twenty splashed water on his face. "This is nothing Twenty." He muttered to himself. "God's will be with you. You're doing this for a reason

179

now." He turned the water off and dried his face. Tech popped in the doorway. "The keys are done. The concepts should be a breeze. Everyone is here now. We're waiting downstairs for you." "Ok," Twenty said. He hung up his towel. "I'll be down in a minute." Tech noticed the look on his face. "You good man?" "I'm cool." he said while walking past heading in the bedroom. Tech turned around to his attention. Twenty said he never wanted to lift cars again. The man just did ten years of a life sentence for what he was about to go out and do again. Knowing the danger of going back to prison. That probably had his mind swimming. Tech had never been to prison or even jail. So he couldn't begin to perceive what he was going through mentally. "Twenty, you'll get through this. Bad things happen to people who do bad. Good things happen to people who do good. You're doing a good thing, just remember that. Janet needs you. So trust me, whatever is bothering you? Shake it off and let's go make this good thing happen." Tech made him feel better about the situation. Janet needed him and by any means necessary, he was going to get her back. "Tech," Twenty patted his shoulder. "You always know how to turn something bad into something good. You're a good friend." He smiled. "At least, this time. If I go to prison all of my friends will go with me," he joked. Tech had a I don't want to go to prison look on his face.

"Um…" "Don't worry, it's not as bad as they say it is." He walked pass Tech and went out the door. Tech was left there thinking about going to prison. He snapped out of it and followed after Twenty, "You got my back right?" He called and exit the room. Paula saw Twenty, first. He was coming downstairs with Tech following. "Hey." She caught him coming down the stairs. "Twenty," Jeff said coolly. "Twenty, bro." Bobby was standing next to the bar. "I'm ready to work." "What's going on," he greeted his team. He got right to business. "Tech and I prepared the lifts for today. The cars are tagged by their area, making it safe for us after the lift. We won't have to visit the particular area again afterward. The vehicles today are located on the south side. Paula, you will lift the BMW 650i and the Porsche 991 today. Bobby, the Mercedes S63 AMG and the Mustang Boss 302. Jeff, the Mercedes CL63 AMG, Dodge Viper and the Porsche 911 Turbo. I will lift the McLaren MP4, Mustang Shelby GT500 and the Porsche 918. We will group up on the Mercedes, Mustangs and the Porsches. Better to hit them together since they're at the same locations. You already know what to do. Do anyone have a question before we crank Atlanta the fuck up?" Bobby was the only one. "Can I take the GT500 and you take the Boss 302?" "Hell no," Twenty said coolly. "I hate that fucking car new and old." "Oh," Bobby muttered to himself remembering what had happened to Twenty in a 69' Boss 302 ten years ago. "That's right." "Anyone else?" Everyone in the room was silent. "Let's do it!" Twenty said with his arms up. "Let's lift!"

# Chapter 32

# MCLAREN MP4-12C

The McLaren MP4-12C was being tested on a racetrack. They were testing the overall performance of the 3 seconds, 205mph sports car. Twenty watched the beautiful machine zip around the track from the bleachers. He had a nice seat at the top out of sight. The testers were busy with the MP4 anyway and they never noticed him. Two testers, a photographer and a cameraman. He noted every detail in his mind. This job was going to be a little tough with the workers around. He thought about waiting until everyone was on a break before he lift the car. What if they locked the vehicle up in a trailer? That would put a bend in what he was trying to do. He watched the car come to a stop in the pit area. The cameraman got a real good close up of the vehicle while the photographer snapped away. The testers were taking down notes from the test runs. That's what it seems like to him from where he was at. I know what I need to do, he thought. He surveyed the track for an opening. He spotted it and got up from his seat to make a move. He walked down the bleachers on the far end and made sure he didn't get noticed. He entered the building and made his way around to where the workers were. They still were busy with the car. He watched them through the glass. This was a private test. He noticed no one was in the building. He noticed two security guards. They were just outside of the building smoking cigarettes while watching the MP4 do its thing. "Excuse me, Sir." The track manager said from behind. "You're not supposed to be in here. The building and track are closed today. You will have to come back tomorrow." Twenty had turned around to the manager's attention. He missed one. He must've been in the restroom or something. He looked the manager over. "I'm with the MP4 team. I came in to get something to drink. The hot sun is making my mouth dry." "You're with the McLaren team?" the manager asked sarcastically. "I didn't notice you when they first came in." he flipped out his phone. "Let me check. What is your name?" he looked down at his phone pressing numbers. Twenty didn't answer. "Sir, what is your-" he was cut off by a mouth full of fist. Twenty knocked the little guy out with one blow. He caught his body in his arms so the man wouldn't have a hard fall and alert the security. "Twenty," he muttered dragging him to a nearby closet. "And I'm not on the list." he placed the manager in the closet standing him straight up. He read his name tag. "Danny." He shut the closet door. He went back to the window. The two security guards were still smoking. He opened the back door. "Hey, guys." He called over to them. The guards looked in his direction. "Danny said go ahead and take an hour lunch break." They put their cigarettes out and walked over to him. One spoke. "Who are you?" "I'm with the MP4 team. I got here kind of late. Danny let me in after he checked out. He told me to tell you. Head to lunch." "Danny said that?" "Yeah, and he's pissed. Both of you keep smoking cigarettes on the job." Twenty lied hoping it would work. "He always gets mad about us smoking." He turned to the other security guard. "C'mon, let's go grab a bit to eat." They walked off. Twenty waited for them to completely leave the building. "Gone," he watched them pull away. He heard a noise behind him. He left to the back area. He peeped around the corner. A tester was getting a drink from the soda machine. He smiled while walking towards him. "I need this racing suit." He had his 9 pointed at the back of his head. "Excuse me," he turned around and met the beautiful chrome. He dropped his drink from being scared to death. "I said I need that suit." Twenty repeated. The tester didn't want to get shot, but the idiot wasn't quite using his head. He gripped his helmet and swung.

*Chapter 33*

# BMW 650I CONVERTIBLE

Paula was dressed to kill. She was wearing a tight mini skirt, her sun hat, Gucci purse and red bottom heels that matched. She had her body lotion and was smelling extremely pleasant. She had a too die for walk, that any man in their right mind knew she's the perfect catch. She walked around the dealership casually looking for the BMW 650i. The dealership had many wonderful cars to choose from. No one came out to help her. She ran her finger along the cars as she passed them while keeping an eye out for the BMW. She wasn't a BMW driver. She thought most of the cars were beautiful although. She needed to get a salesman›s attention. That was the only way this lift was going to work. She didn't want an old salesman. She needed one that wanted her more than she wanted the car. She walked slowly and seductively in front of the dealership trying to get noticed. The way her hips and voluptuous ass moved that wasn't a problem. Three salesmen came out of the building all wanting to assist her. One was an older man, about fifty something years old. The other was a woman and she looked like she dated women by the way she dressed and walked. The last was a young male with a nice haircut and suit. He looked around twenty-four. She didn't want to ruin his career early so she went with the old man. He got his time in, she thought. "Excuse me," Paula waved signaling to the older man. "Can you please help me with a purchase?" she asked nicely. "Told you," he muttered to his co-workers. "The old man still got it." He walked away from them and over to Paula with his hand out. "Yes Ma'am, my name is Brent. How can I assist you today?" Paula shook his hand. "Thank you so much for helping me, Brent. I want to buy a car. There are so many to choose from, though." "Well, Ma'am." Brent was admiring her amazing figure. "You asked for the right guy. I'm guessing your favorite color is red?" Paula knew she had the old geezer where she wanted him. She caught him staring at her chest and well lotion legs. She played it like she didn't notice him. "Yes, it is." she smiled warmly. They turned away from the building and started looking through the vehicles. She knew exactly the vehicle she wanted. She didn't want it to be obvious, of course. "I like convertibles," she told him with a smile.

"That's a start," Brent said following her through the cars watching her ass move side to side. She turned around and he hurried to look up. Not wishing to get caught. "Red and convertible. Check this one out Ma'am." He pointed to a red convertible 3 series. "Nah," She walked away seductively knowing the old guy was checking her butt out. "I don't like that one." She spotted a red 650i convertible. That's the one, she thought. She walked over to it. "What kind of car is this one?" she already knew what it was. He followed her over while covering up the hard on in his pants from thinking about a chance to have sex with her. "That's the 650i. It's a beautiful car, isn't it?" Paula was reading the numbers paper on the window. "What's twin turbocharged?" something she already knew. "Means it has a twin turbo system which makes the car faster." He said coolly. "Ninety-one thousand." She gawked at the price. "I'll take it. Can we test drive it?" she pulled at his tie seductively. "Please, Brent." She whined. "I'll get the key." Brent went off to get the key. He returned and Paula hopped in the driver seat. She pulled out of the dealership. She hit the open road and punched it all the way to 150mph. Brent was scared for his life and the car. "Ma'am, please slow down and take me back to the dealer." Paula started laughing. "You're not having fun Brent?" she skidded the car sideways. She took her hat off and let her hair down. She dropped the top. "Ma'am, please!" She ignored him and put on her red lipstick. "That's better." she grabbed her pistol from her purse and aimed it at him. "I'll take it." She popped the locks signaling for him to get out. "Bye, Brent!" after he exited the vehicle she performed a burnout. She left a cloud of smoke circled around him before she sped off. Brent thought it was fucked up. He was cool, although. He had the experience of a lifetime.

*Chapter 34*

# MERCEDES S63 AMG/ CLS63 AMG

"So you were the best huh?" Jeff asked Bobby while they walked to the Mercedes dealership. "That's what they were saying bro," Bobby responded. "I can't believe your little brother is that smart." Jeff saw the dealership come into view. Jeff parked his truck four blocks down just to be on the safe side. They were the first team to pair up. "Jimmy is the smartest person I know bro." Bobby noticed the dealership. "He takes after our father." "How did you get into lifting cars for a living?" Jeff asked. "With your brother being a genius and all. Don't you think you're setting a bad example for him?" "Bro," Bobby sounded serious. "Jimmy's the one who convinced me." Jeff looked shocked. He was thinking about the kid convincing his older brother to lift cars. The answer took him totally off guard. "How did your brother convince you to lift cars? That's something I have to know if you don't mind." "T.V. bro," Bobby replied. "He loves cars. One day he was doing research on car thieves. He was only eight then. Five years ago to be exact. He pulled up the greatest car thieves of all time. He stumbled across Twenty. He was considered the number one guy. Jimmy researched everything about him. That's how I found out about the Lifters. For some reason, Jimmy wanted to be like Twenty. He wanted to be a tough guy. So I went out and stole my first car and told my brother about it. I wanted him to look up to me like he did Twenty. I wanted to be a Lifter like him. I wanted to be better than him. Jimmy said he could do it. Make me better than him. Twenty was already gone five years before. There was no one else until I stepped up." "Touching," Jeff said sarcastically stepping in front of the dealership. "Still closed." He looked at his watch. "We got one hour until it opens." "More than enough time bro." Bobby stepped next to him. "How you want to do it?" Jeff smirked. "Watch the master." Jeff hopped over the little rail. "C'mon," he walked to the door. "What you're waiting for… the weekend?" Bobby hopped over the little rail. He followed Jeff through the parking lot. Jeff seemed to be walking right up to the front door. I know that's not what I think it is, he thought. Bobby stopped and turned around. "Shit!" somebody was coming through the front gate. "Jeff!" he called. "Somebody's coming!" Bobby ducked off behind a Mercedes. Jeff turned around. "What?" he barely heard Bobby, he had got a good distance away. He noticed the car pulling in. "Damn," he muttered and ducked off in cover. He crept around to Bobby. "I thought you said we had an hour?" Bobby whispered to him. "Someone probably opened the place up an hour ahead to set up." He whispered back. "I got an idea bro." Bobby crept around to get a good view. He was watching the car park. "What you got in mind?" Jeff crept up behind him. "Watch the master," Bobby whispered to him. A male emerged from the vehicle. He walked over to the front door. Bobby pulled out his Beretta. It was time. "Bobby," Jeff whispered. He didn't want Bobby to do anything stupid like kill someone. They wouldn't be able to lift the vehicles. Somebody would probably hear the gun fire. Bobby paid Jeff no attention. He needed to act before it would be too late. The man didn't notice him creeping up. He opened the door and went through. Bobby caught it just before it closed. "Excuse me." Bobby held the man at gunpoint. He dropped everything. "Oh my God!" he looked like he was about to have a heart attack. Jeff came through the door. He noticed Bobby holding the man up. "Good work." He shrugged. "I'll get the doors so we can drive the cars out." "Gotcha, bro." Jeff opened the doors. Bobby tied the man to a chair so he couldn't alert the law after he disabled the alarm for the building. He hopped in the Benz. Bobby spoke with his head out the window of the S63 AMG. "Thanks for the hand bro." then sped out behind Jeff.

*Chapter 35*

# TEST DRIVER

Twenty ducked swiftly and countered with a kick to the tester's stomach. The tester flew backward up against the soda machine. He fell down onto his butt while dropping his helmet and holding his stomach. "Ah." he groaned heavily. He was trying to catch his breath. His stomach hurt like hell and it felt like he had to take a mean shit. Talking about kicking the shit out of somebody, he thought. Twenty had kicked the wind completely from his lungs. He didn't know what was going on. He watched Twenty stand over him with a weapon. "Please don't kill me. I… I have a family." He cried. "Man," Twenty shook his head at the tester. "I don't want to kill you. All I want is the suit you're wearing." "My suit?" the tester was confused. "All you want is this stupid suit and you'll let me go?" "All I want is your suit and I'll let you live, not go." Twenty told him. "I mean, I'll let you go after I'm finished doing what I have to do." "Ok," the tester was ok with that. Take the suit, he thought. As long as I'm going to make it out of this situation alive. "You got yourself a deal." Twenty reached down and helped the guy up. "Sorry about that." That tester came to a full stand. "It's my own fault. No need to apologize. When a guy has a gun pointed at you. The first thing you should do if he doesn't shoot is give him what he wants, right?" he slid off the driving suit. Twenty laughed a little. "I would guess so." The guy had the suit off and gave it to him. "Good man." The tester wondered what Twenty wanted with the suit. He almost got his head blown off for it. It wouldn't hurt to ask. He seemed like a nice enough criminal. "Now what?" Twenty didn't answer. He just fitted himself inside the suit. "Perfect," he muttered zipping it up. "Why do you need the suit?" he was curious. "Is it that important that you had to put a gun in my face?" "You're an investigator now?" Twenty asked. "Yes, it's that important. Come with me," he waved the gun at him. He opened another closet. "Get in." "What?" He had a confused look on his face. "Get in and count to one thousand." He ordered. "When you're finished. You can come out and do whatever you want." "That's it and you'll let me go?" the tester was worried about getting into the closet. "That's it and you can go." Twenty picked up his drink. "Take that with you. You might get thirsty in there." The tester took his drink and got in the closet. Twenty grabbed a chair and prompt it up against the knob just in case. He might get brave and make a run for it. The tester couldn't believe what just happened to him. He was robbed at gunpoint for his racing suit. Then put in a closet and ordered to count to one thousand. The guy was even nice enough to give him his drink. He tried the door knob after he heard Twenty walk off. "Fuck," he muttered. "I knew it." He locked me in, he thought. At least, he didn't kill me. He shrugged and opened his drink. The drink sizzled and exploded all over him. Twenty walked over and grabbed the racing helmet off the ground. He put it on and left out towards the track. He noticed the car was racing around the track. He waited where the other tester was standing. The cameraman came up to him. "It's about time you got back." Twenty nodded at him. Speaking was not an option. C'mon with the damn car, he thought. "What took you so long in there? Bill had to take your turn." Twenty still didn't answer. He gestured his hands and arms like I don't know. The car finally came around. Twenty walked away from the cameraman to greet the other tester as he got out. "What took you so long," he asked? "I had to take an extra lap." Twenty didn't respond to him either. He got in the McLaren MP4-12C and shut the door. The tester walked over the cameraman. "What's his problem?"

"Probably had something bad to drink." He joked. Twenty floored the MP4. He was speeding around the track at 200mph. He saw his opening and the MP4 was gone for good. See ya!

# SECOND RUN

**T**wenty drifted the McLaren sideways onto the road. "Forty yard dash baby," he muttered spotting Tech up ahead with the lift on the eighteen-wheeler down. He shifted back into first gear. The McLaren was a beast. The best car he's ever driven in his life. The McLaren had him ready to lift the other concept cars. He hated thinking about it. He felt his adrenaline pumping as he sped from 0 to 60 in 3 seconds flat. He slowed the MP4 down and the rear wing lifted 32 degrees for an enhanced down force that acted as an air brake. He carefully pulled up the ramp and parked in the back of the trailer. He swept his hand along a flush surface and the insect-wing door opened. "What a car," he shut the door. He exited the trailer and hit the side with a closed fist signaling for Tech to close the lift. Twenty watched the first car disappear inside the trailer. He walked around and jumped in the passenger seat.

"Let's go." Tech fired up the eighteen-wheeler and they headed back to the garage. Twenty told Tech the whole story about the lift on the way back. The lift went perfectly. They had no encounters with the law on the way back. Tech pulled into the garage parking lot at the same time Paula did. "Look at her." Tech was admiring her beauty. Twenty hopped from the truck and watched Paula emerge from the BMW. "Dayum." He muttered noticing her sexy figure. Tech lowered the lift. Twenty and Paula pulled the two cars into the garage. They heard two cars racing in the parking lot. Twenty turned to the Mercedes CLS63 AMG and slowly pulling in followed by the S63 AMG. Jeff hopped out of the CLS63 AMG and hurried over to Bobby emerging from the Benz. "I told you I was going to smoke you! Where's my hundred dollars?" he said while tapping the hood. "You got lucky bro." Bobby reached into his wallet to give Jeff his money. "I'll get you next time." "Yeah," Jeff said coolly. "I had to show this young buck how to drive like a man." Everyone started laughing. Bobby started checking out the MP4. "What a badass looking car bro," he said aloud. "Drives like a Formula 1 car too." Twenty told him walking up next to him. "Watch this," he swept his hand along the smooth surface tucked under the side scoop upper edge. The MP4 dramatic insect-wing door opened. "Insect-wing doors." Twenty told him. Everyone came over to check the car out. "Bro," Bobby was amazed. "That's the coolest ever." Tech looked at his watch. "Guys, it is 9:05 am. The mustang dealer opens at ten. You two need to be on the move." He pointed at Twenty and Bobby. He turned his attention to Jeff. "The Dodge dealer is open. You have to figure out how to snatch one of those new Vipers. A little test drive wouldn't hurt. Paula, you're on break until later so you can give Jeff a lift over. I'll give Twenty and Bobby a lift in the eighteen-wheeler. I want to be ready for when they're on the way out." Tech grabbed the keys for the mustangs. "You're going to need these. You lose them and you'll have to find the other at the dealer. When you get in the building the security code is 9,9,4,2. I'll remind you before you get out." he handed Twenty and Bobby a key. "Let's move." They all locked the place up tight. They covered the cars so no one would peep in and notice them. Tech would look them over later and then move them to El' Nino's garage.

*Chapter 37*

# SHELBY GT500/BOSS 302

Twenty thought it would be a great idea to lift the Mustangs from the dealer he got arrested in ten years ago. He knew the place well and it was a convenience being in the area they were working. The second car of the day, he thought. You get this one and you're two for two Twenty. Get the Porsche tonight and I would say you're on a roll. He thought about the situation he was in while looking out of the passenger side window. He listened to Tech and Bobby talk about how cool the MP4 was the entire way to the Mustang dealer as he thought. They were about two more minutes away from the dealer when his stomach began to turn. He started to feel sick as he got closer to the dealership. Maybe it isn't a good idea to hit the same dealer, he thought. Just thinking about going back in gave him the creeps. He felt like he needed to throw-up. He let the window down. All I need is some fresh air and I'm good.

If Tech knew how to lift cars. He would've sent him in his place. Tech parked the truck. "Y'all ready?" he looked over to the dealer. It only took them fifteen minutes to make the drive over to the Mustang dealer from the garage. Tech checked his watch. "Twenty minutes to make this happen." "Ready bro," Bobby assured him. Twenty got out of the truck. "Let's get this over with. I hate this fucking place." "Remember," Tech said from the driver seat. "The code is 9, 9, 4, 2." "Got it bro," Bobby got out behind Twenty. "9, 9, 4, 2." "Follow me," Twenty ordered. "I know the way in through the back door." "Back door it is." Bobby followed Twenty across the street. If only Jimmy could see me now, he thought. My second job with Twenty, but this time. I actually get to lift a car with him. Twenty and I side by side bro. I still can't believe I'm a Lifter. Nothing can top this. The best working with the Legend. This was the best moment in Bobby's life and he would cherish it forever. Twenty crept up to the back door of the dealership. He used his lock pick tool to enter the exact same way as the last time. The lock clicked with ease. "That was awesome bro," Bobby watched him successfully pick the lock. "You have to teach me how to do that one day." He whispered. Twenty opened the door. No one was home and they only had about fifteen more minutes. In his mind, everything that happened here ten years ago was happening again. This time, he had Bobby with him. They entered and Twenty gave Bobby direct orders. "You go to lift the door so we can drive the cars out. While you do that I'll take care of the alarm. Got that?" "Ten-four," Bobby said and hurried over to the door. Twenty remembered where the pad was. He went right over to it. He remembered the code without any problem. He punched 9, 9, 4, 2 and the pad lit green. Suddenly, he heard noise coming from the front. "Bobby," he called to him. "Somebody's coming, hide." Twenty ducked behind the GT500. "Shit," Bobby had the door halfway open and shut it back down and hid. They watched a man enter. He hurried over to the pad. He entered the code and it didn't light up. He entered it again looking confused. Nothing. "Ah fuck it," they heard him say angrily. "I got to go." He ran into the men's restroom. Twenty pulled out the nine and hurried over to the restroom door. When he got there and was about to open it. He heard the man and froze up. "Ah, that's better. Dropping the kids off at the pool, honey." Twenty smelt an atrocious smell. He backed away. "He's shittin'. Hurry up and get the door." They got in the Mustangs and the keys work without a problem. Twenty burnt out and so did Bobby. Successfully completing the second lift.

*Chapter 38*

# DODGE VIPER

Paula drove Jeff over to the Dodge dealership in her Lexus IS-F. She was silent for most of the ride. She had a lot on her mind and Twenty was one of them. She successfully completed her first lift. That was something she was proud of. She was one step closer to getting her daughter back. As she drove she began to think about her daughter more and more. She was only ten years old. Paula thought about things that happened to little girls that age that got kidnapped. Janet was innocent and the thought brought tears to her eyes. Jeff noticed Paula getting emotional from the passenger seat. He knew exactly what was bothering her. He finally broke the silence. "Honey, please don't cry. You have to be strong. We're going to get her back, I promise." He put his hand on her shoulder to comfort her. Paula pulled into a plaza down the street from the dealer. "How do you know for sure Jeff? Those men could be doing anything to her. She's only ten." Paula couldn't help the tears streaming down her face. Paula was right. Janet was lonely ten and they could easily be taking advantage of her. He couldn't allow Paula to think like that. "You can't think like that. This Mexican they call El' Nino wants the cars. We're doing well so far. We have to keep that up in order to get her back. Twenty, Tech, Bobby, me and I know you most of all you, won't let her down. Three more days and that's it. We'll have our little girl back.""Ok,"Paula whispered.Jeff massaged her then kissed her on the cheek. "Ok," he whispered before he got out of the car. He had a Dodge Viper that was calling his name to be lifted. Jeff hurried over to the dealership. Two Dodge Vipers were parked directly in front of the entrance to the building displaying the new vehicles for sale. He entered the dealership casually. He scanned the room for the perfect sales person to take on the test drive. You, he thought while noticing a pretty young lady at her desk. He walked over. "Excuse me, ma'am. I'm trying to see what I have to do to purchase one of those new Vipers?" he wasn't worried about the cameras in the building. He had his hat low and his mirrored shades on. The sales woman told him to have a seat. "Why sure, I can help you with that." Jeff wanted to make her feel comfortable with him. He softened her up a bit as they casually talked about the Viper and its features. Suddenly, the door flew open and a loud man entered. "Shawdy!" the man yelled through the building. "I'm tryin' to cop one of them mafuckin' new Vipers, shawdy!" Jeff turned to the loud man's attention. He noticed the man had on a lot of jewelry. Diamonds in every piece that made him look like an ice show. He had a huge man with him. Maybe a bodyguard, he thought because the man with the ice on resembled a rapper. Jeff noticed a bag in the large man's hand. "Shawdy!" he yelled again. "I got mafuckin' cash out this bitch! Somebody better come get this money!" The sales person next to them assisted the loud man. Jeff overheard everything. He was definitely buying the car with cash. When the salesman said, let me get the key to your new ride. Jeff had a new plan. "I'm going to think the purchase over." Then he hurried back to Paula. Paula looked confused. "What happened?" "New plan." He told her. "The car is coming to us." He pointed toward the dealer. "Watch." Five minutes later the new Viper pulled out of the dealer. "Follow it." Jeff got his pistol ready. Paula followed the Viper a safe distance for ten minutes before she whipped in front of it. Jeff hopped out and ran around to the driver side aiming his weapon. "Get out!"

he ordered. "Now!" "Shawdy man, I just bought this." He cried. "You gon' do a brotha like this? We supposed to stay down, shawdy." "Get out or catch some hot ones… Shawdy." he aimed at the man through the window. He could see the man was scared to death and he got out. Jeff got in the car while still aiming at the man. "Shawdy don't do me like this!" "Holla," Jeff sped off.

# Chapter 39

# 918, 911, 991

Twenty and Bobby were unloading the Mustangs. Tech opened the garaged for them and Twenty parked the Shelby GT500 next to the McLaren. Bobby pulled in next to him. Twenty got out and he looked at the line of cars. "Looks like we're still in business." He told Tech. Tech was shutting the garage door. "Feel good doesn't it?" Tech loved the idea of lifting cars. He never felt bad about doing it either. He felt like an American badass working beside his main man Twenty. Bobby shut the door to the Boss 302. "I love doing this job. I'm sorry bro, but lifting cars is the job for me." Twenty walked over to the refrigerator and got some beer for everyone. The second run was complete. One more tonight, then on to day two. He tossed them both a beer. "Tech, what's it looking like for tonight?" Twenty wanted to know the details of their next mission. Tech worked on his beer while walking over to the computer. "The Porsches are in a warehouse located in the back of the dealer. After the dealer closes tonight so getting the cars should be a piece of pie." "It's a piece of cake bro." Bobby corrected him. "Same thing," Tech said. "Cake, pie, it's still a piece." "True," Twenty took a gulp of his beer. He heard a car horn at the garage door. "Jeff and Paula are back." Tech put his beer down and walked over to open the garage door. Jeff blew the Viper's horn as he entered. "Jeff," Tech said coolly as he pulled in to park the Dodge Viper. Jeff shut the car off and hopped out. "And this one is paid for. Cash shawdy." He joked. He noticed everyone had beers. "I must be late for the party?" "The way you pulled in on us in that cool ass car. I would say the party is just getting started." Twenty handed him a beer. Jeff gave him a toast. "The celebrity's always show up late anyway." Paula came in through the front door and flopped down on the couch. "So what time are we moving out tonight?" "Best if we go around one in the morning," Tech told her. "The place will be well closed by then." "While we're waiting, let's start inspecting the cars. Then we'll move them to the other garage." Twenty finished off his beer and uncovered the McLaren. "We'll all pitch in and help Tech." They started inspecting the vehicles. All of the vehicles were perfect. They moved the vehicles to El' Nino's garage two at a time. That was all that would fit in the back of the eighteen-wheeler without being bumper to bumper. They finished around five o'clock in the afternoon. Bobby was done for the day. Twenty told him to go home and get some rest. Bobby friend came through to buy the computers when they were inspecting the cars. He paid out $100,000. Twenty gave Tech, Jeff and Paula $5,000 apiece. He made $42,500 and so did Bobby because they actually did the lift themselves. When you're a Lifter, everyone makes money even if you didn't take part. That's the way Twenty rolled. Everyone would eat and stay happy. Twenty watched the news for about an hour. The area was hot just as he thought it would be. Seven cars lifted in the same area all in the morning. The plan had worked out perfect. Now they would strike at night and turn away from that first area completely. Tomorrow would be an entirely new playing field. Tech worked at the computer and Paula took Jeff to pick up his truck. Twenty stretched out on the couch and turned to NBA playoffs. He watched an entire game. The Lakers lose to Dallas. "Dayum," he muttered. He would never have thought. "The Lakers are out of the playoffs." He called to Tech. "Really?" Tech was amazed. "No way." "Yep," Twenty said. He was looking at the stats. "Dallas swept their ass four-O." he finished watching Sports Center until he fell asleep.

***

"You have the cutters?" Tech asked Twenty. They were preparing themselves for the Porsche lifts. It was thirty minutes until one. Paula and Jeff had just arrived. Twenty held up the cutters. "Right here boss. You got the keys?" Tech opened his right hand and revealed three fresh cut Porsche keys. "Can't drive without them." He gave Twenty the key for the 918, Jeff the 911 and Paula the 991. "Can't wait." Jeff looked the key over. "What's the code once we get inside?" Paula tucked the key in her pocket. "That's the trick," Tech gave her his attention. "You have to phone the security team at Porsche and verify that you're the manager. There is no keypad system with this one." "You mean," Twenty spoke up. "You would have to phone a security team at Porsche's main office as the manager to disable the alarm?" "Correct," Tech assured him. Jeff exhaled thinking about the odd situation. "So you're saying there is no way we can disable it and once we get to the cars. We're going to have to make a run for it or go to prison forever?" "Sounds about right," Tech answered. Jeff shrugged. "I'm game." "Twenty," Tech said. "Your car is the fastest one of the bunch. We only have room for two of the vehicles to fit in the trailer so you're going to have to race back here without killing the car or yourself." "Fun," Twenty said sarcastically. "How much time do I have after we get in the warehouse?" "I hate to say it," Tech said seriously. "But three minutes before the alarm sounds and the police come." Twenty knew for a fact that he's the best driver out of the bunch. If anybody was going to get the job done, it's going to be him. "Let's move." Fifteen minutes later, Twenty, Jeff and Paula were at the Porsche dealer. They crept around to the dealer warehouse where the cars were stored for the night. Twenty looked at the lock on the garage door. "Hand me the lock cutter." He told Jeff. Jeff handed him the cutter. "Find the cars quickly and hurry to the trailer. Remember, we only have three minutes." They nodded and he began cutting the lock. The lock popped. "Jeff," he signaled for him to lift up the garage. Jeff turned the hatch and lifted the garage door. "Move." Twenty stepped into the garage. There were over a hundred beautiful Porsche's to choose from. The sight was truly amazing. If you wanted a Porsche, it was in here. "Found mine," Jeff called. He noticed the Porsche 911 Turbo and hurried over to it. There were at least ten lined in the second row. Paula hurried through the cars searching for the 991. It was one of the newer versions and there weren't many of them out. "Bingo," she found what she was looking for. It was on the opposite end of the warehouse. "Where the fuck is it," Twenty mumbled. He was scanning the cars as fast as he could. The Porsche 918 was the newest Porsche to date. The car wasn't even out. There was only one in the warehouse and he spotted it with one minute left to go. It was on the opposite end from Paula. Jeff pulled the Porsche up and yelled. "One minute hurry!" he drove the car out of the warehouse to meet with Tech. Twenty got to the Porsche and stuck the key in the door. What the? The key wasn't working. He wiggled the key and tried again. Nothing. He pulled the key out. "Why in the hell are you not working?" he muttered to the key. Maybe it was cut wrong? How could Tech make a mistake like that? He had about thirty seconds left before the alarm sounded. He needed to abandon ship. He scanned the key. The little piece of paper taped on the back read, 991. "Shit!" Tech handed him the wrong key. He turned to Paula's attention at the other end of the warehouse. She was definitely having her problems trying to open the door to the 991. He ran over. "Wrong key!" Paula looked at her key. "Wrong key?" she read the taped paper on the key, 918. Twenty made the swap with Paula and bolted back to the 918. He heard the 991 fire up while on the move. The keys do work, he thought. He got to the 918 and inserted the key into the keyhole. The key worked. That's one less thing to worry about. He got in and saw Paula whipping the car through the warehouse toward the door. He fired up the Porsche at the same time the red lights in the warehouse flashed on and off with a loud horn sounding. "Fuck." The cops were on the way. He maneuvered the exotic sports car through the garage toward the opening. He floored the pedal exiting the warehouse. The 600hp pumping out of the motor sounded like an animal. He flew through the parking lot ahead of the dealer. He saw the eighteen-wheeler close in Paula as the cops passed. They passed right by, he skidded the 918 onto the main street headed in the opposite direction. They're safe, he thought as the cops automatically noticed him drifting the sports car from the dealer's parking lot. He looked through the rear view and it was just what he thought would happen. The cops were giving chase. There was at least, five of them behind him. They were in the new police Chargers. This run wasn't going to be that easy. The chargers were fast, but they couldn't touch the 918 and there was absolutely no way in hell Twenty was going back to prison. He maneuvered the true mid-engine concept through the road speeding away from the police. He made a quick turn up ahead and drifted the car all the way out of the turn. He shifted into first gear and punched it. The car responded with a 0 to 60 burst in 3 seconds. The 918 was faster than what he had thought. Maybe faster than the McLaren he lifted earlier. He noticed the police bending the corner as he approached

180mph. There was no way they would catch him. He was too skilled of a driver and it was too fast of a car. He turned his attention back to the road ahead. "Don't tell me?" he muttered to himself. The police were two steps ahead. There was a roadblock set up with more police waiting. The officers were shielded and their guns were drawn. Twenty hit the brakes and stopped thirty yards from them. There were no other exits on the straight road. Think, Twenty. He checked the rearview. The police were closing in on him. In five second he would be cuffed and back off to prison. Fuck that, he thought while shifting the car into reverse. He floored the pedal heading straight at the pursuing Chargers. "Do or die," he said one second away from colliding with the first vehicle. The officer swerved off the road and so did the others. Not wishing to test death. Twenty smiled as he rushed through the swerving vehicles clearing the way. He maneuvered the 918 one hundred and eighty degrees and smashed the gas. "Whoa!" he said excitedly looking through the rearview at all of the off balanced vehicles. He felt like Batman or maybe more like the Joker as he made his getaway. He looked back and there wasn't any police in sight. Just to be safe, he bent two more corners. That was a close one, he thought. He felt his nerves beginning to relax, his heart was beating faster than the Porsche. The feeling had him shook. He got back to the garage safely and blew the horn at the door. The door opened for him. He pulled the car in and was greeted by everyone. He shut the car off and exhaled. He opened the gullwing door. "Exciting," he muttered. He emerged from the vehicle. He noticed that everyone had a worried look on their face. They probably thought without a doubt in their minds, he was going back to prison. Twenty smiled at his friends. "Why the worried looks?"

*Chapter 40*

# AVENTADOR/GALLARDO

Yesterday was successful, today is the second day of their mission and it needed to go just as well. The alarm went off and Twenty woke from the sound ringing in his ears. He reached over to the nightstand and turned it off. Time to get Thursday started. It was five in the morning and everyone would be on their way in an hour. He got up and took a nice thirty minute shower and then got dressed. He went downstairs to make a pot of coffee. He was greeted by Tech working at the computer. "Dayum, you're here early." "Better early than late." Tech held up his mug. "Coffee?" "Yeah," Twenty walked over to the pot. "I was just thinking about that." "I talked with everyone." Tech sipped his hot coffee. "They should be here in ten." "Great," he muttered pouring himself a cup. He took a sip. "Um, not bad." They went over today's plan for the next couple of minutes. There was a knock at the door.

Tech went over to answer it. Jeff and Paula had arrived. "What's up?" Jeff greeted Tech. "Hey, Tech." Paula greeted him warmly. "Bobby just pulled up so you might not want to shut the door just yet." "Hey, guys." Tech greeted them. He looked out towards the parking lot and noticed Bobby getting out of his Hellcat. "Hurry up, I don't have all day." He joked. "What's up?" Twenty greeted. He was still half sleep. "Ready for the day," Jeff responded. "Nothing much," Paula walked over to the coffee pot. "Tech made this?" she asked. "Yep," Twenty told her. "I'm good then." Paula sat the pot back down. "He always makes it to strong." "That's the only way I like it," Twenty said. "Strong." Bobby walked in. "Bro's," he said like he was on a strong cup of coffee himself. "Bobby," Twenty greeted him by coolly raising his mug in attention. Everyone else greeted the coolest white boy they had ever met. They all gathered around the computer and Tech informed them about the lifts. Tech filled them all in on what they were lifting. "Twenty, the Lamborghini Aventador, the Jaguar C-X75 and the Nissan-Renault DeZir. Jeff, the Gallardo, Camaro HP-ZL1 and the Aston Martin V-12 Vantage. Paula, Lexus LFA and the Nissan GT-R. Bobby, you're lifting the Corvette C7 and the Hennessey CTS V700." Twenty and Jeff were up first. Tech drove them in the eighteen-wheeler to the Lamborghini dealer. Tech parked the truck a little ways up the street. He didn't want to make it too obvious by parking directly in front of the place. They hopped out and made their way over to the dealer. They broke in through the back door. Twenty found the keypad. "8, 5, 7, 4, 3, 4." He punched the code Tech had given him while Jeff lifted the garage door. Twenty scanned the exotic cars for the Aventador. "Dayum," he was gawking at the fascinating sports car. Jeff stood next to him. "Remind me to lift one of these for myself," he said eyeing the car. "There we go." He turned his attention to the Gallardo. "But I'll settle for one of those if I have to." He made his way over to it. Twenty checked his key. It was the correct one this time. He didn't want to go through what happened last time ever again. He got in the Aventador and drove the car out of the garage follow by Jeff. They hit the road heading towards Tech. One more light ahead and they were good. The light turned red and Twenty didn't care. He was going to run it anyway until he saw a cop parked at a store nearby. "Dayum," he had to stop at the light. He slowed down. He was hoping it would turn green, but it didn't. He stopped at the light and Jeff stopped behind him. Two fresh ass Lambo's at 6 o'clock in the morning, at the same light, obviously the cop would try them. Twenty prepared to smash the gas and bolt. That cruiser couldn't catch them with two motors in it. He glanced over at the cop car. "What?" he noticed the cop getting down with what seemed to be a naked lady. The cop was getting his groove on with a prostitute. She was all over him. She was riding him like a bull in the driver's seat. The light turned green and he pulled off and safely made it to Tech. Jeff pulled in behind him. "You see that?"

*Chapter 41*

# CAMARO HP-ZL1 CORVETTE C7

Tech pulled the eighteen-wheeler around back. That lift could've turned out to be an all-out chase if the officer would've been on his job. They unloaded the exotic cars into the garage. Bobby lifted up the garage for them. "Sweet wheels bro," he said as Twenty pulled the Aventador into the garage. Twenty parked the vehicle and got out. "I love the sound of that motor." Jeff had lined the Gallardo right next to it. "I need some more coffee," he said emerging from the vehicle. Tech closed the lift on the truck and got out. "Home sweet home." He said walking into the garage. "Yes, it is and the day is only getting started. "Paula watched the geek close the garage door. "That is true," Tech agreed. He walked over to his workstation. "There's more work for us to do." he clicked the mouse searching for the address for the Camaro and the Corvette. "Jeff you're up and you will be working with Bobby. The good thing is that we're done with dealerships and the bad thing is these cars are in a rich neighborhood. The cool thing is that the cars were given to the MVP of MLB. He plays for the Atlanta Braves and he won't be home because they're on the road this week. I've made keys for both vehicles." Tech handed them the keys. "Let's get a move on." "Cool bro," Bobby said excitedly. "We're about to lift cars off the MVP. This is the coolest job ever bro." "Remind me to keep Bobby on the team if I decide to continue lifting after this." Twenty whispered to Paula. "He really likes doing this for a living." He said sarcastically. Paula smiled at Twenty. "Me too," and winked at him. Paula, Jeff and Bobby pulled up outside of the rich neighborhood. Paula drove the eighteen-wheeler so Tech could start inspecting the Lamborghinis. Paula shut the truck off. "Be safe and hurry up. I hate rich folk." "Why is that?" Bobby asked while getting out of the truck. Paula smirked. "Cause I'm not, now go." "Bye honey," Jeff said while kissing her on the cheek. He exited the truck. They hurried through the neighborhood following the mailbox numbers. The houses were huge and beautiful. "One more," Jeff walked pass a mailbox while counting the address. They stepped in front of a huge mansion. "Bro," Bobby was amazed by the wonderful mansion. "This is his home? We're in front of the league's MVP mansion bro." "Um hum," Jeff answered with sarcasm. "And we're about to lift his cars too. C'mon." Jeff led the way. They stepped in front of a huge backyard garage. "Watch my back while I pick the lock." "Got you bro." Bobby turned around and surveyed the scene. Ten minutes later, Jeff got it. They were in. "Shit, ya boy got some nice cars." "Baseball money, bro," Bobby replied. "Why didn't I play sports?" Jeff said skeptically. "Camaro, anyone?" he asked himself stepping in front of the new HP-ZL1. "Bro, it has the split back window like the 65' Sting Ray," Bobby said stepping around the Corvette C7. Bobby went to lift the garage door. "Bro!" Jeff turned to his attention. He noticed the baseball player had step out on his back porch. He's home? Jeff got a good look at him. The MVP had a cast on his leg and a shotgun aimed at them from forty yards away. He started limping towards them. "Get off my property!" he yelled while slowly limping. "Bro!" Bobby yelled. "Help!" two baby pit bulls were locked on Bobby's pant leg. He tried his best to shake them off. They were around four months old. Jeff noticed Bobby struggling with the dogs. He ran over and grabbed one by the tail and swung him off. He looked back and saw the baseball player closing in. He grabbed the other and swung him off as well. "Get your filthy hands off my dogs!" he yelled from 25 yards out and fired a shot. "Bobby!" Jeff ran to the ZL1. "Hurry!" he hopped in and fired the motor. Bobby got in the Corvette just in time. He sped out of the garage behind Jeff and almost ran over the MVP. He fell to the ground as his cars sped off. "My cars!"

# LEXUS LFA

"You should have seen him," Jeff told Twenty. "He was screaming for is life." he acted out Bobby struggling with the baby pit bulls. "Help Jeff, help!" he joked. They all started laughing. "Hey bro," Bobby tried to defend himself. "Those little critters were vicious. I have teeth marks to prove it." Bobby lifted up his torn pant leg and showed them what he was talking about. "See bro?" Paula looked at the marks. "Awe, poor Bobby got some little baby marks." She joked in a whining voice. They all were getting a good kick off Bobby and the baby pit bulls. "I use to like baby dogs bro," Bobby put his pant leg back in place. "Paula," Tech spoke up. "You're up." "Ready for service captain." She joked saluting him. "The Lexus LFA is in a neighborhood not far from here," Tech tossed her the key to the vehicle. "I don't know who owns the vehicle or anything about the neighborhood.

All I know is the car gets washed every two days. That's how the vehicle was spotted. At least, that's what my sources say." "Great," she stood up. "Let's go." Tech got Paula to the neighborhood in no time. They were four cars in and it was only ten in the morning. "This is the place," Tech looked over at the neighborhood. "Don't look too bad of a place to stay either." "Be back," Paula hopped out of the truck. She got herself in the zone as she hurried through the neighborhood. "This is nothing." She told herself. "You've done much harder lifts than this one." One thing about a beautiful woman walking through the neighborhood in a sports bra and sweats is no one would care. Her morning workout disguises fit perfect every time. Paula is one of the best car thieves there is. She was a monster in disguise and she loved it. She got close to the house that owned the LFA. She stopped two houses down. "Damn," she noticed the LFA backing out of the driveway. Not good, she thought. She turned around and sprinted back to the entrance. She didn't want the LFA to beat her to the front, but it did. She hopped in the eighteen-wheeler. Tech looked confused. "I thought you lost your mind. I thought that was you in the LFA taking it for a nice little spin." "Think again," Paula caught her breath. "Follow the car." Tech already had the truck running. "You still want to try?" "Wouldn't hurt." She shrugged.

"Whoever is driving the car might slip up." Tech pulled out following the Lexus. It was kind of hard to keep up with the vehicle because the truck was slower and the turns were wider. He managed to get the job done. "What's going on over here?" He gawked at all the pretty women wearing two pieces. "Victoria Secret car wash." "That's where it's heading," Paula slipped off her sweats. Paula had a banging body. "Not Victoria Secret but it'll do." she hopped out of the truck and hurried over to the car wash. She had to catch the Lexus driver before one of the other girls flagged the car down. The girls had the car wash jumping so it wasn't difficult for her to mix right in. Paula was by far the prettiest girl and had the best body there. The Lexus parked and a handsome man emerged from the vehicle. Paula tried her best to beat the other girls over to him. It was too many of them pushing and shoving other girls out of the way. "Forget it." She muttered and begun to walk away. "Hey miss," the man called. "You, with the red two piece." Paula stopped. Is he talking about me? I got red on but three other girls do too. She turned around and noticed that the other girls didn't wear a two piece. She was to only one with a red top and bottom. She saw the guy pointing at her. She pointed to herself signaling to him that he was indeed talking to her. "Yeah, you." he said. "Can you please be the one to wash my car?" he asked. He was clearing the other girls out of his way. "I'll be glad to." She showed him a bright smile. "Thank you very much," he handed her a fifty dollar tip. "You're beautiful and you didn't hound me like the other girls," Paula smiled. She held it until he walked inside the building. She pulled the key from her bra. The man walked inside and paid the owner for the service. "That's one beautiful woman you got working for you, Sir." The old man smiled. They all were beautiful to him at his age. "Which one is yours?" The man pointed to the Lexus. "The LFA." The old man put his glasses on. "That's a fine car you got but that young lady doesn't work for me." The man turned around and watched his car speed away from the lot… lifted.

*Chapter 43*

# JAGUAR C-X75

"What you think about this suit?" Twenty asked Jeff while coming down the stairs. The next lift was going to be at an Atlanta concept car show. The Jaguar C-X75 was one of the cars on the list. Jeff examined him as he came down. "You're going to a car show, not a wedding. Lighting up." "Yeah, I know." Twenty responded. "But I like to be clean, though. I haven't worn a suit in ten years." He turned his attention to Bobby. "What you think Bobby?" "I like the suit bro. Us brochunskis's rock the pinstripe." The horn from the eighteen-wheeler sounded. Jeff got up. "They're back," he walked over to the garage door. He lifted the door for them. He noticed Paula pulling the LFA from the back of the trailer. Paula pulled the Lexus in the garage. She shut the car off and got out. "That's another one down." She saw Twenty looking himself over. The man was truly stunning to her in the suit. Why does he always have to look so damn good to me? He filled the suit well. She only saw him in a suit one time in her life and that was the night he took her to the prom. He looked different now, he was more of a man than a boy. "You look great," she uttered standing next to him. "Let me help you." She fixed his tie. "That's better," she whispered. "Thank you," he answered quietly. He stared into her eyes. He wanted to kiss her so bad but knew he couldn't. Somehow he gained the power to control himself. Luckily, Jeff went to go meet Tech at the truck. He didn't witness the moment at hand. Bobby on the other hand, did. He watched them stare into each other eyes passionately. What's going on between these two? For all he knew, Paula was Jeff's girl and if he saw this it could mean trouble. "Ok then," he wanted to interrupt them before Jeff walked back in and caught them. "Twenty's suit is nice," he said sarcastically. They both snapped out of the trance they had on each other. Twenty spoke first. "Um, yeah, thanks." "Yeah," she shook it off. "Anytime." They both walked in separate directions. Paula went to the bar and Twenty went outside to greet Tech. "Twenty," Tech looked at his suit. "You look nice man." "Thanks," he said. "You grab the key for the Jaguar?" Twenty showed him the key. "Then we got a car show to rain on." Tech went over the plan with Twenty as he drove him to the

Atlanta concept car show. There's going to be a lot of people there so he needed to create the perfect diversion. He had one and it would happen at one in the afternoon. Tech parked the truck down the street from the building. Everything was set. "You got it right?" "Got it," Twenty assured him. "One o'clock." "I'll be waiting." Tech held his hand out and Twenty gave him some dap. Twenty hopped out of the truck. "Let's get this show on the road." He muttered to himself. He made his way over to the car show. He showed his fake invite that Tech created for him. It worked perfectly and he went through. He noticed that a bunch of business people had shown up to the car show. Companies were there showing off their new development or checking out what the competition had. The competition was though because all the cars were worth having. Twenty looked at all of the future concepts that were coming out. He wanted to lift all of them and keep them for himself. If only, he thought. He finally came across the Jaguar C-X75. "Dayum." It was one of the coolest cars there. Whoever was buying the cars from that Mexican they call El' Nino had taste. From the McLaren to the Jag he was standing in front of. All of the cars were fast, fun and exotic. He stood next to the car fascinated by its unique curves and wet paint job. "Beautiful car, isn't it?" a man from the Jaguar team walked up on him. "Yeah," Twenty responded. "I'm diggin' it." "Who do you work for?" he asked. "This is my first time seeing you here." "I'm with the Lamborghini team." He lied. "Tom hiring new people again?" he asked. Who the hell is Tom? "Yeah, short staffed." "Of course," he noticed what Twenty had in his hand. "Might I ask, what is the umbrella for?" "It's supposed to rain." Twenty checked his watch. Thirty seconds. "I check the weather regularly. I didn't see that it was going to rain." Twenty opened the umbrella and the water system showered the building. Pandemonium broke out. "Told you." People cleared the building. He hurried over to lift the garage up. He removed the red velvet rope from the car's driving path. He pulled the key from his pocket and got in the car. He revved it up a couple of times just to hear the sweet sound of the motor. As he drove out, he noticed the man that questioned him trying to give him a hard time. He pulled the car next to him and rolled down the window. He tossed the guy his umbrella. "You might want to check your weather report again." He winked at the guy and sped off.

*Chapter 44*

# HENNESSEY CTS V700

They got the eighteen-wheeler back to the garage. Bobby opened the garage door for them. Twenty pulled the super sports car into the building. He parked it next to the Lexus LFA. The Jag drove smoothly. It's too bad he didn't get the chance to push the exotic car like the McLaren and the 918. He thought about taking the Jag for a quick spin. He decided that would be extremely hot. Being a hot boy is not Twenty at all. Bobby met him at the driver door. "Bro," he watched Twenty emerge from the vehicle looking like he owned it. "That suit with this car bro. You could be the first black James Bond." "Well, I'm a little bit more handsome than him and a little bit better." Twenty responded adjusting his suit jacket coolly. Tech walked through the door. "Bobby you're next." "I'm ready bro," Bobby responded excitedly. "The Hennessey CTS V700 is the newest version. There's only two in the state. One was given to a federal agent after he retired and the other was given to a lawyer two blocks from here so which one do you think we're going after?" he said with sarcasm. "The fed one." Jeff joked. Everyone looked at him like he was insane. He shrugged his shoulders. "Excuse me for joking. I thought it would be a little more exciting." "I'll give you a lift in my car," Tech told him. "We won't need the truck for this one. It's too close. By the time we load the car up you would've made it back by then. The lawyer has his own office so the lift should be easy enough since the car is left unguarded outside." "How did he manage to get one of the cars anyway?" Twenty asked. "They're test cars. The most expensive rides are put on the road for a year before they come out to see how they manage. Not to mention, his brother owns the company." "That's some major chips," Jeff muttered. "C'mon," Tech told Bobby while grabbing his keys to his Lancer." He should've taken a lunch break. Let's go get this over with. You guys got me tired already for the day." "That's cause you're the man Tech." Paula praised him from the couch. She was lying down with her feet kicked up on the armrest watching Jimmy Neutron and getting some rest before her next lift tonight. Tech and Bobby left the garage to go make the move on the Hennessey CTS V700. The lift would be the easiest one of the day. It couldn't have been sweeter. The car was basically waiting for them in the parking lot. Bobby noticed that the lawyer's office closed at 4 o'clock. It was 3:30pm on the dot. They needed to hurry. The lawyer would probably leave work soon. Thirty minutes is more than enough time for Bobby. It's only going to take him two minutes to lift the car. They finally spotted the CTS V700 parked double spaced. People who had nice cars always double space parked. People were scared a reckless driver would hurt their baby. That's a shame because Bobby is going to do more than hurt the CTS. He's going to make the entire car disappear from both spaces. Tech parked and Bobby got out and made way to the CTS. He patted himself down for the key Tech made for the car. "Damn." He muttered checking every pocket. "I left the key?" he hurried back over to Tech hoping he had the key. He opened the door. Tech looked at him confused. "Tech, please tell me you got the key bro?" "No, you forgot it?" Tech answered. "Let's hurry back then." "No way bro," Bobby answered. "He'll be gone by then. I got an idea." Bobby shut the door and went into the lawyer's office. It was just him and the lawyer. The lawyer spoke while grabbing his coat. "Sorry, I'm done for the day." "Please," Bobby cried. "I need a lawyer for my brother. It's a murder case." The lawyer loved murder cases. They were the highest paid cases. "Well, I guess I got a little time." he sat his coat around his chair. "Give me one minute." The lawyer went into the back room to receive his laptop. Bobby ran around the desk when the lawyer vanished. He searched the jacket frantically for the key. Bingo, must be my lucky day. The lawyer came back with his laptop and the guy was gone. He shrugged it off and put his jacket on. The security system was already off and all he had to do was lock the front door. After he locked the door from the outside. He turned around and saw a CTS V700 speeding by. "Um, he has a car like mine."

*Chapter 45*

# V-12 VANTAGE

**B**obby pulled the car into the garage. He shut the CTS off and got out. "You forgot something." Twenty tossed him the key for the CTS. Bobby caught it. "The lawyer was kind enough to let me borrow his bro," Bobby smiled. Tech came in behind Bobby. "Bobby just made himself a new lawyer friend." He joked patting him on the back as he walked by. Tech walked over to the computer. He sat down in his chair and looked over the next assignment. Jeff was looking over the Jaguar. Every detail on the car was magnificent. He went to the bar and made himself a drink. "Anybody want a drink while I'm back here?" Twenty was checking out the Hennessey blacked out badges. "I like this bad boy, this me right here." He muttered to himself. "I'll take whatever you're having bro," Bobby answered Jeff. Twenty opened the door to the Hennessey. He got in and noticed the car had 200mph on the dash. This CTS was faster than the McLaren, the Porsche 918 and the Jaguar C-X75. Twenty got out of the tuner. "Tech, this car can hit 200mph plus." "Yes, it can and I bet you didn't know it could do 0 to 150 in 16.4 seconds. Its max is said to be 211mph." Twenty shut the door. "This here, is a fuckin' monster." He joined Jeff and Bobby at the bar. They spent the next three hours talking about the lifts and what they went through to get the cars. There wasn't a story that could top Paula's Victoria Secret car wash. The boys went crazy because they weren't a part of something like that. Tech backed Paula up by bragging about all the pretty women there. Bobby wished he could've brought his Hellcat through. The women loved his car and always fell for his brochunski surfer boy swag. Tech came downstairs after his nap. He met them at the bar. "Mr. Bartender." He called Jeff. "Let me get a beer?" "Coming right up." Jeff got him a beer and popped it open for him. "Here you are my man. That will be six dollars plus a tip." Jeff joked. They all had a good laugh. "What's next on the list?" Twenty sipped on his beer. "The Aston Martin," Tech took a drink. "Jeff's on." "Love it when you call my name," he said sarcastically. "V-12 Vantage right?" "Nothing better than a V-12." Tech handed Jeff the key. "Let's get er done." He said like a redneck. Tech and Jeff made their way over to one of the nicest neighborhoods in the area. Tech set the truck up and Jeff went to the target house. Jeff walked four houses down. It was starting to get late. People were home so he needed to make this happen fast as possible. The car was at a rich old man's house. Wife died and he had no kids. He was told all he did was sit in the house and watch TV. The car was given to him from his wife's cousin. He worked for Aston Martin and wanted the old man to enjoy the rest of his life instead of being cooped up in the house all day. Too bad the old guy had never driven the car. It stayed in the same spot as it did when it first arrived. Right there lonely in the driveway waiting for a guy like Jeff to come and lift it. Jeff stepped next to the car. "Easy," he pulled the key from his pocket. When he was about to put the key in the door someone called to him. "Peter?" the old guy called from the porch. Jeff swiftly put the key in his pocket. He turned around and noticed the old man sitting on his porch in a rocking chair. "Peter, c'mon up here and talk to me, son." The old man waved him over. This old guy must think I'm Peter? He decided to walk onto the porch. "Have a seat." The old man said. "If you were coming to take the car back you could've at least you can say hello to me." Jeff looked confused. This old man must have Alzheimer's. He thinks I'm Peter and that I was coming to take the car back from him. Jeff took a seat next to the old man. They talked for the next ten minutes. The old guy kept referring to him as his wife's cousin, Peter. Jeff had found out him while they were talking. "Alright George," Jeff got up. "Nice seeing you again." He walked to the Vantage. Easy as pie, like my man Tech would say.

# Chapter 46

# RENAULT DEZIR, GT-R35

"The old man was cool," Jeff told Twenty and Bobby. He was watching Twenty tear Bobby apart in a game of pool for the second time in a row. "I'm telling you it was the easiest lift in my life." he took a big bite of pizza Paula had ordered for everyone. "Pretty soon that's going to be you sitting on a porch, Jeff. Someone is going to come along and lift your ride." Twenty aimed the pool stick. "Eight ball corner pocket." "That's it for me, bro." Bobby handed Paula the pool stick. "I can't beat this guy." "Bobby," Paula said as he tried to walk away. "Rack 'em up." Bobby came back over to racked the balls. "What is it for tonight, Tech?" Twenty called while waiting for Bobby. He was working on his third pizza. "The Nissan's," Tech walked over to watch the game. "I got fifty on Paula." He threw the offer out there. "I'll take that bet bro," Bobby wanted to make some of his money back from the race he loss to Jeff. Paula broke the balls. Two of the stripes went in and then she finished off the rest of her balls. She aimed at the eight ball and signaled her pocket. "Game." she took the shot and the eight ball went in the side pocket. "Bro," Bobby was shocked at what just happen. Twenty didn't get a chance to shoot. "I'm through with gambling." He handed Jeff his money. Paula stood next to Tech with her hand out. "I think you owe me some of that." Tech put $25 in her hand. He knew that Paula is a pool shark and would win if she went first. "When did Paula become a pool shark?" Twenty leaned closer to Jeff and spoke among themselves. "When you went in," Jeff answered. "That's all she did." He took a bite of his pizza. They continued to enjoy themselves for the next few hours. They listened to music, drank beers, played cards, video games, Paula danced a bit before she snuck off to smoke some weed. No one noticed and when she came back. She smashed a bag of popcorn. The extra butter had her taste buds going. When 1:30am rolled around it was time. The Nissans were waiting on them. "It's one-thirty," Tech informed them. "We got a warehouse to hit." Twenty was upstairs. He acted like he was going to sleep. Instead of doing that. He secretly talked to Rosa on the phone. He didn't want Paula to find out. She probably wouldn't be able to take it and screw up the lift for tonight. Twenty needed love and Rosa to him, was alright. He actually liked her, too bad Paula didn't. "I'm ready." "Me too," Paula got up from the couch. The weed made her crash, but she slept it off. "That's good you two will be able to make it to tonight's service." Tech joked like a pastor in a church. He gave them both a key. They loaded up in the eight-wheeler. Tech drove them to the Nissan warehouse. They got there in ten minutes. The place was huge. Nissan made a number of different vehicles. The front of the building had tinted windows. If you put your face close to it. You can see the cars inside. Twenty and Paula crept up to the building. Twenty surveyed the scene. When he felt it was clear. He led the way around back. "You like her don't you?" Paula asked. The question came out of nowhere. Twenty was stunned by it. He kept walking. "Like who?" he asked like he didn't understand who Paula was talking about. "The Spanish girl," Paula caught up to him. "Don't try to act like you don't know what I'm talking about." Twenty started to lock pick the back door. "I don't know what you're talking about. Now let me handle this lock." He popped the lock. She followed him in. "I heard you talking to her on the phone." He ignored the statement. "You got your key?" he went over to the glass doors to open them. "Yes, I got my key." She said chasing after him. "I know you like her. You don't have to hide it from me." Twenty was searching for a way to open the doors. Paula was getting on his nerves about Rosa. He was frustrated because it was making his job harder than what it was supposed to be. "I'm not trying to hide anything from you. He stood there looking the glass doors over. They must be automatic, he thought. Paula kept going on about Rosa. He blocked her out. What the hell is that? Lights were coming at them straight towards the glass doors. Paula wasn't paying attention. Twenty shoved her out of the way just in time. A vehicle had crashed through the doors.

Chapter 47

# REPORT

El' Nino sat in his restaurant turned club. When 10 o'clock came around every Thursday, Friday and Saturday night. The restaurant would go ham. El' Nino sat next to two beautiful women. Nacho was standing behind the roped off area. He was making sure his boss was safe. Mexicans would get drunk and too out of control and he would straighten them out before it caused El' Nino problems. El' Nino is a man who never sleeps. He is always about his business. He told The Spokesman to spy on Twenty and make sure he was doing his job. If The Spokesman wanted to get paid he had to do it anyway. He told El' Nino Twenty was the man and wanted to secure his job with that Mexican they call El' Nino. A lot of money was on the line and The Spokesman wanted to get paid. That's all that mattered to him. El' Nino puffed on his cigar. He signaled for his personal VIP waitress. She came over. "Another bottle of champagne for me and my guest." She disappeared to get what her boss ordered. He picked up a golden plate that rested on a table in front of him. There was a mountain of cocaine on it. He took a sniff and gave it to the model on his right. He leaned back and watched everyone have a good time in his club. His eyes were sharp when he was on the drug. Everything moved in slow motion just for him. Nacho turned to his boss. "The Spokesman has arrived Boss." El' Nino signaled for Nacho to let him through. "Bring him over. Gracias Nacho." Nacho is the only person El' Nino thanked. Why not, he was the protector of his life. Nacho undid the rope and let The Spokesman pass. "He's in the back." he guided him to El' Nino. El' Nino spoke. "My friend." He signaled for The Spokesman to have a seat. "Have a seat and enjoy yourself with me and these beautiful women. The champagne is on the way." El' Nino puffed on his cigar. He pointed to the golden plate. "Coke?" The Spokesman took a good drag of cocaine. He set the plate on the table. "How are you doing today?" "Better my friend, now that you are here." El' Nino puffed on his cigar. The waitress came back with the bottle and popped it for them. She everyone a drink. "Tell me, is Twenty been taking care of my business?" he sipped his champagne. "Yes, he's doing what needs to be done." The Spokesman answered. "I've been watching him closely. He's been getting the job done with an eighteen-wheeler. That's how the cars are hidden after the lifts and are transported to your garage." "An eighteen-wheeler is a god idea." El' Nino watched the crowd sharply. "That Twenty is a smart man." "Yes, he is." The Spokesman watched the coked up models dance seductively in front of him. "He has about twenty of the cars done on the list." "That's good progress." El' Nino signaled for Nacho. "Is that Paco?" Nacho looked where El' Nino was pointing. He noticed Paco dancing with a pretty Spanish woman. "That's him, Boss." "You know what to do Nacho." El' Nino continued with The Spokesman and the girls. Nacho signaled for two of the soldiers to come with him. He walked through the crowd casually until he got to Paco. He tapped him on the shoulder. When Paco turned around he knocked his lights out. "Get the girl." He told the soldiers. Nacho and his men dragged them all out back. He violently tossed Paco against a dumpster. Paco fell to the ground. "Please." He cried. "I got half the money now." He owed El' Nino for ten keys of cocaine he got fronted from him two weeks ago. The due date is today. "I just need one more night and I'll have the money." The girl kicked and screamed. "Help!" "Kill her," Nacho ordered. The soldier put two in her head. "Please, Nacho!" Paco began to cry. He knew he was going to die. When you give El' Nino a date, that's it. No extensions. "Kill him and dump the bodies in the dumpster. Nacho heard five pops as he entered the club. He went back to El' Nino to report. "Done Boss."

*Chapter 48*

# REPO MAN

"**C**'mon," Twenty ordered Paula. They ducked for cover as they hurried behind a 350z. "What's going on?" Paula whispered. She covered herself behind Twenty. "I don't know." He whispered back. He peeked from behind the Nissan 350z. He noticed two rednecks in jumpsuits. They had assault rifles in their hands. "This isn't good." He said in a low voice. Paula didn't see what was going on. Her vision was shielded behind Twenty. "What can't be good? What is it?" she whispered and came from behind him trying to get a view of what had almost killed them. "Stay low," he told her. "Two guys with assault rifles." Both of the rednecks didn't seem like car thieves to him. They were doing it all wrong. They drove a truck through the front of the warehouse. That made Twenty think. "Shit, the police will come soon. We need to get the hell out of here." Paula scoped out the rednecks. "What are they doing?" Paula noticed what type of truck they were driving. "That's a repo truck isn't it?" That didn't spring up in his mind. He was too busy trying to figure out what they were doing. She's right, he thought. That is a repo truck. "Yeah." He answered. "They're probably going to lift a car." She suggested. "That's what I'm thinking." He watched one of rednecks back the truck up while guided by his partner. "What you think they're going to take?" she whispered while watching them. "There isn't any telling with these two." He watched the redneck load a car up. No, they can't be. "Twenty they're–" "I know, I know." He said cutting her off. The rednecks were lifting the only Nissan-Renault DeZir in the warehouse. It was the only concept of its kind in the entire state. "We got to do something." She cried. "What?" he knew they needed that car badly. Janet depended on it. "They have assault rifles." The rednecks loaded up the car and burnt out of the building shooting their AK's in the air. "Yee Haw..." "C'mon," Paula ordered Twenty. She ran over to the Nissan GT-R35. "What are you doing?" Twenty asked following her. "We have to get the hell out of here." "I'm not letting them get away with that car. My daughter's lift depends on it." She hopped in the GT-R35. "You coming or not?" Twenty knew they were outgunned but he had to try for Janet. He got in the passenger seat. He pulled his chrome 9 out and cocked it. "Catch'em." Paula smashed the gas. The Nissan had amazing speed. The $90,000, twin turbocharged, intercooler DOHC 24-valve V-6, aluminum block and heads with port fuel injection could do 0 to 60 in 2.9 seconds and a max out at 191mph. The rednecks wouldn't stand a chance. There wasn't a doubt they would get caught. The repo truck supported extra weight from the Nissan-Renault DeZir that slowed the heavy truck down. "Left or right?" Paula approached the road from the warehouse. The rednecks were out of sight and they needed to make the correct turn. Twenty went with what his gut told him. "Right." Paula drifted the car onto the road heading right. She shifted the 6-speed into gear and accelerated pushing the car to the max. "There they are." She said seeing them up ahead. "Pull up next to the driver." Twenty told her. "I need to take him out first." Paula maneuvered into the opposite lane. She punched it and got next to the truck. Twenty aimed the 9. "Bubba!" the redneck in the passenger seat called. Bubba fired his AK out of his window while still trying to handle the truck. Paula hit the brake a little. She didn't want Twenty or the car shot up. She gained on them. Twenty aimed the nine. He let off on the door and connect with Bubba. The truck swerved off of the road. "Bubba!" the other redneck cried. He fired his assault at them. He ran around to the driver side. "Bubba," he whispered. Paula skidded the car to a stop. She hopped out with her pistol. She snuck up on the redneck attending to his cousin. "Put the weapon down." He turned around and to face an angry Paula. "Twenty get the car."

*Chapter 49*

# THE SHAKE DOWN

The redneck didn't give them any problems. He was busy holding his cousin. He got shot twice in the side and in the leg. He was bleeding quite well, but he survived. After Twenty and Paula got the Nissan-Renault DeZir off the truck. He rushed his cousin to the local hospital. Paula and Twenty couldn't race the Nissan's back to Tech because he was in a hot zone. The police probably are swarming all over that place. Paula called Tech on the phone and told him to meet them back at the garage. The chances would be better if they just headed back. They made it back safely and ten minutes before Tech. They had pulled the cars in. They told Tech the story about what happened. He couldn't believe the wild manner rednecks would do something that crazy and stupid. It was kind of funny because if it wasn't for Twenty and Paula the rednecks would've successfully got away. Twenty suggest that first thing in the morning they would move the cars to El' Nino's garage. It would be safer because the police would be out all night. They'll be looking for the cars after seeing the warehouse. Paula went home. She lived two minutes from the garage and if she didn't, Jeff would be worried about her. Tech stayed at the garage with Twenty. He was looking the cars over. The DeZir had a little scratch from the repo truck in the front. It wasn't something he couldn't handle. He gave the GT-RS35 an oil change too. Twenty called it a night and went to bed. The day had taken a toll on him. After Tech finished and cleaned himself up, he crashed on the couch downstairs. Twenty woke at 9am the next morning. Friday, he thought. The last day of the lifts. They would move on to Saturday with the greatest challenge of all. Lifting the President's Land Rover. He cleaned himself up and went downstairs. He heard the eighteen-wheeler pull around back. He noticed that the cars were gone. Tech must've woken up early and took the cars to El' Nino's garage, he thought. He went out of the back door. Tech was getting out the truck. "You finally up?" he walked over to him. "You were dead tired. I said fuck it and moved the cars." Before Twenty could respond. He heard a loud beating on the door. He turned around. "Who the hell is banging on the door this early in the morning like they're crazy?" "Beats me," Tech said following him in. Twenty went to the door. The person at the door kept beating. "Hold on!" he checked the peephole. "Shit." It was Daverson and his partner. "Tech, hide everything." He whispered. Tech ran over to the computer to shut it down. Everything else that had anything to do with the lifts he got rid of. "Good," he whispered. Twenty opened the door and Daverson came barging in. "Hold up old guy before you kill yourself." "Where are they!" Daverson roared "Where's what?" Twenty asked like he was confused. Daverson grabbed Twenty by his shirt. "The cars, son." he said angrily. "Get off me," Twenty brushed him off. "I don't know about any damn cars." "Well, I have the warrant to search the place." Daverson showed him the warrant. "Search it." Twenty shrugged. "Doesn't look like any cars are here to me." Daverson could tell the garage was empty. He still had the feeling Twenty had something to do with it. He asked questions while he looked around. "New McLaren, stolen right off the track. BMW, taken from a test drive. Jaguar, from a car show. Mustangs, stolen while a manager was shittin' at the same place I busted you." "Well, he should've been shittin' around on the job." Twenty joked. Daverson had got what he wanted. "It's clean." He walked to the door. "Don't forget who caught you last time." he stepped out. He got in his car. His partner got in the passenger seat. "Look at this?" It was a shredded piece of paper that read, Ferra-. Daverson got it from the trash. His partner signed. "What's this supposed to mean?" he asked confused. "They're going after a Ferrari." He pulled away smiling.

*Chapter 50*

# 16.4 SUPER SPORT

"He's on to us. He doesn't know if it's us for sure," Twenty told Tech from the doorway. He was watching Daverson and his partner Matt Gains pull away. Tech went over to the bar. He needed to get himself a drink after what just happened. It was a close call. If he hadn't decided to take the cars over early they would've had some serious problems on their hands. Lucky us, he thought. "Why do you suggest he's on to us? The garage was empty and he didn't take us to jail." Tech poured himself some Grey Goose. "Not yet," Twenty walked over. "He doesn't have any hardcore evidence. He wants to catch me red handed, but without any good evidence. He knows I'll be out in no time. I know he's planning something. I can feel it. They might try to come back. They didn't catch us this time and they might put the dogs on us. They will be watching us from here on out. I'm sure of it. We need to be more cautious with our steps. The best thing for us to do is not bring the cars back here. Instead, we'll just take them straight to El' Nino's garage. It's safer that way. We'll just have to do our best to inspect the cars there." Tech poured him a shot. "Thanks. When are the others arriving?" Tech downed his second shot. "Jeff and Paula will be here around ten. Bobby will be in around one. Everyone is working solo until we lift the Ferrari's tonight." "Ok," Twenty poured himself another shot. "When they get here we'll let them know the new plans. Until then, let's start the day." He threw the shot back. "Ugh." He signed. Tech walked to the computer and booted it back up. He made a couple clicks of the mouse. "Today you only have two cars to lift. You have the Bugatti Veyron 16.4 super sport and the Ferrari 599 Replacement. It's a light day for you since you have the Land Rover tomorrow." "Where is the Bugatti located?" Twenty walked over to the workstation. "It's at a compound thirty minutes from here. It will be a test getting to it. There's a huge gate around the compound. You'll have to find a way to open it. There is a keypad. The passcode is unbreakable. The compound is on a mass amount of land and the owner is unidentified to my sources." Tech turned around in to face Twenty. "Sounds fun?" "Great," Twenty said sarcastically. Why does it sound like I'm going to die trying to lift this

Bugatti?" he sighed. "Why we have to lift this one? There's a couple easier ones around here I'm sure. "It's the only carbon fiber Bugatti in the state. The others are at a dealer in Cali. Unless you want to try your luck out there, be my guest. I don't think we have the time for a two-day trip." "Let's go." They got in the truck and hit the highway. They got to the compound in twenty five minutes. The place looked like it was worth millions. The gate was about eight feet tall all the way around the estate. It was black with gold spikes for the tips. There was a huge lion's head on the gate's entrance and it is solid gold. The compound is at the least, two football fields away from the front entrance. "Keep driving," Twenty told Tech. They stopped about fifty yards from the front gate. Twenty noticed a side area of the gate that was covered with trees. "Tech,"Twenty side seriously. "Let me get your gun."Tech pulled out his Desert Eagle and handed it to him. "Dayum, and I thought you were just a skinny geek." "Take care of her," Tech grinned. "I'm off."Twenty got out of the truck and hurried back down the road. He looked through the enormous gate. Something just didn't sit right about the place to him. He shrugged it off and crept around to the trees. He found a good one and climbed up and jumped over the fence. He stayed low and hurried over to the house. He crept along the house until he heard a voice. He paused and ducked lower. He thought someone was on to him. It was coming from the window up ahead. He crept over to it. The voices became clearer to him. It was two men talking. Twenty stood there a moment and listened. He wanted to know what kind of people he was dealing with. He heard a harsh male voice. "How much for the fifty kilo's?" "Give me $15,000 apiece." The second male voice came through the window. "That's a total of $750,000. I'm sure you can live with that." He thought, kilos, $750,000? He was at a cartel's compound. A world of alert went through his body. This is the worse place this Bugatti could've been. These were the type of people you wouldn't want to fuck with and Twenty was on their land… fuckin' with them. "Damn," he muttered. He pulled out the biggest gun he had on him. Tech's Desert Eagle. Thank you Lord. He peeped into the window swiftly. Man oh man, he thought. There were about ten guys in the room. One guy was behind a desk with fifty keys on it. Another guy with a leather jacket on was facing him. The other guys surrounded them. This was bad because Twenty knew the men were armed. How many soldiers were in the drug trade did you know weren't? He ducked low and continued to creep to the front of the mansion. He remembered seeing a number of cars and trucks. They were too hard to make out from the far road. Maybe he would have some luck and one of the vehicles would hopefully be the Bugatti. He made sure the Desert Eagle was cocked and ready. He got to the front of the mansion. He stooped low looking at the vehicles carefully. "Please be out here," he said to himself. There it was. He noticed the carbon fiber Bugatti parked at an angle. "Hell yeah." He whispered excitedly. Now he just had to find a way to get out of the front gate. He had a plan. The first thing he's going to do is find one of the other vehicles that's unlocked. Drug dealers always left their cars unlocked at their house. Hotwire it and run it through the front gate. Then hopped in the Bugatti and hightailed it the hell out of there. It wasn't the best plan, but it was all he could come up with unless the drug dealers were going to be kind enough to let him have the Bugatti. Then open the gate for him and say, good luck with Janet. We're praying for you. What a dream, but that wouldn't happen. On to the plan A. He crept over and the second vehicle he tried was unlocked. Good so far. He retrieved one of the heavy stones from the front garden. He sat it next to the truck and took his belt off. He tied one end to the steering wheel and the other end to the brake pedal. He didn't want the truck to brake. The goal was to keep the steering wheel straight. That's the biggest issue. He popped the truck steering column. This wire here, that wire there and the truck roared to life with the damn alarm. "Shit." It was over.

They're coming for sure. He knew if they found him. They would try to kill him. He continued through with the plan, anyway. He pressed the brake pedal and put the truck into gear. He pulled the emergency brake up and then he tightened the belt. He swiftly place the stone on the gas pedal. The truck revved with a redline RPM. The truck was burning out in place. Suddenly, he heard gun firing. The sound made him duck for cover. He swiftly lowered the emergency brake and the truck sped off towards the gate. He ducked behind a Lamborghini. He peeked out. All of the men came storming out and took firing positions. He pulled the Deseret Eagle and the 9 out. "What have you got yourself into Twenty?" he said as the bullets whizzed by the exotic car. The Bugatti is four cars away from him. If he could get to it. He would be good. He watched the truck. "C'mon, hit the damn gate." The truck swerved a little. He almost thought the truck wasn't going to make it, but it crashed right through the front gate. It worked, he thought. It fuckin' worked! Now all he had to do was manage to stay alive while getting to the Bugatti and fighting off the drug dealers. The bullets had slowed down and a harsh voice spoke. "Come out essay!" Twenty crept around a Lamborghini and got behind a Bentley. He only wanted to shoot if he had to. His bullets were limited and he didn't want to give up his position. He needed to come up with another plan. He was trying his best to remember the name that was at the window. What was that damn name? "I said come out essay!" the harsh voice commanded. "I wanna see who is crazy enough to try and come for me at my own home. Tell me, who sent you essay!" he fired some shots at the Lambo. Twenty thought long and hard about the name. He heard the gunfire and the bullets ricochet off the Lambo. What the hell is this guy talking about? That's it, he thought. He had some type of plan. Hopefully, it would work. Drug dealers were always paranoid about who's out to get them. Twenty was going to keep this guy talking and use that tactic against him until he remembered the name. "Hey," he yelled. "You want to know who sent me!" The drug lord held his men down. "Speak to me, who sent you after me, essay!" he wanted to know. If he found out which one of his enemies were after him. He would go at them full blast. "We have to make a deal if I tell you!" Twenty yelled back at him. He knew that he wouldn't be good on the deal. All he wanted was to stall a little while he tried to remember the name. "I don't know essay!" he yelled. "You fucked my gate up, homes! Who's going to pay for that!" Twenty stayed low and crept to the next vehicle. "You worried about the gate or more about who sent me after you and the fifty kilo's!" He looked around his men and the buyers. They were the only people who knew about the kilos. Now he was starting to get suspicious and believe someone among them sent this man after him. "Ok, you have a deal! I'll let you live essay if you tell me who sent you!" That's the name! Himis, he thought. "It was your boy, Himis!" Twenty yelled from behind the car. He wanted to see the reaction. He came from cover just a little. The guy in the leather jacket looked shocked. "He's bullshitting! Why would I send someone after you!" Twenty had them. He kept it up. "He sent me to kill you! He told me I would get ten of the kilos!" "He's fuckin' lying!" Himis yelled angrily. "Let's kill this motherfucker!" The drug lord turned his gun on Himis and five other men did too. Himis men turned their guns on them. It was only four of them all together. The drug lord spoke up. "How does he know about the cocaine!" He roared furiously. This entire deal was a setup, he thought. "The first person I'm going to kill is you Himis! Tell me, essay!" "I don't fuckin' know!" Himis answered frantically. "But it wasn't me or my men." Twenty watched in cover. "You're fuckin' lying Himis. You sent me to kill him!" "Kill them!" the drug lord took the first shot and it smacked Himis in the head. Himis fell to the ground dead. Both sides started attacking each other. Twenty had their attention off him and he crept the rest of the way to the Bugatti. He pulled out the key and opened the door. The drug lord noticed. "Chase him!" the men started firing instead. "Don't shoot up my Bugatti essay!" he held them down. "I mean chase him in another vehicle!" by then the drug dealer saw his 2.4 million dollar car speeding off the property. No way were they catching a 256mph car. One thing about being a drug dealer, whatever is stolen, was stolen. He pulled out his phone and punched a number in. "Joe, this is M. I need another Bugatti essay." Lifted One More Time Daverson sat in his office. He was looking over every single car theft in the last two days. He was trying to figure out the pattern while he sipped his coffee and smoke a cigarette. He thought about what if Twenty was clean? What if he didn't have anything to do with the thefts? What if there's someone new? He shook the thought from his head. There couldn't be anyone as good. One week after Twenty was released the GTA'S picked up. The thefts weren't random either. These people were professionals. He started back at the first file. McLaren MP4-12C, stolen right off the test track. The test driver was held at gunpoint and was robbed for his racing suit. BMW, 650i convertible, stolen while on a test drive. A beautiful woman held an older salesman at gunpoint. Mercedes S63 AMG and CLS63 AMG, stolen from the dealership. Two men held a manager at gunpoint and tied him a chair. Mustang Shelby GT500 and BOSS 302, stolen from the same dealer he caught Twenty ten years ago. Would Twenty really go to the same dealer? Dodge Viper, a rapper was held at gunpoint right after he purchased it. Three Porsches, 918, 991 and a 911 all stolen from the same warehouse. Chase was given after the 918 but the person driving was too skilled of a driver to be apprehended. The subject got away without a trace of him or the vehicle. Sounds like Twenty, he thought. He moved on to the next file. Jaguar C-X75, stolen from an Atlanta Concept car show. The shower system was somehow activated. When it was finally cut off the Jaguar team found their concept missing. Camaro HP-ZL1 and Corvette C7, stolen from an baseball player's mansion. The MVP to be exact. He saw two males, one black and the other white. Lexus LFA, stolen from a sponsored Victoria Secret car wash. A beautiful woman disguised as a worker drove the car right off the lot. Two Lamborghini's, Aventador and a Gallardo, stolen under a cop's nose. He described the two vehicles as joy riding. He was unaware the vehicles were stolen. Hennessey CTS, stolen from a lawyer at his office. He said a white male came in late and the next minute he was gone. Aston Martin v-12 Vantage. This was the worst one to Daverson. How could anyone be so cruel? Stolen from an old man with Alzheimer's. His wife's cousin reported the car and the old man kept suggesting it was taking up too much space. He checked the very last file he had. Last night, the front entrance to a Nissan warehouse was broken into. They got away with a Nissan-Renault DeZir and GT-R35. The scene was reported to have truck tread marks and assault rifle shells everywhere. The front windows were shattered. No blood or bodies on the scene. What was being shot at? This was the only job that didn't sound like Twenty had something to do with. The theft was reckless and Twenty wasn't that type of guy and Daverson knew that. What's this person next move? He looked at the shredded piece of paper. The ripped word, Ferra. Was this a part of a list of cars? There wasn't any Ferrari's stolen and there isn't going to be, he thought. He picked up the phone and dialed the Chief of police. "The Chief speaking." He answered in a raspy voice. "Chief, this is private investigator Daverson." He said then sipped his coffee. "Detective Daverson," said the Chief. "I haven't been bothered by you in a long time. This must be important?" "It is," Daverson answered seriously. "I have a lead on the car thefts. I believe their next theft will be a Ferrari." Lifted The Breakdown Twenty zipped the car up into the eighteen-wheeler. He hurried from the back of the trailer. He slapped the side of the trailer for Tech to close the lift as he ran to the front. He opened the door frantically and hopped in. "Drive, drive!" he ordered

Tech. Tech could tell by the way Twenty was acting that something was wrong. He cranked the truck and smashed the gas without any questioning. He noticed Twenty checking the side mirror as he got further down the street. He was at a safe distance and he checked his side mirror himself. There was no one following them. "What happen back there?" he focused on the road while asking the question. "Drug dealers," Twenty looked through the side mirror one more time just to be absolutely sure no one was following them. "We were at a drug dealer's compound." "The Bugatti belongs to a drug dealer?" he made a wide turn. "Yeah," Twenty exhaled and leaned back in his seat. "Some serious drug dealers were making a deal and I had no choice but to get in the middle of it." Tech was really interested. "How that come about?" "Well, when I jumped the fence." Twenty elaborated. I crept to the side of the compound. Then I overheard two voices. I thought they were coming for me. They were tending to some business. I looked through the window that was up ahead. I noticed a group of men. They were standing around a desk with fifty kilos of cocaine on it." "That's some major r weight." Tech cut in. "Yeah, I know." Twenty continued. "Then I crept around to the front of the mansion where I saw the vehicles from the far road. That's where the Bugatti was. I had to come up with a plan to open that damn gate so

I hot-wired one of the trucks that were out front and ran it through it." "That was a pretty good idea." Tech said casually pulling into El' Nino's enormous garage. "You think?" Twenty hopped out of the truck. "Well, it worked. On the other hand it almost got me killed." Tech lowered the lift so they could get the Bugatti off the truck. "Almost got you killed? The dealers found out?" Tech stood in the back of the truck. "The damn truck alarm went off on me." Twenty hopped up onto the truck. "Dayum," Tech watched Twenty pull the Bugatti off of the lift and then he got the door from him. Twenty pulled the Bugatti in with the other exotic cars. It made number 21. He shut the car off and got out. Tech met him by the car. Twenty leaned against the Bugatti. "All the men that were in the compound came storming out." he continued the story. "They took firing positions and let loose on me." "You superman or something?" Tech joked. "I don't see any bullet holes in you?" "They stopped firing because their leader wanted to know who sent me." Twenty walked towards the door. Tech followed. "Who sent you?" he asked confused. "He kept going on and on about who sent me to kill him and steal his drugs." Twenty locked the garage up and they walked back to the truck. "I remembered the name I overheard by the window. I told him a guy named Himis sent me." "Himis," Tech said starting up the truck. "Himis turned out to be the guy he was dealing with." Twenty relaxed back in his seat as Tech pulled off. "Oh lucky guess," Tech said. "Did he believe you?" "Did he," Twenty assured him. "They turned their guns against each other." "Oh shit," Tech said excitedly. "Yeah, oh shit." Twenty echoed. "The dealer shot and killed the guy and his men. It gave me just enough time to get away." "Yeah," Tech said casually. "You're superman." Lifted Bentley Mulsanne Twenty and Tech made it back to the garage. Jeff's truck was parked out front. He had arrived when they were out on the Bugatti mission. Tech opened the front door. He noticed Jeff seated in front of the TV watching the sports channel. "Jeff." He said coolly. "Tech, Twenty. "Jeff turned to their attention. "What's going on? You guys were out too long. So I made myself at home." He held up a bag of chips. "I got dip." "I'll take your offer on that." Twenty took a seat next to Jeff. He kicked back and helped with the chips and dip. He almost got killed. Just to make it out alive and be sitting here eating chips and dip is a pleasure and a blessing. "You know the Lakers got swept?" Jeff popped a chip in his mouth. "Oh yeah," Twenty popped one in his mouth. "I saw it the other day. I couldn't believe it, crazy." Tech went over to his workstation. The only place he ever goes in the garage beside to bed. There's work to be done and this is when he was at his best. When Twenty and

Jeff get a chance to watch sports. It's easy for their attention to easily get occupied. He would be the one to tell them that there was work to be done. Hey, we still have to rescue Janet remember? That's funny how a sports broadcast will totally make a man forget the task at hand. Tech clicked his mouse. The next lift is the Bentley Mulsanne. "Jeff," he called keeping his attention on the screen. "Where's Paula and Bobby? They were supposed to be here by now." Jeff finished gulping his Kool-Aid. He signed, "Ah. Paula left, she forgot something at home. I think it was her purse or something. I don't know, some girl shit though. Ah, man!" Jeff jumped up and so did Twenty. They both got excited over the basketball highlights. "Did you see that dunk!" Twenty had his hands on his head in disbelief. "He dunked right over his tall ass. Tech!" he called. "You got to see this shit! It's crazy." Tech shook his head. I can't ask a simple question, he thought. "Jeff." He called calmly. "And Bobby?" "Oh yeah, um Bobby…" he thought still amazed by the dunk. "Bobby, um… had to pick up his little brother Jimmy Neutron. He um… got suspended for teaching class again because the teacher didn't show up. He played substitute." "He taught the class?" Twenty dipped a chip while thinking about the genius 13-year old teaching an entire 12th-grade class. "Bobby said Jimmy told the substitute to go home. That she was at the wrong place and he is the sub for the day." Jeff told him. "Really, she believed him?" Twenty inquired. "I guess so because he taught the class and seven other periods before he got caught." "Dayum." Twenty said. "Jimmy the truth." "Funny thing is," Jeff added. "The kids were actually learning something." Even Tech paid attention to what Jeff was talking about. He likes the kid Jimmy Neutron. The fact that a 13 year old could convince a real teacher that he was the substitute. Then turn around and teach eight classes is astonishing. He didn't deserve to get suspended. He deserved the right to finish teaching for the rest of the day. Tech focused on the computer. Bentley Mulsanne. "Jeff." Tech called. "Yo." Jeff answered coolly without turning around. "You have to lift the Bentley Mulsanne. A man named Jason Grey owns it. My sources say he has a meeting today at the Four Seasons hotel. They have valet parking so you know what you'll be disguised as?" "The mat that's rolled out when his rich ass steps out that muthafucka." He joked. "Right now," Tech said seriously. "I wish that were possible. Unfortunately, you weren't clean enough for that job. "Oh man." Twenty laughed. "Not the geek trying to sneak one." Jeff jumped up and turned to Tech. "You wanna get some! You wanna joke?" Tech smiled. "Nah Jeff, you got it." Jeff sat back down and popped a chip in his month. "He doesn't want none." He told Twenty. "You'll be one of the valet parkers." Tech continued. "He will arrive at the hotel around twelve. So let's keep in mind that we don't have that much time wasted… you emotional bastard." Jeff walked into the Four Seasons hotel. His plan is to get one of the valet parking suits. He watched all of the people in the massive building carry on with their business casually. Little did they know, the snake was in the jungle and it's about to strike. He walked through the crowd noticing everything around him. He noticed a woman with a small dog in her hands. She looked to be complaining about something to one of the hotel managers. All he could read was her lips and from the distance she seemed to be angry. He noticed three kids running around the resting area. The mother was having a hard time controlling them. He watched that scene play out and knew that would never be Paula. Paula would beat the hell out of them kids until they understood that she's the boss and what she says goes. That's where he's going to meet, he thought. He noticed a group of well-educated men standing around an older one. They all had on nice suits and each a briefcase. The scene looked like a private event. Their area was roped off leading to the back. He wondered what type of meeting they were having. He didn't think too long about it. Maybe later, they could have a meeting about how one of the members getting his Bentley lifted. He stood at the front desk behind a man with an all brown suit on. He observed the valet workers coming from a back room while he waited his turn in line. He overheard the man in front of him talking about how much it would be for a week. The desk worker had told the man it was a special going on and he could stay for $1,500. Wow $1,500. That's special? He continued watching the workers go in and out of the room. He looked up at the enormous clock on the wall. Fifteen minutes before the Bentley would show. He had to make his move. "Sir," the desk worker called getting his attention. "Can I help you?" "Fifteen hundred for a week, right?" Jeff threw out there. He needed to break the conversation fast and head to the back room. "Yes sir," the front desk worker said nicely. "That is our special for the week. Would you like to purchase it?" "I'm alright for now." Jeff said. "Let me check my bank account. I'll be right back." He walked away. He made his way through the crowd over to a busy backroom that the workers were coming in and out of. He checked the area to make sure nobody will notice him slip into the room. Everyone seemed to be still carrying on about their own business. Now, he thought. He swiftly pushed through the backroom door. He noticed a few workers were still in there. He carried on like he worked there himself. He went over to the valet parking suits. They were all hanging in a row, different sizes. He grabbed one that was about his size and swiftly put it on and then he hurried outside to where the other workers were servicing. He stood out there nonchalantly waiting for the Bentley. "You're new here?" One of the guys on the unit stopped him. "Yes, I am." He said. "Just started today." He noticed the Bentley pulling up. "How long ha- Jeff cut him off. "Sorry, can't chat. Got to work." He said walking off to the Bentley. He stood there patiently waiting for the rich man Jason to emerge from the vehicle. Jason got out of the Bentley. "Hey," he said coolly. "Don't fuck my baby up." Jeff smiled and walked around to the driver side. "I promise I won't, sir." He got in. "I'm telling you." He said harshly. "This my baby. I'll fucking kill you over her." Jeff spoke coolly. "I got you." "Here's the key." He tried to hand it to Jeff. Jeff smirked at him. "Don't need it." He started the car and sped off. Jason looked shocked. "Bring back my fucking car!" Lifted Lotus Esprit "Tech." Jeff said. He was amazed after driving the very smooth Bentley Mulsanne into El'Nino's enormous garage. Even though the luxury car could only do zero to sixty in 4.9 seconds. He was fascinated with its other amazing features. "Check out these leather seats, the trimming leather into the panels for the wall and ceiling. Leather wrapped around these motorized blinds. Polished burl-walnut crown molding, baseboard, and door and window trim. Man, the wall-to-wall Wilton wool carpeting and the custom-designed lighting. Dayum, a desk, bookcase and filing cabinets and they match the veneered fold-down tables. The Naim audio system and it matches the thumper. Tech, I'm about to take this car back home with me." Tech smiled. "Is a $330,000 luxury car really worth it?" He said looking through the window at Jeff. He looked at Tech like, yeah… this one is. "I can lift another one." "Jeff," Tech said seriously. "Get your ass out of the car and let's go. We got a long day. This car isn't all that." he walked away. "Tech growing some balls." He said to himself. He got out and shut the door. He made his way back to the truck and hopped in with Tech. "You know I was just bullshitting right?" Tech started up the eighteen-wheeler. "Yeah, right. I'll lift one of them baby's if I knew how." They got back to the garage. Twenty and Bobby were outside kicking it. They were talking about Bobby putting 22' inches on his Hellcat. Twenty suggested putting 24's on it. Might as well ride big. Jeff walked up. "Put the fo's on it. Black on red would look nice." "Ho's love the fo's bro?" Bobby asked. They all laughed. They went inside after a couple of minutes. Jeff was telling them how cool the Bentley is and that one day he's going to buy one. He had to, the car is a retired man's dream. "I would live in that thang."

Jeff told them as they entered the garage. Paula was sitting on the couch. She turned to their attention. "Live in what?" "Somebody's in trouble..." Tech said coolly. "Nothing." Jeff spoke. "At home, of course. We were talking about a car." Paula walked over to Tech by the computer. "It figures." She answered softly. "What's up next, Tech. I'm ready to work. It's getting boring sitting around here." "Well, actually." Tech clicked the mouse and went to the Lotus Esprit file. "It's almost time for the Lotus convention. It will be starting in the next hour." "Finally." Paula said. "I get to lift a car that hasn't come out yet. This is going to be a challenge isn't it?" "You sound like you want it to be." Twenty walked pass heading to the couch. "Maybe I want it to be." Paula said eyeing him. "You don't get to have all the fun." "Bro," Bobby said. "I've been having fun with my lifts." "You always have fun." Jeff said. "You actually love doing this shit for a living." "That's right bro." Bobby assured him. "Although," Jeff said. "When I was your age. I loved lifting cars too. I guess when you get older and have a family, things change." "Or go to prison for life." Twenty added from the couch. "Paula." Tech got her attention. "The Lotus will be a challenge if that's what you were asking for. There will be different groups that will be listening and learning the new vehicle from top to bottom. It will be your job to hide among the group unnoticed and then somehow work your magic to get the car lifted safely. The building will be crowded with study groups working on different Lotus. So driving the car out of the building through the people will be a task. Don't run anyone over. So… Is that fun enough for you?" Fifteen minutes later. Tech and Paula were down the street from the Lotus convention. The building looked like a school. Many people were going into the building. They watched the scene carefully. Paula turned to Tech. "Get in, hide among the study group. Somehow lift the Lotus and drive the car safely out the building without killing anyone." "That's it." Tech answered. "Piece of cake." Paula hopped out of the eighteen-wheeler. She hurried down the block towards the building. She was going through different options in her head about how to get the car out of the building. Getting into the study group wouldn't be a problem. That's the least of her concerns. She got to the front of the building. She waited until a group of people got on her. The group crowded around the door and started to enter. She slipped right into the group of people casually. She entered the building behind a heavyset guy who was sweating profusely. Maybe he just finished the mile run? Paula thought as she hid behind the sweaty man. He provided great cover even though she wasn't really hiding from anyone. She just didn't desire to stick out. She came from behind the guy and scanned the building taking in everything around her. Tech was right. This is going to be a challenge. There were people everywhere in different groups. Each group had a teacher. She noticed because every group had someone in a long white professor's coat. How in the hell am I going to get the car out with all of these people in here? She continued searching for the Lotus Esprit. There were test cars everywhere. Some on the ground. Some on alignment machines. Some on lifts so you can see the underbody of the car. Some were hooked up to test machines and running. Hopefully the Esprit wasn't one of them. You can't run the miles up on a car and then ask someone to buy it from you is a big no, no. El' Nino wouldn't be happy with that. She slowly started walking toward a crowd around what seem to be a black Lotus. Someone tapped her on the shoulder. "Excuse me, Miss." She turned around. "What study group are you with?" The man in front of her was one of the teachers. "I'm with the Esprit group. I lost track of them a minute ago." She said sadly. "Ma'am, the group is right over there." He pointed to the large group of people behind her. "And where are your study books that were assigned to you?" My books? Paula thought. "My friend Heather has them. I had to go to the ladies room and she was just standing here with them. When I came out I lost her and the entire group." The teacher looked at her skeptically. "Ok, well hurry up and be on your way. The session has already begun." Paula nodded and turned toward to study group. She hurried over and mixed in with them. The car in front of her was the Lotus Esprit. The car is absolutely beautiful to her. She listened to the teacher. "This is a mid-engine, aluminum bodied supercar designed to take on the Ferrari and the Lamborghini. This is a huge gamble for our brand. Our new alloy structure shares a number of components with the less extreme Lotus Elan. Our main competition will be the Ferrari 458 Italia, Lamborghini Gallardo and the Porsche 911 Turbo. Our Esprit offers mid-engine, rear-wheel drive platform with a V-8. Our V-8 can produce as much as 550 horsepower. We also offer a hybrid system such as this one." He pointed to the Esprit and continued. "The hybrid version will lift the output to 620 horsepower." He paused. He spotted the only person around him that wasn't taking notes. He also noticed the very attractive female didn't have any books with her. "Where are your books young lady?" he pointed to Paula. "Are you that smart that you don't have to take any notes or am I just teaching for my health?" People started mumbling among the group. Paula built up her act and busted out crying.

*Chapter 51*

# ONE MORE TIME

Daverson sat in his office. He was looking over every single car theft in the last two days. He was trying to figure out the pattern while he sipped his coffee and smoke a cigarette. He thought about what if Twenty was clean? What if he didn't have anything to do with the thefts? What if there's someone new? He shook the thought from his head. There couldn't be anyone as good. One week after Twenty was released the GTA'S picked up. The thefts weren't random either. These people were professionals. He started back at the first file. McLaren MP4-12C, stolen right off the test track. The test driver was held at gunpoint and was robbed for his racing suit. BMW, 650i convertible, stolen while on a test drive. A beautiful woman held an older salesman at gunpoint. Mercedes S63 AMG and CLS63 AMG, stolen from the dealership. Two men held a manager at gunpoint and tied him a chair. Mustang

Shelby GT500 and BOSS 302, stolen from the same dealer he caught Twenty ten years ago. Would Twenty really go to the same dealer? Dodge Viper, a rapper was held at gunpoint right after he purchased it. Three Porsches, 918, 991 and a 911 all stolen from the same warehouse. Chase was given after the 918 but the person driving was too skilled of a driver to be apprehended. The subject got away without a trace of him or the vehicle. Sounds like Twenty, he thought. He moved on to the next file. Jaguar C-X75, stolen from an Atlanta Concept car show. The shower system was somehow activated. When it was finally cut off the Jaguar team found their concept missing. Camaro HP-ZL1 and Corvette C7, stolen from an baseball player's mansion. The MVP to be exact. He saw two males, one black and the other white. Lexus LFA, stolen from a sponsored Victoria Secret car wash. A beautiful woman disguised as a worker drove the car right off the lot. Two Lamborghini's, Aventador and a Gallardo, stolen under a cop's nose. He described the two vehicles as joy riding. He was unaware the vehicles were stolen. Hennessey CTS, stolen from a lawyer at his office. He said a white male came in late and the next minute he was gone. Aston Martin v-12 Vantage. This was the worst one to Daverson. How could anyone be so cruel? Stolen from an old man with Alzheimer's. His wife's cousin reported the car and the old man kept suggesting it was taking up too much space. He checked the very last file he had. Last night, the front entrance to a Nissan warehouse was broken into. They got away with a Nissan-Renault DeZir and GT-R35. The scene was reported to have truck tread marks and assault rifle shells everywhere. The front windows were shattered. No blood or bodies on the scene. What was being shot at? This was the only job that didn't sound like Twenty had something to do with. The theft was reckless and Twenty wasn't that type of guy and Daverson knew that. What's this person next move? He looked at the shredded piece of paper. The ripped word, Ferra. Was this a part of a list of cars? There wasn't any Ferrari's stolen and there isn't going to be, he thought. He picked up the phone and dialed the Chief of police. "The Chief speaking." He answered in a raspy voice. "Chief, this is private investigator Daverson." He said then sipped his coffee. "Detective Daverson," said the Chief. "I haven't been bothered by you in a long time. This must be important?" "It is," Daverson answered seriously. "I have a lead on the car thefts. I believe their next theft will be a Ferrari."

# THE BREAKDOWN

Twenty zipped the car up into the eighteen-wheeler. He hurried from the back of the trailer. He slapped the side of the trailer for Tech to close the lift as he ran to the front. He opened the door frantically and hopped in. "Drive, drive!" he ordered Tech. Tech could tell by the way Twenty was acting that something was wrong. He cranked the truck and smashed the gas without any questioning. He noticed Twenty checking the side mirror as he got further down the street. He was at a safe distance and he checked his side mirror himself. There was no one following them. "What happen back there?" he focused on the road while asking the question. "Drug dealers," Twenty looked through the side mirror one more time just to be absolutely sure no one was following them. "We were at a drug dealer's compound." "The Bugatti belongs to a drug dealer?" he made a wide turn. "Yeah," Twenty exhaled and leaned back in his seat. "Some serious drug dealers were making a deal and I had no choice but to get in the middle of it." Tech was really interested. "How that come about?" "Well, when I jumped the fence." Twenty elaborated. I crept to the side of the compound. Then I overheard two voices. I thought they were coming for me. They were tending to some business. I looked through the window that was up ahead. I noticed a group of men. They were standing around a desk with fifty kilos of cocaine on it.""That's some major r weight." Tech cut in. "Yeah, I know." Twenty continued. "Then I crept around to the front of the mansion where I saw the vehicles from the far road. That's where the Bugatti was. I had to come up with a plan to open that damn gate so I hot-wired one of the trucks that were out front and ran it through it." "That was a pretty good idea." Tech said casually pulling into El' Nino's enormous garage. "You think?" Twenty hopped out of the truck. "Well, it worked. On the other hand it almost got me killed." Tech lowered the lift so they could get the Bugatti off the truck. "Almost got you killed? The dealers found out?" Tech stood in the back of the truck. "The damn truck alarm went off on me." Twenty hopped up onto the truck. "Dayum," Tech watched Twenty pull the Bugatti off of the lift and then he got the door from him. Twenty pulled the Bugatti in with the other exotic cars. It made number 21. He shut the car off and got out. Tech met him by the car. Twenty leaned against the Bugatti. "All the men that were in the compound came storming out." he continued the story. "They took firing positions and let loose on me." "You superman or something?" Tech joked. "I don't see any bullet holes in you?" "They stopped firing because their leader wanted to know who sent me." Twenty walked towards the door. Tech followed. "Who sent you?" he asked confused. "He kept going on and on about who sent me to kill him and steal his drugs."Twenty locked the garage up and they walked back to the truck. "I remembered the name I overheard by the window. I told him a guy named Himis sent me." "Himis,"Tech said starting up the truck. "Himis turned out to be the guy he was dealing with."Twenty relaxed back in his seat as Tech pulled off. "Oh lucky guess," Tech said. "Did he believe you?" "Did he," Twenty assured him. "They turned their guns against each other." "Oh shit," Tech said excitedly. "Yeah, oh shit." Twenty echoed. "The dealer shot and killed the guy and his men. It gave me just enough time to get away." "Yeah,"Tech said casually. "You're superman."

# Chapter 53

# BENTLEY MULSANNE

Twenty and Tech made it back to the garage. Jeff's truck was parked out front. He had arrived when they were out on the Bugatti mission. Tech opened the front door. He noticed Jeff seated in front of the TV watching the sports channel. "Jeff." He said coolly. "Tech, Twenty. "Jeff turned to their attention. "What's going on? You guys were out too long. So I made myself at home." He held up a bag of chips. "I got dip." "I'll take your offer on that." Twenty took a seat next to Jeff. He kicked back and helped with the chips and dip. He almost got killed. Just to make it out alive and be sitting here eating chips and dip is a pleasure and a blessing. "You know the Lakers got swept?" Jeff popped a chip in his mouth. "Oh yeah," Twenty popped one in his mouth. "I saw it the other day. I couldn't believe it, crazy." Tech went over to his workstation. The only place he ever goes in the garage beside to bed. There's work to be done and this is when he was at his best. When Twenty and Jeff get a chance to watch sports. It's easy for their attention to easily get occupied. He would be the one to tell them that there was work to be done. Hey, we still have to rescue Janet remember? That's funny how a sports broadcast will totally make a man forget the task at hand. Tech clicked his mouse. The next lift is the Bentley Mulsanne. "Jeff," he called keeping his attention on the screen. "Where's Paula and Bobby? They were supposed to be here by now." Jeff finished gulping his Kool-Aid. He signed, "Ah. Paula left, she forgot something at home. I think it was her purse or something. I don't know, some girl shit though. Ah, man!" Jeff jumped up and so did Twenty. They both got excited over the basketball highlights. "Did you see that dunk!" Twenty had his hands on his head in disbelief. "He dunked right over his tall ass. Tech!" he called. "You got to see this shit! It's crazy." Tech shook his head. I can't ask a simple question, he thought. "Jeff." He called calmly. "And Bobby?" "Oh yeah, um Bobby…" he thought still amazed by the dunk. "Bobby, um… had to pick up his little brother Jimmy Neutron. He um… got suspended for teaching class again because the teacher didn't show up. He played substitute." "He taught the class?" Twenty dipped a chip while thinking about the genius 13-year old teaching an entire 12th-grade class.

"Bobby said Jimmy told the substitute to go home. That she was at the wrong place and he is the sub for the day." Jeff told him. "Really, she believed him?" Twenty inquired. "I guess so because he taught the class and seven other periods before he got caught." "Dayum." Twenty said. "Jimmy the truth." "Funny thing is," Jeff added. "The kids were actually learning something." Even Tech paid attention to what Jeff was talking about. He likes the kid Jimmy Neutron. The fact that a 13 year old could convince a real teacher that he was the substitute. Then turn around and teach eight classes is astonishing. He didn't deserve to get suspended. He deserved the right to finish teaching for the rest of the day. Tech focused on the computer. Bentley Mulsanne. "Jeff." Tech called. "Yo." Jeff answered coolly without turning around. "You have to lift the Bentley Mulsanne. A man named Jason Grey owns it. My sources say he has a meeting today at the Four Seasons hotel. They have valet parking so you know what you'll be disguised as?" "The mat that's rolled out when his rich ass steps out that muthafucka." He joked. "Right now," Tech said seriously. "I wish that were possible. Unfortunately, you weren't clean enough for that job. "Oh man." Twenty laughed. "Not the geek trying to sneak one." Jeff jumped up and turned to Tech. "You wanna get some! You wanna joke?" Tech smiled. "Nah Jeff, you got it." Jeff sat back down and popped a chip in his month. "He doesn't want none." He told Twenty. "You'll be one of the valet parkers." Tech continued. "He will arrive at the hotel around twelve. So let's keep in mind that we don't have that much time wasted… you emotional bastard." Jeff walked into the Four Seasons hotel. His plan is to get one of the valet parking suits. He watched all of the people in the massive building carry on with their business casually. Little did they know, the snake was in the jungle and it's about to strike. He walked through the crowd noticing everything around him. He noticed a woman with a small dog in her hands. She looked to be complaining about something to one of the hotel managers. All he could read was her lips and from the distance she seemed to be angry. He noticed three kids running around the resting area. The mother was having a hard time controlling them. He watched that scene play out and knew that would never be Paula. Paula would beat the hell out of them kids until they understood that she's the boss and what she says goes. That's where he's going to meet, he thought. He noticed a group of well-educated men standing around an older one. They all had on nice suits and each a briefcase. The scene looked like a private event. Their area was roped off leading to the back. He wondered what type of meeting they were having. He didn't think too long about it.

Maybe later, they could have a meeting about how one of the members getting his Bentley lifted. He stood at the front desk behind a man with an all brown suit on. He observed the valet workers coming from a back room while he waited his turn in line. He overheard the man in front of him talking about how much it would be for a week. The desk worker had told the man it was a special going on and he could stay for $1,500. Wow $1,500. That's special? He continued watching the workers go in and out of the room. He looked up at the enormous clock on the wall. Fifteen minutes before the Bentley would show. He had to make his move. "Sir," the desk worker called getting his attention. "Can I help you?" "Fifteen hundred for a week, right?" Jeff threw out there. He needed to break the conversation fast and head to the back room. "Yes sir," the front desk worker said nicely. "That is our special for the week. Would you like to purchase it?" "I'm alright for now." Jeff said. "Let me check my bank account. I'll be right back." He walked away. He made his way through the crowd over to a busy backroom that the workers were coming in and out of. He checked the area to make sure nobody will notice him slip into the room. Everyone seemed to be still carrying on about their own business. Now, he thought. He swiftly pushed through the backroom door. He noticed a few workers were still in there. He carried on like he worked there himself. He went over to the valet parking suits. They were all hanging in a row, different sizes. He grabbed one that was about his size and swiftly put it on and then he hurried outside to where the other workers were servicing. He stood out there nonchalantly waiting for the Bentley. "You're new here?" One of the guys on the unit stopped him. "Yes, I am." He said. "Just started today." He noticed the Bentley pulling up. "How long ha- Jeff cut him off. "Sorry, can't chat. Got to work." He said walking off to the Bentley. He stood there patiently waiting for the rich man Jason to emerge from the vehicle. Jason got out of the Bentley. "Hey," he said coolly. "Don't fuck my baby up." Jeff smiled and walked around to the driver side. "I promise I won't, sir." He got in. "I'm telling you." He said harshly. "This my baby. I'll fucking kill you over her." Jeff spoke coolly. "I got you." "Here's the key." He tried to hand it to Jeff. Jeff smirked at him. "Don't need it." He started the car and sped off. Jason looked shocked. "Bring back my fucking car!"

*Chapter 54*

# LOTUS ESPRIT

"Tech." Jeff said. He was amazed after driving the very smooth Bentley Mulsanne into El' Nino's enormous garage. Even though the luxury car could only do zero to sixty in 4.9 seconds. He was fascinated with its other amazing features. "Check out these leather seats, the trimming leather into the panels for the wall and ceiling. Leather wrapped around these motorized blinds. Polished burl-walnut crown molding, baseboard, and door and window trim. Man, the wall-to-wall Wilton wool carpeting and the custom-designed lighting. Dayum, a desk, bookcase and filing cabinets and they match the veneered fold-down tables. The Naim audio system and it matches the thumper. Tech, I'm about to take this car back home with me." Tech smiled. "Is a $330,000 luxury car really worth it?" He said looking through the window at Jeff. He looked at Tech like, yeah… this one is. "I can lift another one." "Jeff," Tech said seriously. "Get your ass out of the car and let's go. We got a long day. This car isn't all that." he walked away. "Tech growing some balls." He said to himself. He got out and shut the door. He made his way back to the truck and hopped in with Tech. "You know I was just bullshitting right?" Tech started up the eighteen-wheeler. "Yeah, right. I'll lift one of them baby's if I knew how." They got back to the garage. Twenty and Bobby were outside kicking it. They were talking about Bobby putting 22' inches on his Hellcat. Twenty suggested putting 24's on it. Might as well ride big. Jeff walked up. "Put the fo's on it. Black on red would look nice." "Ho's love the fo's bro?" Bobby asked. They all laughed. They went inside after a couple of minutes. Jeff was telling them how cool the Bentley is and that one day he's going to buy one. He had to, the car is a retired man's dream. "I would live in that thang." Jeff told them as they entered the garage. Paula was sitting on the couch. She turned to their attention. "Live in what?" "Somebody's in trouble..." Tech said coolly. "Nothing." Jeff spoke. "At home, of course. We were talking about a car." Paula walked over to Tech by the computer. "It figures." She answered softly. "What's up next, Tech. I'm ready to work. It's getting boring sitting around here." "Well, actually." Tech clicked the mouse and went to the Lotus Esprit file. "It's almost time for the Lotus convention. It will be starting in the next hour." "Finally." Paula said. "I get to lift a car that hasn't come out yet. This is going to be a challenge isn't it?" "You sound like you want it to be." Twenty walked pass heading to the couch. "Maybe I want it to be." Paula said eyeing him. "You don't get to have all the fun." "Bro," Bobby said. "I've been having fun with my lifts." "You always have fun." Jeff said. "You actually love doing this shit for a living." "That's right bro." Bobby assured him. "Although," Jeff said. "When I was your age. I loved lifting cars too. I guess when you get older and have a family, things change." "Or go to prison for life." Twenty added from the couch. "Paula." Tech got her attention. "The Lotus will be a challenge if that's what you were asking for. There will be different groups that will be listening and learning the new vehicle from top to bottom. It will be your job to hide among the group unnoticed and then somehow work your magic to get the car lifted safely. The building will be crowded with study groups working on different Lotus. So driving the car out of the building through the people will be a task. Don't run anyone over. So… Is that fun enough for you?" Fifteen minutes later. Tech and Paula were down the street from the Lotus convention. The building looked like a school. Many people were going into the building. They watched the scene carefully. Paula turned to Tech.

"Get in, hide among the study group. Somehow lift the Lotus and drive the car safely out the building without killing anyone." "That's it." Tech answered. "Piece of cake." Paula hopped out of the eighteen-wheeler. She hurried down the block towards the building. She was going through different options in her head about how to get the car out of the building. Getting into the study group wouldn't be a problem. That's the least of her concerns. She got to the front of the building. She waited until a group of people got on her. The group crowded around the door and started to enter. She slipped right into the group of people casually. She entered the building behind a heavyset guy who was sweating profusely. Maybe he just finished the mile run? Paula thought as she hid behind the sweaty man. He provided great cover even though she wasn't really hiding from anyone. She just didn't desire to stick out. She came from behind the guy and scanned the building taking in everything around her. Tech was right. This is going to be a challenge. There were people everywhere in different groups. Each group had a teacher. She noticed because every group had someone in a long white professor's coat. How in the hell am I going to get the car out with all of these people in here? She continued searching for the Lotus Esprit. There were test cars everywhere. Some on the ground. Some on alignment machines. Some on lifts so you can see the underbody of the car. Some were hooked up to test machines and running. Hopefully the Esprit wasn't one of them. You can't run the miles up on a car and then ask someone to buy it from you is a big no, no. El' Nino wouldn't be happy with that. She slowly started walking toward a crowd around what seem to be a black Lotus. Someone tapped her on the shoulder. "Excuse me, Miss." She turned around. "What study group are you with?" The man in front of her was one of the teachers. "I'm with the Esprit group. I lost track of them a minute ago." She said sadly. "Ma'am, the group is right over there." He pointed to the large group of people behind her. "And where are your study books that were assigned to you?" My books? Paula thought. "My friend Heather has them. I had to go to the ladies room and she was just standing here with them. When I came out I lost her and the entire group." The teacher looked at her skeptically. "Ok, well hurry up and be on your way. The session has already begun." Paula nodded and turned toward to study group. She hurried over and mixed in with them. The car in front of her was the Lotus Esprit. The car is absolutely beautiful to her. She listened to the teacher. "This is a mid-engine, aluminum bodied supercar designed to take on the Ferrari and the Lamborghini. This is a huge gamble for our brand. Our new alloy structure shares a number of components with the less extreme Lotus Elan. Our main competition will be the Ferrari 458 Italia, Lamborghini Gallardo and the Porsche 911 Turbo. Our Esprit offers mid-engine, rear-wheel drive platform with a V-8. Our V-8 can produce as much as 550 horsepower. We also offer a hybrid system such as this one." He pointed to the Esprit and continued. "The hybrid version will lift the output to 620 horsepower." He paused. He spotted the only person around him that wasn't taking notes. He also noticed the very attractive female didn't have any books with her. "Where are your books young lady?" he pointed to Paula. "Are you that smart that you don't have to take any notes or am I just teaching for my health?" People started mumbling among the group. Paula built up her act and busted out crying.

*Chapter 55*

# MASERATI MC-12

Twenty was driving Bobby to the neighborhood where the Maserati MC-12 is located. Tech had informed him on all of the details after he briefed Paula on the Esprit. The distance from the Lotus convention was only about five minutes. The drive for Bobby wouldn't take long. He offered to knock the job out. This is his last job until tonight. The Ferrari 430 Scuderia would be the last lift. Twenty would lift the Land Rover and then get Janet back. The Lifters would be done, he thought. He wanted to continue lifting cars. He wanted to continue as a Lifter. He wanted to be with Twenty and the rest of the crew. He understood that Twenty was doing this for a reason. That was the only way he became a Lifter. Just a little experience he had with the team. He was grateful for. How many car thieves can say they were a part of the greatest team of car thieves of all time? He looked out of the window and thought about what he would be doing on Sunday morning when all of this was over. Twenty noticed that Bobby was quiet on the ride over. He looked like he really had something bothering him. Bobby was an up-tempo kind of guy. Why the long face? He was about to lift a Maserati MC-12. One of the most exotic cars in the world. This was something he thought Bobby would be excited over. He thought he loved lifting cars. Did he have a bad feeling about this one? "What's up Bobby?" Twenty made the turn into the neighborhood. "What are you looking all down for? You're about to lift a Maserati MC-12. You worried or something?" Bobby exhaled. "No way bro, that's not it." "What is it then?" Twenty inquired. "You bro," Bobby said. "After Saturday, you're going to be done. The Lifters will be done." Twenty was silent for a moment. He could understand what Bobby is talking about. "Bobby, the Lifters will never be done. We'll always be together. We'll always be a team. Rather, we're lifting or not. One day you'll feel like me. You'll get older or either go to jail. You have to get out when the time is right. The time may not be right for you, but it is right for me." "Bro," Bobby nodded his head. "I can understand that. Maybe after Saturday it will be the right time for me. Jimmy's too smart to be left alone. All we have is each other." Twenty smiled. "And us." He held his hand out. Bobby smiled and gave him some dap. "Go get that Maszi." Twenty said coolly. "Gotcha, bro." Bobby hopped out of the car. He made his way through the neighborhood. He didn't realize how huge the houses were back at the car. These were mansions. The houses were at least three to ten million dollar homes. Expensive cars, trucks, SUV's, bikes and limousines were in everybody's yard. One mansion had a helicopter on top of it. Talking about breaking the bank, he thought. He stepped in front of the house that had the target vehicle. The mansion was enormous. Three limousines were parked out front, a Rolls Royce and a stretch Bentley coupe. There was a 15 car garage next to the mansion. Even more exotic and luxury cars were in it. He surveyed the scene. Long driveway, no fence. Easy. This looked like the type of place that would have security running all around it. He noticed that every single vehicle was dressed in all black paint with dark tinted windows. The President would ride one these rides. He crept around to the garage. No big deal. He gawked at every car he passed. He finally found the Maserati MC-12. It resembled a street formula one car. The car looked like the word speed. He walked over to it and tapped the dark window. No alarm. He pulled the key out. Suddenly, he heard a voice call to him. "You like that car?"

*Chapter 56*

# THE BREAK UP

The teacher came over to Paula. "Ma'am, are you ok?" he asked concerned. What is this woman's problem? She starts crying during a study session. Is she upset about the way I spoke to her in front of the study group? This never happened to me before. I've seen it all. "Ma'am?" He gently touched her shoulder. Paula jerked away and yelled throughout the building loud enough to stop the other study groups. "Just leave me alone, you mean man!" she began to cry louder. She made sure everyone's attention was on her. "Ma'am," the teacher spoke. "What is wrong with you? Will you please speak to me so I can help resolve this situation?" he now was kind of embarrassed. He was used to being the center of attention with his students. He's never been the center of attention in front of a thousand people with a crying woman although. "I don't want to speak to you!" Paula cried. "You don't like me!

All I wanted to do was come to class and learn something new today." "That's not a problem." The teacher noticed the student were mumbling to each other. It made him feel uncomfortable. Were they talking about him? Maybe because all of the woman wanted to do was learn and he somehow preventing that? "We'll just get you some new books and then I'll start back from the beginning." Paula dropped her head in her hands. She secretly smiled to herself. She had the teacher going. He was such a fool. Now it was time for the switch up. "All you care about is them stupid books and not my emotions! You're the worst teacher ever!" she started crying wildly. Oh dear God, he thought. What is wrong with this woman? What have I done to make this woman feel this way? Her emotions? Can't she see I'm doing the best I can? Maybe I should break the class for a short recess while I figure this out. He looked around. They were whispering to themselves and other study groups joined in. "Everyone take a 10 minute recess. There is nothing to see here. The food court will be open if you want to grab a quick bit to eat." He felt some of the pressure easing. He bent down on one knee in front of Paula. "Ma'am, can you please explain to me what is going on? The other students are not around if there is something important going on please feel free to let me know. I'm listening whenever you're ready. If it's personal and you want it to stay between me and you, it will. If you need help. I'll do my best and if I can't. I'll find the best person for you." Paula smiled in her hands. This guy is supposed to be a teacher. He's not even smart enough to realize that I'm faking. She lifted her head from her hands. She wiped the fake tears from her eyes. She scanned the area. The students were gone and some of the other student groups were taking breaks also. Out of the thousand people that were in the building. There were about three hundred people left. That was good enough for her. "My boyfriend," she sniffled. "He dumped me and I'm here to get him back." "He's in one of the study groups? This boyfriend of yours?" "Yes," she sniffled. "What's his named?" he asked. "Lotus." she smiled. The teacher looked confused. "Lo-" She cut him off by putting her pistol under his chin. He never saw it coming. "Where is the exit for the vehicles?" the teacher pointed to the direction. "Thank you," she whispered. "Lay down." The teacher did and she fired shots in the air. People broke in every direction. She casually unhooked the Lotus from the test machine. She got in and drove off while people were scrambling for safety. People were dodging the vehicle not trying to get hit or shot. She shot out the glass doors from the vehicle. She put on her Prada Shades as the glass shattered while driving away in the sports car.

*Chapter 57*

# IT'S BEEN A WHILE

**B**obby turned around swiftly. His mouth dropped. He couldn't believe what he saw. This is going to be his last lift without a doubt in his mind. What was standing in front of him is worse than the law. This is the end, caught red handed. Five enormous Italian looking men in black suits with sub-machine guns all aimed at him. There's an elderly woman standing in the center of them. She looked about eighty years old. Bobby noticed that the elderly woman was still kind of attractive for her age. Must've been all the money keeping her healthy? He couldn't think about that though. He was too busy trying not to take a shit on himself. The elderly woman spoke. "Answer me boy. Do you like this car?" Bobby did the only thing he could do. He answered. "Yes Ma'am, I do." Please don't let that get me shot. The enormous men stood in front of him without breaking a sweat. They were her bodyguards.

The men looked serious and like they wouldn't have any problem killing him. "What are you doing on my property boy?" The elderly woman ask. "Were you going to take from me? Don't be afraid to answer me." Little did Bobby know about this woman. She's one of the most dangerous women in the world. She's used to dead bodies. Bobby is just another Joe but for some reason. She likes him. This woman is about to have my head bro. Bobby exhaled. He was still alive and that's all that mattered. This was a difficult question to answer. She wanted him to admit his wrongdoing. Maybe if he did, she would let him go. "I'm sorry Ma'am, I should've been on your property. I was wrong. Please forgive me. I'm only nineteen years old. Still young and dumb." The elderly woman smiled. At least he wasn't begging for his life like a coward. That earned more point for him. He wasn't weak. "I said was you going to take from me boy? That's what I want to know." Bobby felt his legs shaking. The armed men were statues aiming at him. They wouldn't speak or move. The elderly woman was the boss, obviously. They were waiting for her command to blow him away. Would she really kill him over the car? Did the vehicle mean that much to her? Twenty said there would be a time to call a quit. Was my time back at the car? Looking at the situation he was in. Maybe, it is? "Yes," he answered bravely. "I was going to steal this

Maserati. Not because I wanted to because I had to and if I had the chance again, I would. A little girl's life depends on it. She was kidnapped and this car was on the list. I have to have it for her safe return." The woman smiled. The boy was truthful. She dealt with a lot of scum bags who cried for their lives. She could tell when someone was lying. "Come with me boy." She ordered. She turned and walked towards the house. The black suited men lowered their weapons. One waved him over and spoke in a deep harsh voice. "C'mon." What was going on? Were they going to torture him in the mansion? He went with them inside the mansion. The inside was absolutely astonishing. Pictures were everywhere trimmed with gold frames. The stairwell and all of the trimmings around the house were in gold. "Up the stairs." The elderly woman called to him. He followed her into an enormous room about the size of his house. There was a picture over the bed. There was an elderly man sitting in a gold chair and she was behind him. Fat "My late husband." She noticed him looking at the picture. "He was the last great Mafia Boss. He left me with all this. Even his business. I call all the shots. I am the first Mafia Queen. The only thing he didn't leave me is someone to be with. Everyone is scared to love me because of the fear of death. Do You want the car? Make love to me and the car is yours. I never liked it and I'm too old to drive it." Better than death, he thought. He dropped his pants and gave the elderly woman the business.

*Chapter 58*

# MOSLER PHOTON

obby left the mansion in the Maserati. He felt alive and great. The elderly woman actually was an old freak and she had some good. He even asked the woman for her phone number and promised to call and come back to see her. If he didn't have to give the Maserati up for Janet. He would've had a free brand new exotic ride. He smiled as he pulled away. He asked himself what he would be doing Sunday. Now he knew. He would be visiting the Mafia Queen Maria. Maybe when she died, she would leave everything to him? Maybe he would be the first brochunski Mafia Boss. He didn't bother to meet up with Tech and Paula. The law wouldn't be after him so he was safe. He drove the exotic car around for a minute. The car was technically his why not enjoy it for a moment? He pulled up to the garage and blew the horn. The garaged opened and he pulled in. He cut the car off and got out. He noticed that Tech

310

and Paula were back. He also noticed that everyone had worried looks on their faces. "Where have you been Bobby?" Paula was concerned. "We thought you were off to jail or got yourself killed." Twenty spoke up. "We tried your cell phone several times why didn't you answer?" Bobby smiled at them. "Us brochunski's bro." he spoke to all of them. "Know how to charm the ladies." "Bobby what the hell are you talking about?" Paula fired. "You've been joy riding? Probably, picking up girls or something?" she crossed her arms. "Bobby," Tech said. "You've been riding around getting' girls and you didn't bring any back?" Twenty smiled. "Tech!" Paula straightened him. "Right." Tech agreed. "Bobby you've been picking up girls in the car? Are you crazy?" he tried to sound serious. Twenty and Jeff smiled at each other. Twenty didn't really care anymore as long as Bobby was ok. He was straight with that. "Bro's, bro's, bro's." Bobby looked at Paula. "And bro-ats. What we have here is a big misunderstanding. I wasn't joyriding around picking up girls. That's insane bro. This car here before us." He pointed to the Maserati behind him coolly. "Was given to me." "The person gave you the car?" Paula asked. "What, a Maserati?" Twenty asked shocked. "Dayum." Jeff shrugged, shit happens. "Wow," Tech muttered to himself. "Not just a person." Bobby added. "The Mafia's Queen." "This dude lost it." Twenty said. "A Mafia

Queen?" Paula asked confused. "No way," Tech was amazed. "A Mafia Queen gave you this million dollar car for free without you getting killed?" Jeff said. "Don't believe it." "A Mafia Queen gave me this car bro," Bobby said. "Better believe it." "What did you have to do?" Paula asked. "Kill someone?" "Yeah," Tech said excitedly. "Did you feed the bastard to the pigs like a wise guy?" "Tech!" Paula straightened him again. "Right." Tech sounded somewhat serious. "Bobby, I know you didn't kill anyone did you?" Twenty smiled and shook his head at them. "Bro's and bro-at's." Bobby spoke. "No way would I kill anyone. Us brochunski's bro, only kill unless we have to. I got laid for it." "Wha..." Twenty said coolly. "Dayum," Jeff was shocked. "You're dead." Tech said. "The Don is going to whack you. That's what wise guys do when you sleep with their women." "Laid by a Mafia Queen for the car?" Paula asked. "He's dead and yes by the Mafia's Queen." Bobby explained the entire story to them. "Eighty-six!" Twenty said. "You like that old whipped pussy?" They all laughed. "And it was awesome bro." Bobby assured them. "That-is-nasty." Paula walked off. They talked for a few more minutes before Tech got down to business. "Jeff." "Yo." Jeff said coolly. "My turn?" "That it is. The Mosler Photon is owned by a bank manager. All he does, is work long hours. He drives only to work and home, work and home." "Let me guess." Jeff joked. "He's probably at work or… home?" Tech and Jeff drove to the owner's house and the car wasn't there. Jeff had searched the garage thoroughly. The car wasn't there or nowhere else on the property. Their next move was to the owner's job. They drove up to the bank and Tech parked the eighteen-wheeler in a large plaza behind the bank. Far enough for the owner not to be aware of what will happen if he was to come running out. He would actually have to chase Jeff, which is impossible. The distance is too far and the car was too fast. Jeff hopped out of the truck. "Be back in a flash." "You have the key right?" Tech asked before Jeff could shut the door. Jeff showed him the key. "C'mon, I'm a vet. Do I look like Bobby?" he flipped the key up in the air coolly and it landed in his front pocket. "You got to teach me that." Tech said. "Be back." Jeff shut the door. He walked through the parking lot towards the bank. It was a nice day outside for a good lift. After the Ferrari FF he had to grab tonight. He might throw a couple of burgers and ribs on the grill. They all would drink a few beers. They'll relax while talking shit about the past. Hell, he might even hit some of the weed Paula's been sneaking off to smoke. Yeah, he knew about that. He let it go because he knew it would ease her mind about Janet. "Oh shit!" he shouted while falling to the ground. He had tripped over something. The key had flown from his pocket. He reached for it as he was falling. It was like the key and his body were floating through the air in slow motion. He fell all the way flat on his stomach without catching it. He immediately looked up to catch where the key would bounce to a landing spot. "No…" he scrambled to a crawling position while trying to catch the bouncing key. The key had bounced over a sewer and fell in just before he almost caught it. "Damn!" he was frustrated. That was the only key. He got up from the ground and brushed himself off. "Ok, you're ok." He told himself. "You've been in worse situations than this Jeff. You just have to go in there and take the key off the manager." He made his way over to the bank. He exhaled and opened the door. The manager was there. He definitely noticed the orange and black custom stripped Mosler Photon double parked before he walked in. He scanned the bank. He saw a guy working his ass off in his office. That's got to be him. He told himself. He walked right into the guy's office and took a seat. Manager, Rocky Jones. He read the badge on the desk. "I'm busy Sir. Please find someone else to help you." Rocky asked nicely. "I've found him." Jeff said. "I only want to deal with you. You're the brotha in the bank." "Sir," Rocky said seriously. "As in myself, being a brotha doesn't matter. Everyone in this bank is more than qualified to help you." "Fuck it," Jeff stood. "I'll just take my ten million dollars and go somewhere else." "Whoa, whoa, whoa." He stood. "I'm sorry. Have a seat." He couldn't let 10 M's walk out of the bank. "If you're serious. I'll be more than happy to help you my brotha." "Serious?" Jeff sounded frustrated. "Man, I'm gone." Rocky came around the desk and pleaded with Jeff. "Ok, you're serious. Just let me go get the paperwork. Have a seat. I'll be back in a minute." He left the room and shut the door. Jeff smiled. He tore the office apart and finally found the keys in the bottom drawer. He snuck out of the office and went straight to the car. Rocky noticed Jeff leaving and followed out behind him. "Sir please, I got the papers my brotha!" Jeff didn't turn around. He's getting in my car, he thought. He took off after Jeff. "My car!" Jeff started the car and began a mean burnout. Rocky chased Jeff the entire way to the next lot. He cut Jeff off and hopped on top of the car. Tech noticed a man on top of an orange sports car. "That's Jeff?" he muttered. The car was swerving all through the parking lot. After a long minute. The guy was finally thrown from the vehicle and rolled about ten feet before coming to a stop. When the Mosler pulled up. He knew it was Jeff. Wow, the guy is a track star.

*Chapter 59*

# THE VISIT

Jeff had loaded the Mosler Photon in the trailer in front of the Maserati. Bobby had taken up so much time with the Mafia Queen that he had to bring the car back to the garage. He didn't have access to El' Nino's garage. They unloaded both of the exotic vehicles. They headed back to the garage where everyone was waiting for their return. They pulled into the parking lot and parked the eighteen-wheeler in the back. Twenty met them in the back. "Where's the old women?" he joked with his arms out. "Not this time." Tech walked over to him. "We couldn't find any. They must've gone to bed early." Twenty laughed. "But it's only sex." They went into the garage. Jeff got behind the bar and made everyone some drinks. Tech seated himself in front of the TV. He gave the computer a break. Everyone already knew their last assignment. The Ferraris tonight and the job would be 95% complete. The final vehicle, the Land

Rover on Saturday. Twenty, Paula and Bobby sat at the bar. Jeff slid them all a straight shot of vodka. "To the Lifters." Jeff held his glass up. Tech ran over and he slid him a drink. "Ok, one more time guys. Tech was late." They all laughed. He raised his glass a second time. "To the Lifters and our last job tonight. May everything work out for us tomorrow." Everyone raised their glass and spoke at the same time. "The Lifters!" they all threw the shot back. Twenty spoke up first. "I think I'm about to go pay El' Nino a visit." "What's the visit for, bro?" Bobby asked. Tech knew what Twenty was thinking. He wanted to let El'Nino know that the job will be complete tomorrow and everything has been going according to plan. That way, there will be no excuses about handing Janet over to him. He thought it was a great idea. "He wants to let El' Nino know that the business is being taken care of. He wants everything in order after he lifts the President's Land Rover." "That's correct." Twenty said. "C'mon," Tech said. "I'll drive." Twenty and Tech made their way over in the Lancer. They talked about their plan for tomorrow. They had had an idea, but it still wasn't full proof. I little more thought and it would be good. They pulled in front of the Mexican restaurant. Tech spoke. "You want me to go in with you?" Twenty smirked. "You afraid to die?" he joked. Tech answered by getting out. He made his way in the restaurant. "Tech, when you grow some nuts?" He got out and hurried up to Tech. They both went in. The first person he saw at the door was the waiter. The same waiter, he had busted in the nose. The guy had a face mask covering his nose protecting it. His eyes were still black and purple. When he noticed Twenty he became very frightened. Twenty held his hands up. "I didn't come here to start trouble. I just want to speak with your boss." The waiter hurried off and came back after a minute. "He'll see you." he pointed to the office. The guy seemed scary to Tech. Twenty is a tough guy and he wanted to be a tough guy too. As he walked passed the waiter, he flinched at him. "Punk." The waiter was frightened and had stumbled back into a table. He slid off of the table cloth and all of the food fell on top of him. The guest had jumped from the table to attend to him. They walked into the office. El' Nino was behind his desk being that Mexican they called El' Nino. "Please be seated." Twenty waved the offer off. "This won't take long. I just want to tell you the cars are in the garage and after the lift tomorrow on the Presidents truck. We'll meet back here to pick-up the girl and the money." El' Nino smiled. That's what he wanted to hear. "Good my friend. It will be done. I'm a man of my word. I want you to meet some of my friends tonight Twenty. I will be hosting the Mexican Ball. Come see what I'm about. You might think differently about me. Bring a nice young lady with you and enjoy yourselves. Please don't say no." "Nacho, give him invites." Twenty and Tech walked back to the car. "Tech, two points for the flinch." Getting some balls, Tech thought.

*Chapter 60*

# 599, 458,430, FF

"A Mexican Ball?" Jeff asked. "He wants you to go to a Mexican Ball?" "Yeah," Twenty sipped his beer. "He wants me to bring a girlfriend or something." "What about that little Spanish girl I've been hearing about?" Jeff asked. "For one," Twenty spoke. "I don't have her number. Second, I'm not about to bring her around people like that. I›m not putting anyone else in danger." "Take Paula. "Tech threw out there. "Nah," Twenty said. "Too dangerous." "No way!" Jeff fired. "I already lost my daughter." Paula stood from the couch. "I want to go." She said warmly. Everyone stared at her silently. "Paula," Jeff turned to her. "You can't." "Jeff, please." Paula said. "I can make my own decisions. I want to meet the man who kidnapped my daughter. I want to get a good picture in my mind of him. So when I get my baby back and all this is said and done. I will know what he looks like so I can kill him."

"Paula," Jeff said concerned. "Jeff there's no changing my mind." She said cutting him off. She turned to Twenty. "When are we leaving?" Twenty had no choice but to agree with her. She's a mother and this was her child. "I think it's best if we leave after the lifts on the Ferrari's. We won't have any distractions after that. There is no telling how long he will want us to stay." "That's a great idea." Tech added. "Lift the Ferrari's then head over." Jeff walked to the bar. "I can't believe this." He muttered to himself. He poured himself a double shot of vodka and threw it back. Twenty walked over. "Jeff," he said softly. "I won›t let anything happen to her. I put my life on it. All El' Nino wants to do is convince me to join him after this job. That's it. It's better I befriend him then be against him. It will make the chances better for Janet if he thinks I'm on his side." Jeff took another shot of vodka. "Don't let anything happen to her." The rest of the day was long. They went over the plans for the Ferrari lift, the Land Rover lift and the chances of something happening at the party. The time was approaching. Thirty minutes until midnight. Thirty minutes until the lift. "Here are the keys." Tech said. "Twenty, the Ferrari 599 Replacement. Paula, the Ferrari 458 Italia. Bobby, the 430 Scuderia. And Jeff, the Ferrari FF." everyone checked their keys before he continued. "There's a twist to this one. The eighteen-wheeler will only hold two of the vehicles. Twenty, the 599 have to be one. The other one is up to y'all. The other two will have to race the cars back to El' Nino's garage unharmed." "Bro," Bobby spoke. "I'll race." "That leaves Jeff or Paula." Tech said. "I'll race," Jeff said quietly. He was still upset about the situation earlier. "It's safer. Twenty and Paula can head to the ball while we finish up with the cars at the garage." "Ok," Tech said. "Twenty and Paula, eighteen wheeler. Jeff and Bobby, racers. Let's get it." They all rode out in Jeff's truck except Tech. He took the eighteen-wheeler. Jeff parked the truck up the street at a friend's house. They walked the next two blocks quickly. The Ferrari warehouse was up ahead. Twenty had something telling him they should creep over one at a time. Four people walking up to the building would be suspicious. They all took the back way. Creeping one at a time and watching each other back. They got in through the back door swiftly. All of the Ferrari's were absolutely astonishing. They hurried to their target vehicle.

***

The agent was sitting outside the bus stop. They never noticed him sitting there. On the other hand, he almost let them slip by. They were fast. He dialed Daverson's number. Daverson picked up. "Daverson speaking." "Detective, four suspects just entered the Ferrari dealer." "Is Twenty one of them?" he asked. "Too hard to tell." He said. "What you want us to do?" "Don't let them get away." He snapped. "We're loading up."

# THE ULTIMATE CHASE

Twenty, Jeff, Bobby and Paula all came racing out of the Ferrari warehouse. Twenty was ahead of the group. He was the first to be greeted by the helicopter. He skidded the car to a stop. What the hell, he thought. Everything went perfectly. Did someone set me up? Jeff stopped behind Twenty. "Oh shit!" he said to himself. Bobby slid next to Jeff. "Bro," he was shocked by the helicopter. Paula skidded the 458 next to Bobby. "Oh my God." She muttered to herself. The police began to flood the area. Someone spoke through a megaphone from the chopper. "Get out of the vehicles and give yourselves up!" Twenty looked in his rearview. His team was behind him. Waiting for his decision. Their engines were revving. They would follow until the end. Twenty shifted into first and burnt out towards the cops. "That's what I'm talking about!" Jeff shifted to first and took off right behind him. "Lifters bro!" Bobby yelled excitedly peeling out behind them. Paula kissed the air seductively and smashed the gas. Twenty glanced at the rearview. He smiled. His team was right behind him. He paved the way by driving right through the team of police cruisers. The cruisers drove off to the side not wanting to crash head on. He skidded out onto the open road. Heading towards Tech would be dangerous. He needed a new plan. "Behind you," Jeff skidded the FF right behind Twenty. Bobby shifted back into first after sliding onto the road behind Jeff. "Still here bro!" Paula was pushing the 458. She was the second best driver out of the bunch only to Twenty. She drifted onto the road and overtook Bobby speeding past him. "Here I come." Bobby watched Paula drifted right past him. "She's good." He shifted into second and got behind her. Daverson was in one of the Chargers. "Chase them! We can't let them get away!" he yelled over the radio turning the Charger onto the road. The police was pursuing them. We need to get to the highway, Twenty thought. He noticed the helicopter. It swooped down in front of him and he maneuvered the 599 around it. "What the fuck!" Jeff jerked the wheel and swerved around the chopper. "Desperate." Paula muttered and skillfully maneuvered around the chopper and sped ahead of Jeff. Bobby maneuvered around it. "This is the best bro!" Twenty dialed Tech from his new cell phone. "Tech," he was frantically as he answered. "Where are you guys?" Tech asked worriedly. "I saw the cops rush the warehouse." "Listen." Twenty ordered. "I need you to get to the highway. When I dodge the cops. You can pick me and Paula up on the move." "Gotcha." He hung up with Tech and called Jeff. "Jeff we have to split up. You and Bobby head right at this next turn. Paula and I will head left toward the highway." "Right, be safe." Twenty called Paula. "Follow me." He hung up and smoothly went into an astonishing drift heading left. He punched the gas. Paula drifted right on his tail. They were almost bumper to bumper. "I'm behind you baby." She shifted and pulled up next to him and rolled down the window. Twenty rolled down his. He looked so sexy to her driving the 599. He belongs in that car. "Highway?" Twenty nodded. She blew him a seductive kiss and sped ahead of him.

***

An agent called Daverson from the chopper. "Two heading towards the highway and two heading west." "Where is the 599 heading?" Daverson asked. He knew if this was Twenty and his team. He would be in the Ferrari 599. He would surely drive the most expensive car. "The highway." The agent told him. "Then follow that car!" Daverson ordered. "That's the one we want.

Send some cruisers west to cut the other two off. Let's not fuck this up!" he hung up the phone and sped towards the highway. Here I come Twenty. Twenty drifted onto the highway behind Paula. Paula stepped her game up, he thought. He noticed the helicopter was still on their tail. We need to somehow dodge this helicopter. Paula pushed the 458 maneuvering through traffic. She noticed the helicopter flying over them. "Twenty we need a plan." She said to herself gripping the wheel.

***

Jeff skidded the FF right. He noticed Bobby make the same maneuver. The helicopter went after Twenty, he thought. He checked the rearview. Flashing lights were behind Bobby. He maneuvered to the opposite lane. Bobby noticed police cruisers behind him. He's never been on a high-speed chase. He dodged a cop or two. There were fifteen to twenty cops and a helicopter. That's a whole new experience. He watched Jeff shift to the opposite lane and he speed up next to him. "Bobby!" Jeff yelled over to him. "We need to split up at this next turn!" Bobby nodded. "Then we'll meet under the bridge!" Jeff knew if they both split up the cruisers would have done the same and that would make their numbers low. They would be easier to dodge that way. "Ok bro!"

Bobby shifted the car into neutral drifting right simultaneously with Jeff left turn.

***

Daverson pulled onto the highway. "They're heading south on highway 85!" he called over the radio. He could see the Ferrari's up ahead. "I'm not letting you get away Twenty." He said through clenched teeth. He smashed the gas pushing the super Charger to the max. Twenty maneuvered into the next lane and he sped up next to Paula. "Take the far lane and when you see my lights flashing! Head in the opposite direction!" "Ok!" Paula shifted over to the far lane. I don't know what you're thinking Twenty but I hope it works. Daverson watched from the far. "What the hell are you doing?" he watched the 599 take the far right and the 458 take the far left.

***

Twenty shifted the FF coming off a sweet drift. "Woo!" he pushed the vehicle. Cops… three of them. "Bring it.'" He shifted into fifth gear. Bobby shifted into sixth gear. Seven cops were behind him. "That's how I like it bro!" he had a plan. He made a quick turn into an open parking lot and sped through. He jerked the wheel and skidded to a stop facing the direction the cops were coming.

***

More cops flooded onto the highway. Tech noticed them up ahead. They sped up ahead towards Twenty and Paula. About thirty of them. They left his sight. The eighteen-wheeler was too slow to keep up. Twenty was way ahead of him. How is this plan of his supposed to work? He dialed Twenty. Twenty answered the phone. "Tech, where are you?" "I'm way, way, way behind you." he answered. "About thirty cops are on your tail." "Don't worry." Twenty told him. "Keep driving, we're coming to you." he hung up with Tech. He looked over at Paula and she was parallel to him. He checked the rearview. Tech was right. The cops had grown in numbers. He flashed the lights. Paula flashed her lights back then drift 180 degrees simultaneously with Twenty. She sped down the opposite direction towards the cops.

***

"Shit!" Daverson yelled. "They're heading backward in the wrong direction!" he radioed his team while watching them bolt pass him. He turned the cruiser around and continued the chase.

***

"I got this!" Jeff said. He gunned the FF further

ahead and then spun the car swiftly at the next turn all the way into a parking garage. The maneuver was so amazing he couldn't believe he had pulled it off. He pushed through the garage. "Chase me in here muthafuckas! He raced to the top. He thought the cops were going to chase him and… they did. Bobby revved the engine waiting for the cops to enter the large parking lot. This next move is going to determine rather he make it or not. There were parking meters and light poles all over the area. His plan is to use the objects around him to take the cops out. Were they good enough to keep up with him was his only question? He revved the engine as they entered. Let's see.

*Chapter 62*

# THE LIFTERS

Bobby punched the pedal. The 450 Scuderia burnt out drifting a little sideways before straightening out. Bobby was headed straight to the cruisers. The Scuderia had amazing power and Bobby was amazingly crazy. He lived for danger, this is what he did and what he was good at. He weaved in and out of the tolls and the light poles. He zipped right past the first cruiser. The cop dodged him and spun out of control and smashed into a parking meter. The cop that was behind him smashed directly into his cruiser. The other cops began chasing Bobby through the lot. Bobby drifted the 430 smoothly around a light pole. While drifting he noticed two more cops had smashed into each other. The collision was brutal, they had to be dead. When he came out of the drift he almost ran head on with another cruiser. The cop swerved out of the way and uncontrollably hit a light pole of his own. Bobby pushed through. Two cops were on his tail maneuvering behind him. He pushed the Scuderia in a full circle like he was on a race track. He sped in laps. The cops split up. One kept up and the other was too slow. Bobby drifted 180 degrees and the cop that was on his tail performed the move. "Bad move bro." he shifted into second gear heading back around for the slower cruiser. Before he was about to crash head on with him. He swiftly maneuvered the 430 out of the way. The cop behind him was unsuccessful. He collided into his partner head on. Bobby watched the last two cops explode in his review mirror. "Told you bro." he sped out of the parking lot and headed to the bridge.

***

Jeff looped around the next level. One cop was right on him. He drifted out of that turn into the next level. The cop pursued him. He raced through the fifth level. There was a sharp turn up ahead. Impossible to make at the speed he was pushing. He spun the wheel right, then swiftly left making the FF perform a wide fishtailed turn. He took the sharp turn in the drift barely making it. Unfortunately the Charger behind him didn't. The cop smacked directly into the wall full speed. Jeff looped around to the next level. The second cop was on him. He was trying to ram him, but Jeff kept swerving away.

"Ok," Jeff said coolly. He timed the next attempt perfect. The cop tried to ram and Jeff maneuvered out of the way from an upcoming wall he was speeding towards. The cop ran into the wall totally crushing the Charger before it exploded. Jeff made it to the top. The last cop had got on his tail just like he wanted. Jeff raced the Charger, heading towards the edge. The cop got next to him and aimed his weapon. He never noticed the upcoming cliff. Jeff looked towards the Charger and smirked at the cop. He pointed forward coolly and then skidded the FF right before the edge. The cop went flying off and crashed front end first with the ground. The Charger exploded. Jeff smashed the gas burning out towards the bridge.

***

Twenty pushed the 599 Replacement full speed. He bolted through the gang of upcoming cruisers. They all tried to perform 180-degree turns, but some weren't that skillful. They crowded the highway and some hit the wall. Most of them made it. How far Tech was he didn't know. The first plan he had to carry out is to ride way past Tech. Then comeback towards him. He weaved through oncoming traffic. The cars were frantically swerving out of the way as he zipped down in the wrong direction. Every car he passed blew their horn at him.

They probably had a few curse words to say too. He noticed the eighteen-wheeler up ahead. "Tech," he said to himself as he zoomed by his friend. It was him. He continued pushing the 599 far past getting a good distance away. He needed room and the chopper was still bird watching over him. "I got something for you." he 180 the sports car and continued driving backward. Paula noticed Twenty spin the vehicle 180 degrees and drive backward down the highway. He skillfully maneuvered in and out of oncoming vehicles. What is he doing? She had seen Tech when they passed him a half mile back. Maybe he's getting a good distance away from Tech? Then gun it forward? Whatever it is, she didn't know. Fuck it, she 180 the 458 Italia her damn self and raced through the cars backward waiting for Twenty's next move.

***

Daverson pushed the Charger to 175mph. There was a pileup. He skidded the police cruiser to a stop. He would've wrecked into his fellow officers if he didn't. There were cops slowly turning around to head in the opposite direction to pursue the Ferrari's. Some of the cruisers ran into the wall. Daverson was beginning to become frustrated. He needed to get around the mess. He blew his horn frantically at the cruisers. He got on the megaphone and yelled at the top of his lungs. "Get the hell moving!" we're going to fucking lose them. These Ferrari drivers were the best drivers he's ever seen. The only person that was this good is Twenty. They were in the much faster cars, but they were performing stunts without damaging the vehicles. "Shit!" he slapped the steering wheel. All he could do was wait until the police cruisers cleared.

***

Twenty saw Paula 180 the 458. He smirked. He watched her through the front windshield. He quickly looked backward. He wanted to make sure he wouldn't crash into anybody. The highway was clear for a moment. He had a clear vision of the helicopter. He fired several shots at the chopper. The helicopter maneuvered side to side, making it more difficult. Paula saw fire coming from the 599. At first she thought the helicopter was firing rounds at Twenty but it was Twenty firing rounds at them. He wants to get rid of the helicopter, she thought. She pulled out her Simi automatic Tech 22. She checked her rearview. The traffic behind her was clear. She faced forward and ripped at the chopper. "Way to go Paula!" Twenty said excitedly. The helicopter was still managing to dodge them. There was no sense in wasting bullets on the bird. If they couldn't take the helicopter out. It would see them drive the Ferrari's into the eighteen-wheeler. Twenty continued driving backward down the highway. There was the bridge. He quickly formed a new plan. He pushed the 599 and skidded to a stop under the overpass. He jumped out of the Ferrari. "What the hell?" Paula saw Twenty stop the 599 under the overpass. She skidded to a stop and hopped out. "What the hell are you doing!" she yelled over to him. She was on the opposite side. "The helicopter can't come in here!" he yelled. "We'll get a better shot!" he aimed in the direction the entered. When the pilot noticed they didn't come from under the passage. He would lower the chopper. It happened, the helicopter lowered and Twenty and Paula fired. The pilot was caught by surprise and he frantically raised the chopper back up. The blade struck the edge of the bridge and broke off. It spent out of control and crashed in the center of the highway before exploding. They were on the move now. Twenty maneuvered around the burning helicopter. The cops were coming and he sped past them. Twenty gunned the 599. Tech noticed Twenty and lowered the lift so he could drive in. Paula maneuvered around the chopper. The cops were already turning around to pursue her. She needed to lose them. She 180 the 458 and aimed at another eighteen-wheeler. She shot the tire out and the truck swerved sideways and blocked the entire highway penning the cops on the opposite side from her. She drove up the ramp backward, not bothering to turn back around. Tech shut the lift and drove them away safely. Paula couldn't take it anymore. Her blood was flowing and her hormones were jumping. She got out of the vehicle and went over to Twenty. She started kissing all over him. She went for his belt and he didn't try to stop her. She opened the door to the 599 and let the seat back. She pushed him in and got on top of him. When she felt his manhood fill the inside of her. She knew then this was what she needed and had been missing.

*Chapter 63*

# THE MEXICAN BALL

Twenty couldn't believe he just made love to Paula in the front seat of the Ferrari 599. The chase the police gave them made her horny. She needed Twenty and he needed her. She couldn't resist him any longer and he couldn't resist her. The feelings between them had grown in the last week. They knew they belonged together. The eighteen-wheeler stopped. They were at their planned destination. They hurried to slipped their clothes back on. If Tech caught them. There would be questions they wouldn't be able to answer and changes they were unprepared to go through. Tech lowered the lift and walked around to the back. "You guys still alive back there." He joked as the lift fully opened. Paula was standing in front of the 458. She hopped out. "Of course." she patted him on the cheek twice. She was feeling better than ever. Twenty hopped down behind her. "Tech, if I died. Who would be there to teach you about women?" he smirked and met Paula at her Subaru Impreza WRX STI. He grabbed the dress clothes out of the trunk. They had a ball to attend. He swiftly got himself dressed. "I wish I could go. Unfortunately, I have to deliver these cars to the garage. Jeff and Bobby are already there waiting on me." "A'ight Tech." Twenty watched him enter the truck. The lift closed and he blew the horn before pulling away. "C'mon." Paula called from the driver seat. She was dressed and waiting on him. "Almost done." Twenty had the tux on and looked like he jumped out of the GQ magazine. He folded up his clothes and placed them in the trunk. He closed it and got in the passenger seat. "Nice tux." Paula floored the Subaru and burnt out towards the Mexican Ball that is being held at the Gwinnett Place Arena. They made it to the Ball in thirty minutes. They pulled into the enormous Gwinnett Place Arena parking lot. There was an extreme amount of vehicles in the parking lot. There were at least ten thousand people attending the Ball. That Mexican they called El' Nino is that known and that powerful. Paula finally found a parking spot. "I can't believe this many people are here." Twenty looked over the invites. "Yeah, me either. I'm glad we didn't miss out. I'm kind of in the mood to party." They made their way to the front. They showed their invites and the huge Mexican at the door gave them 14k gold arm bands. "These are special invites." He told them. "The gold band means VIP. You're allowed in the private areas, enjoy." He moved and allowed them to pass. "He might be an evil son of a bitch." Paula said. "But at least he knows how to treat his guest. 14k gold arm bands. How many people you think made that list?" "He does." Twenty agreed. "Looks like a few." He pointed to the crowd. Every other person had a gold armband. Out the ten thousand people attending. Five thousand wore the custom $2,000 armband. The ten million dollars that Mexican they call El' Nino spent on them was nothing. That's how he partied and that's just how he rolled. They made their way to the bar. They needed a shot of something. It didn't matter. The Mexican music was killing them. They never saw so many Spanish people in their lives. "Let me get whatever." Twenty told the bartender. The bartender looked at him confused. "Que?" "Let-me-get-a-drink?" Twenty asked. "Que?" he raised his arms up. "He doesn't speak English." Paula told Twenty. She turned to the bartender and told him something in Spanish. "You speak Spanish?" Twenty asked amazed. "A little." Paula said. "Spanish one and two, remember?" "High school." Twenty said. "Damn, I shouldn't have skipped that class." The bartender came back with their drinks. Paula told the bartender, thank you in Spanish and Twenty repeated what she said. They began to talk about how nice the ball was and it would've been even nicer if they weren't the only black people there. Twenty offered her a dance after they finished their drinks. Might as well enjoy it while they're here. "Dance?" Paula smiled. "To this type of music?" Twenty smiled back. "Well, you can speak Spanish. I'd figured you could dance to their music." He grabbed her by the arm and pulled her towards the dance floor. She resisted while smiling. "No..." She said shyly. "C'mon," he continued to pull her towards the dance floor. They were in the center of the dance floor. "Ok, Ok." Paula said smiling. She has never been to a ball in her life. Jeff didn't go out to parties or dances so she didn't. After Twenty went to prison and Janet was born. Things got more serious. No more play, just work. This is a new experience for her. "Since you already got me out here." The music began to pick up and it was more of a fast pace tempo. Paula smiled and started shaking to the music. Twenty did his thing too. They were doing the salsa. She smiled and Twenty spent her around. They both were having a wonderful time. All of the people around them were dancing in rhyme with them. Twenty had never done the salsa in is life, but he was a quick learner. They were moving better than the Spanish people. Everyone began to join in and switch dates. Twenty spent Paula and she went to another man who was dancing and he picked up a beautiful Spanish woman. They danced the salsa with their new partners then the switch happened again and they were back together. After the salsa went off. Some slower music came on and Paula looked at Twenty shyly as he held her close. This is where she wanted to be, in his arms. When the song ended. They were stuck looking into each other eyes. When he lowered his head to make the kiss, someone interrupted. "My friend." The man tapped him on the shoulder. Twenty turned around. It was that Mexican they call El' Nino. "El Nino." "Twenty." El' Nino smiled and patted him on the back. "I'm glad to see you make it to my 8th annual Mexican Ball." "I figured I wouldn't be busy tonight." Twenty said. "This is a wonderful party." El' Nino nodded. "I see you brought the most beautiful lady here." He said looking at Paula. "The Wife?" Paula put on a fake smile. Deep down inside. She wished she had her pistol. She wanted to put one in the center of the man who kidnapped her daughter, head. She took her mental picture. Twenty smiled. He knew himself what Paula was thinking. "A friend." "A beautiful friend you have." El' Nino said. "She needs to be made a wife. Someone will want to have her for sure. Come, my friend. I want you to meet some people." They followed El' Nino to a back room. There were four men in the VIP private room. El' Nino introduced Twenty and Paula to the men. They were the men buying the cars. El' Nino praised Twenty by saying many great things about him. The four men were surprised that Twenty was the one getting the cars for them. El' Nino also mentioned the ten million dollars a year payroll Twenty would be on if he decided to join El' Nino. No More than one hundred cars a year. Twenty thought it was great. Only if he really wanted to continue lifting cars. Unfortunately, he didn't. He didn't let El' Nino know that, of course. All he wanted to do was get Janet back to Paula. Take the little money and get the hell out. El' Nino sipped his drink. He noticed his wife walk into the room. "Twenty." El' Nino stood. "I want you to meet my wife." Twenty and Paula turned around. They were shocked at who they saw. El' Nino continued. "Rosa, this is Twenty and his wonderful lady friend Paula."

*Chapter 64*

# THE BIG DAY

"**I** can't believe the woman you're messing around with," Paula yelled hurrying through the parking lot. "Is married to the monster that kidnapped my daughter!" Twenty hurried behind her. He was just as surprised as she was. He sure as hell didn't know Rosa was married to El" Nino. That would've been dealt with. "Paula… Paula!" he caught up to her. "I didn't know she was married to him." "Twenty." She turned around angrily. "I'm not trying to hear that bullshit!" she turned around and continued to her car. Twenty followed. "If I was aware of something like that. I would've said something or done something about it." Paula opened the door to the Subaru. "Yeah, but you're fucking in love with her! Don't lie to me! I heard you all lovely, dovey and shit while you were speaking with her on the phone!" Paula got in the car and swiftly locked the doors so Twenty couldn't get in. "You back on that?

Twenty tried to open the door. "You know I don't care about her. Remember what happen in the back of the trailer? Please unlock the door?" "Fuck what happened in the back of the trailer!" Paula smashed the gas. She peeled all the way out of the parking lot leaving him there alone to find his own way. "Paula!" Twenty called after her. "Damn." He said softly. He watched her pull away. He was hurt. He really cared about Paula. How could something like this happen? What are the odds of that? Rosa is El' Nino's wife. He knew she was married, but DAMN, El' Nino's wife. He began to walk home. Thinking about everything that just happen. How could Paula be upset with him? It wasn't his fault she was attracted to him and happened to be the bastard's wife. Then he began to think about what if El' Nino sent Rosa? What if Rosa was like, a spy or something? Was she? She didn't act like it back at the ball. She pretended like she knew nothing about me. She played the best acting role I've seen since I got out. He walked down the long road. It was going to take him forever to get home. He was taken by surprise because lights began to flash on him. Had Paula come back for him? The light got brighter and the vehicle didn't seem like Paula's. A Lamborghini LP570-4 Superleggera pulled up next to him. He stopped. The exotic car was all black, black 22's and black tint. He didn't have a clue who was behind the dark tint. Maybe someone from the Ball? The window rolled down. "Get in." said a woman with an accent. "Rosa!" Twenty knew who she was. "What the hell were you thinking! Your husband is a fuckin' monster!" he walked off. She pulled up following him slowly. "Get in Twenty. It's too cold and too far for you to walk." Twenty stopped. She had a good point. Plus, Rosa had some explaining to do. He got in the Lambo. He explained to her what was going on with him and that Mexican they call El' Nino. Rosa never knew her husband had kidnapped a little girl. The things her husband did, he kept to himself. She promised him she would do whatever she could to get her back and Twenty knew she meant it. They got back to the garage and she kissed him goodnight. Twenty walked towards the door. "What the fuck!" someone grabbed him from behind. It was Daverson. "You're fuckin' under arrest!" he yelled. "For what?" Twenty fired. "Four Ferrari's asshole!" he snapped. "Ferrari's?" "Stolen," Daverson pulled out a pair of handcuffs. "Three hours ago." He tried to put them on Twenty and got his arm twisted. Twenty held him down. "You're going to stop putting your hands on me!" "Let him go!" Matt yelled. "I was at a Mexican Ball." He pushed Daverson away and showed them his invite. Twenty woke up the next morning. He had caught the biggest break. Since the Mexican Ball was a highly advertised event. Daverson had little evidence that it was Twenty and his team behind the Ferrari's. All he knew was that the drivers were skilled. Twenty also had proof that he attended the Ball. When he produced the invites. There was nothing Daverson could do. The invites were official. Last day, he thought. He took what seemed to be the longest shower in his life. He needed to enjoy every moment of it. The showers in prison aren't that nice and there was a high possibility he would be back there after the Land Rover lift. He thought about Paula. She was really upset with him. She must've been really emotional after what happened in the trailer. Then to see Rosa and not to mention she's married to that Mexican they call El' Nino made things a hell of a lot worse. He couldn't think about if Paula will forgive him or not. He had to focus on the Land Rover lift. That's the Presidents ride we're talking about here. Twenty and Tech had mastered the best possible plan. They would use transmitters to communicate with each other while they were out in the field. Bobby would set up at one end of the block. He would transmit when the President and his team would hit the block. Tech would set up at the other end with the eighteen-wheeler. When Twenty lifts the Land Rover, he would head in Tech's direction. After he passed, Tech would pull the eighteen-wheeler out into the middle of the street long ways. He would block any chance of a chase. Jeff would set up in the building across the street. His job is to watch Twenty's back. That's because Twenty would take the place of one of the security guards who would be waiting for the President to arrive in the front of the embassy. They security guards would be wearing black suits and shades. Twenty had his best suit picked out. Paula job is to walk down the street and distract the other guard while Twenty made his move on the Land Rover. After the President and his men went inside. The vehicle would be left for them to guard. Hopefully, Paula would show. If not, he would manage to figure something out. He is Twenty, the greatest car thief of all time. He got out of the shower and dried himself off then took a long look in the mirror. He put his game face on. He finished up and went into the bedroom. He put the suit on that was laid out perfectly on the bed. He fixed his tie in the mirror. It made him think about when Paula fixed his tie the last time. "Twenty!" Tech called from downstairs. "It's time man!" It was time. After they went over the plan one more time they would move out. This was dangerous and the dumbest thing anyone could do. The only problem is, he had to do it. He cared about Paula too much. She needed her daughter and he wouldn't let that little girl down. Prison meant nothing to him anymore. All that mattered was Janet. "Twenty!" Tech yelled again. "C'mon man we're waiting on you!" Twenty left the mirror after saying one last prayer. He went downstairs and scanned the room. There were only three faces that met his. Tech, Jeff and Bobby. Paula didn't show. It hurt his heart even more. She probably hated him more than ever. He sat down with the rest of his team. The plan would have to work without her. They gathered and finalized the plan. There was a knock at the door. Tech opened the door and Paula walked through. That showed how serious this situation is. She showed. This is for Janet.

*Chapter 65*

# MIDDLE EAST

Sayyid walked to the back of the barn. He was staying with his brother in Winder, Georgia. His brother was away at the moment buying some last minute supplies. Sayyid loved spinning time with his brother in the states. His brother moved over ten years ago. Sayyid has been wanting to move, but it is hard because he loved the Middle East so much. Even though his country has experiencing the worst type of hell. He still loved it dearly and would do anything for his country. The Americans would never understand the type of things the Middle Eastern people went through. Here, was a good life. There, was the life no one wanted. If your family wasn't rich in America you would still have a chance of making it in life. You still had good schools and sports. If your family wasn't rich in the Middle East. Things could turn out for the worst. Although, there is some type of school. Sports was not an option, not happening. There were none where he's from. Your family had no type of power and without that. You could end up in their army or some type of suicide bomber. The army ran the streets. All of that stuff the Americans talked about. The Bloods, the Crips, the Mexican Cartels and all the other type of Spanish gangs taking over North America was a tickle to Sayyid. Try waking up every day seeing tanks and soldiers on the streets with assault rifles and other heavy artillery. Kids running up to you with bombs strapped to them. Missiles being fired at the houses and building around you. A constant hostile environment of everyday life endangerment. The gangs of America had nothing on the terrorist and their armies. They wouldn't stand a chance. The terrorist would obliterate the gangs. Sayyid looked out towards the field. The sun was beautiful. The sun is always beautiful to him. That's something he rarely had the chance to enjoy. Here in America, it's nice and quiet. This was a feature he could enjoy without threat. If only there were peace in his homeland. If only his people weren't at war with themselves, the government, the terrorist, the rebels, the Americans and other terrorist that were against them. There's so much one man could do for his country. There's so much one man could say for his country. That's why he needed a change. It's time for that change and change would happen today. "Brother." Al bin Sodd called from behind. He was back from the store. Sayyid turned around. "Brother, you're back." "Yes, brother." Al bin Sodd handed his brother the bag with all the items he had requested. "I have returned with everything you asked for." Sayyid looked through the bag. Everything he had asked his brother was there. The bag is a part of that change. "Everything is here. You have done very well with what I asked for, brother. We must hurry. We have very little time to spare. Come, let's get started." Sayyid and his brother walked to the back of the barn. Al bin Sodd cut the light on in the dark room. The light flickered and cut on. Sayyid sat the bag on the table. There's much work to be done. He took all of the items out of the bag and laid them on the table. The next step was to bless the items. "Brother," Sayyid slipped his sandals off. "We must pray to Muhammad." Al bin Sodd slipped his sandals off. They bowed to their knees and began to pray.

# PRESIDENT'S LAND ROVER

Twenty and his team were moving into position. The President of the United States of America would be arriving in the next fifteen minutes. Bobby transmitted to Twenty. "I'm in position bro." Bobby parked his Hellcat on the side of the road. He got out and pretended to be on the phone in a phone booth that was located on the corner. "Roger," Twenty responded. He had tricked the security guard that was in position waiting for the President. He put a good whooping on him and placed him behind the dumpster. He lured him back there by telling him the back needed to be checked out before the President arrived. All of the surroundings of the embassy must be secured. Too bad for the security guard Twenty was the one who was the threat. Twenty stepped into position. He smirked at the security guard on the other side. "I just stepped into position myself." Jeff made his way to the top floor. He

353

had a bird's-eye view of Twenty. "The bird is in position." He transmitted down to Twenty. "Ten-four on the bird." Twenty transmitted to Jeff. "The blocker is in position." Tech transmitted to Twenty while backing the eighteen-wheeler up on the opposite end of the block. He parked on the next block so he could pull straight out. "Ten-four on the blocker." Twenty transmitted to Tech. The other security guard kept staring at him funny. Hopefully he wouldn't cause any problems. That would be another person he had to deal with. Luckily, Paula would distract him in about ten minutes. That's all the time he needed. "I'm in position." Paula transmitted to Twenty from the news stand. She was pretending to read the paper until it is her time. "Check." Twenty answered. Everyone was in position. Bobby, the alert. Jeff, the eye. Tech, the blocker and Paula, the distraction. Everything is good so far. Twenty stood there casually waiting for the President to arrive like that really was his job. The other security guard kept giving him a funny eye. He checked his watch. About five more minutes to go. This is the last five minutes until the last lift. This is it. The moment that mattered most. Twenty-nine cars down and there is only one vehicle left. The only truck on the list. The Land Rover. The President's Land Rover. Twenty checked his watch again. Three minutes left and the President would be arriving. He transmitted to Jeff.

"Bird, what's the view?" "The coast is clear." Jeff transmitted to him. He scanned the entire area around Twenty. Twenty and the security guard were the only two people around the embassy. "Check." Twenty felt the pressure. Especially from the security guard with is eyeing. One minute left. He transmitted to Paula. "Move." "Twenty." Bobby transmitted." The President and two black SUV's just turned on the block, bro." "Copy." Twenty was about to get approached by the other security guard. Paula bumped into the security guard and dropped her purse. "Oh, my." The President Land Rover pulled up to the curve with the two SUV's. Twenty exhaled. This was the big moment. The guards emerged from the SUV's and surveyed the area. It was clear and the President appeared from the SUV. Paula did her job and vanished. Twenty made his move. He shook the President's hand before he was escorted into the embassy. Twenty walked around to get the door for the first Lady. That was his job before they escorted her in as well. He opened the door. Suddenly, he heard assault fire and was pushed inside the Land Rover.

*Chapter 67*

# FOR MY COUNTRY

"What the hell." Twenty groaned in agony. He was popped in the back of his head with an assault rifle. He fell over on the First Lady of America. "Brother!" Sayyid yelled. "Come, the President is in the vehicle!" He fired assault rounds at the guards as they ran out of the embassy. Al bin Sodd fired at the guards. He hopped in the driver seat of the Land Rover. This was his time. The time he spent in America is for this very moment. He fired out of the window. He started the Land Rover. He got the key for the SUV by shooting the driver to death. Sayyid fired a couple more rounds before he hopped in the passenger seat. "Drive brother!" His brother pulled back into the SUV and crashed the backend of the Rover before he pulled away. Sayyid pulled a cell phone from his pocket and watched the rearview. The guards piled into both of the SUV's and Sayyid pressed zero on the phone. Both of the SUV's exploded. Black smoke engulfed the air after the thunderous explosion. It gave him and his brother the clear. Sayyid pointed his assault rifle at Twenty. The First Lady kept screaming at the top of her lungs. "Be quiet!" He ordered as his brother wildly made the next turn. She kept screaming and he smacked her across the face. He aimed his assault rifle at her head. "Now be quiet or I will shoot!" This made her quiet. He turned his weapon on Twenty. He poked him with the head of the gun. "Mr. President." He called Twenty and poked him again. "You'll meet all of my demands and the demands from my country. Do you understand me?" Twenty slowly picked himself up and noticed the two Middle Eastern men with long beards and turbans on their heads. He figured they were Muslim terrorists. He had an assault rifle pointed at him. What the hell is going on? The First Lady of America was still in the vehicle. Where was the President? He kept hearing the Middle Eastern men call the President. The President is not in the vehicle. So why were they calling him? They're not on a phone, neither. The next voice answered his question. "Mr. President." Sayyid looked Twenty dead in the eyes. "You will meet our demands." "He's not my husband." The First Lady cried. "Now let us go!" "Don't tell me your American lies!" Sayyid yelled. "Brother." Al bin Sodd called from the driver's seat.

"What is she talking about?" He made a sharp turn. "She lies brother." Sayyid said. "She is trying to protect her husband." They think I'm the President of the United States? How could they make a mistake like that? "I'm not the President." Twenty told them. "She's telling you the truth. I'm not her husband." "Lies!" Sayyid struck Twenty in the chest with the butt of his assault rifle. Twenty grabbed his chest and bent forward. On any other day he would've attempted to grab the weapon. He didn't want to endanger the First Lady. He still had his chrome 9 on him. He would wait until the perfect time to pull it out. "I'm not… the President." He choked out. "You look like the President." Sayyid suggested. "You were in the President's SUV. You're with the President's wife. You were guarded by the President's men. You are the President and you will meet mine and the demands made by my country." Twenty did resemble the President a little. Jeff used to crack on him about that. These terrorist men were not going to let up. He had one decision… run with it. "Ok, I'm the President." "What?" The First Lady said confused. Twenty looked at her for understanding. "I will meet your demands but first you must let my wife go. She has nothing to do with this. It's me, you want." All Twenty needed to do was for the terrorist men to release the First Lady. Then he would take the chance. I can't believe this happened to me, he thought. Damn, kidnapped and took for the President of the United States. If I make it out of this. I'll have the best story ever and… I'm definitely done lifting. El' Nino can kiss my ass. Sayyid smiled. "We will release her after you do what we wish." Al bin Sodd made the next turn. He checked the rearview and eyed who he thought was the President. "We're almost there brother." "Please let me go?" The First Lady cried. "You have my husband. He will cooperate and do as you wish." She didn't wish to leave Twenty stranded, but he kept pleading for them to release her. She will remember to honor him for his bravery if she made it out of this situation. "Be quiet!" Sayyid ordered, he pointed his assault rifle at her. "We will release you when our demands are met!" "What are your demands?" Twenty asked. "Peace," Sayyid said. "We need more American soldiers to stop the terror and terrorist in our Country. We need you to fix the economy. We need better schools for our children. The armies removed from our streets. The consisted threats of death. We also demand a trillion dollars sent to our Country to start the rebuilding of our land, homes and buildings that were destroyed by WAR. We need the right leaders put into our government and President office to lead us into the future." Twenty exhaled. Damn, he thought. I'm glad I'm not the President. The type of shit they have to go through. He had to think like the President because for now, that's who he is. "How can I meet those demands? Our Country struggles too. Our soldiers are fighting a war of their own. We owe money to other Countries. We're trying to better our economy. There are barely jobs for the people here. No health care for the poor." "Lies!" Sayyid struck him in the chest a second time. "Your Country know of such things!" "My husband is telling you the truth!" The First Lady cried. She was feeling sorry for the man who was pretending to be her husband. She knew he was trying his best to protect her from the terrorists. "What did I tell you!" Sayyid yelled and aimed his assault rifle at her. "Now you die!" That was all Twenty needed to hear. The terrorist are going to kill the First lady. He couldn't allow that to happen without a fight. He swiftly bent up. Sayyid had the automatic on the First Lady. Twenty push the terrorist back toward the front seat while grabbing hold of the weapon. He knew the terrorist was about to let loose. He penned the weapon on the driver. Sayyid let the assault rip and sent a full clip into his brother. He noticed what he had done. "Brother!" Sayyid struggled with Twenty as his brother slumped over on the steering wheel. The Land Rover drove out of control as Al bin Sodd foot stayed pressed against the gas pedal. The Land Rover wrecked against a line of cars damaging the driver's side as it trailed along. The First Lady screamed for her life as the gunfire erupted and the vehicle spun out of control. Twenty got the advantage over Sayyid and smacked him in the nose backhanded with a closed fist. Blood shot from his nose like water pressure being released from a water hose. The Land Rover wrecked into a pole and Sayyid smacked his head against the dashboard. Twenty slowly got out of the Rover. He pulled his 9 out. Sayyid reached for his brother's assault rifle. He aimed at the First Lady. Twenty caught him from behind and burnt him with several shots. Sayyid slumped in the front seat. He uncontrollably fired shots into the dashboard before dying.

*Chapter 68*

# MY BABY!

Twenty lowered his pistol. It's over. The terrorists were dead. The First Lady was still screaming. "Miss," He called to her. "It's ok now." She calmed down. She was just a little shocked at what had happened. He pulled Sayyid from the passenger seat and let his body fall to the ground and shut the door. He ran around to the driver side and opened the door. He pulled Al bin Sodd from the seat and let his body fall to the ground. He hopped in the driver seat and put the SUV in reverse. "Where are… you taking me?" The First Lady stammered. She knew he wasn't a threat. For all she knew he was one of the security guards at the embassy who is supposed to escort her into the building. Plus, he just saved her life from two terrorists. "Back," he looked into the rear view mirror. He knew she was scared for her life. Blood had spattered over her face and clothes. He noticed her hands were shaking. She probably never seen a dead body in her life before outside a funeral. Yet alone, someone getting shot to death up close. He made the next turn. He was pushing the land Rover 120mph. He still had to deliver this vehicle. "You're taking me back to the embassy?" The First Lady asked. "Something like that." Twenty assured her." He couldn't take her all the way back. The police will be everywhere and they would ask questions about why he was a security guard. Not to mention, they wouldn't let him keep the SUV. "What?" She was confused. He wasn't taking her back made her worry a little. "I'm going to drop you off close by." He told her swerving through traffic. "Why?" She wanted to know. Twenty was silent for a moment. Should he really tell her the reason? She is the First Lady of America. "Because a little girl's life depends on me and this SUV. I must deliver this vehicle to an evil man who kidnapped her in order to get her back." "This SUV?" The First Lady asked. "Were you with the terrorist men?" "No." He pushed the SUV. "I wasn't with them. This SUV was a part of a thirty car list. I had to steal thirty vehicles for the bad man. If I didn't he would've killed my family and the little girl. This is the last vehicle and if I take you all the way back. They wouldn't let me keep it." "Why didn't you go to the police?" She asked. Twenty pulled up next to a curve. This was the closest he was going to take her to the embassy. The police and every other kind of law enforcement were up ahead. He could see them from the far. "The police got nothing on this guy. I wanted to go to the police so bad, but he threatened to kill her. The man I'm doing this for is very powerful. I had no choice. He would've known. He would've found out the police have been alerted and then he would've killed her. I just couldn't take that chance. Maybe it happened this way for a reason. This could've been your husband instead of me." He got out and opened the door for her. "Well, this is your stop." The First Lady emerged from the SUV. She was grateful for all this man had done for her. "What is your name?" "They call me Twenty." He shut the back door never taking his eyes off her. "Twenty." She said softly. "I will never forget you saved my life. You're a very brave man. My husband will know your name and what you did for me and our country. Thank you." She smiled and gave him a hug. "Go save that little girl." "Thank you." He hopped in the Land Rover and sped to El' Nino's restaurant. He skidded the truck to a stop directly in front of it. He noticed Paula's car was parked out front. What? Paula jumped from her vehicle. "Twenty you're ok!" She said worriedly. "What are you doing here?" he asked. "I knew if you made it. You would come here. Your transmitter cut off. Jeff saw the men from the roof. He tried to warn you. These men have my baby. If you didn't make it. I would've had no choice but to try and fight my way to her. I couldn't let them keep my baby." She cried. Twenty thought about what Paula was saying. If he didn't make it. There would've been no hope for Janet. "Where are the others?" "Bobby took off trying to find you." She said. "Jeff was too high up. I couldn't wait for him. He should be on his way. Tech got stopped by the police for pulling the truck out into the road. He was gone from the truck before they got there. I hurried here. I was going to give you five more minutes before I was going in." "Ok." Twenty said. "Wait right here. I'm going to handle this." He turned toward the entrance. Paula turned him back around. "No! I'm not letting you go in there alone!" "It's too dangerous!" He told her. "This is my baby and I'm not letting you go in there alone!" She told him. "You won't be able to stop me and someone has to have your back!" "For what?" He said. "The last vehicle is here. He should give her back like he said." "Twenty." Paula pointed to the Land Rover. "Look at the damn SUV! He's not going to take that!" Twenty looked at the Land Rover. With everything that had happened. He failed to realize the SUV had been totally destroyed. He exhaled. "Damn." El' Nino isn't going to take that. Then he remembered. There still was a chance. "He said he didn't need the Land Rover. He needs what's inside it." "Well." Paula said. "What's inside?" "The GPS system." Said a harsh voice. They turned and looked toward the door. It was that Mexican they called El' Nino. He was with the massive Nacho and three other Mexican gunmen. "She is right." El" Nino said. "I will not accept that. Luckily, I only wanted the GPS. So here's the new deal. That GPS is very important to me. It tracked all of the Presidents moves and secret meeting locations. I can learn where all of the prominent men and women are in America my friend. After I pull the information from it. The vehicle is no use to me. The GPS system works. You get the girl back and Twenty has to come work for me." Twenty exhaled. The SUV may have been damaged, but the GPS still worked. The screen was on when he pulled up. "Ok, deal." "Nacho." El' Nino said. The massive Nacho nodded at his boss. He walked passed them to the Land Rover. All eyes were on him. He opened the driver side door. He started the SUV. The screen cut on. The deal was done. He was about to signal to El' Nino that it works. Suddenly, the screen started flickering and a few sparks flew. The screen went black. Nacho tapped the screen twice with his finger. The screen flicked on then completely went black. Never coming on again. Nacho groaned. He emerged from the vehicle and walked back to his boss. He shook his head no. "What the hell!" Twenty went to the Land Rover and tried himself.

Nothing. The system was completely dead. He put his head back on the headrest. "Why God?" He muttered. "There is no deal my friend." El' Nino said. Paula pulled out her Glock. "Where is my daughter!" She yelled at El' Nino. El' Nino stopped. He had the restaurant door halfway open. He smirked while turning around. He looked Paula in the eye. "Dead." Then he slipped in before Paula could shoot him. Twenty took cover by the Land Rover. Paula continued to fire in their direction. She took one of the soldiers out. They returned fire and Paula dove behind a car. "Paula!" Twenty yelled. "You ok!" He fired and took one of the soldiers out. Just Nacho and one remained. "Ok!" She responded. She dropped her clip and reloaded. She fired at Nacho. He took cover behind the restaurant door. She then aimed at the soldier and shot him in the arm. Twenty came out of cover and finished him off by the door. He never knew Nacho took cover where he was at. "Twenty!" Paula yelled and bolted his way. She dove to protect Twenty from the gunfire. They both fell to the ground. Nacho vanished into the restaurant.

*Chapter 69*

# THAT MEXICAN THEY CALL EL' NINO

Twenty rolled over before he slowly got to his feet. He held his hand out to give Paula a lift from the ground. "Paula." He called to her with his hand out. Paula didn't reach for his hand. She just stared him in the eyes. "Paula." He called again. "C'mon, let me help you." he kept his hand extended. She didn't reach for him and she had the same look. What is going on with her? "Paula, were you shot?" He asked worriedly. He was unaware there was two bullet holes in her back. Paula smiled at Twenty. "You look just like her." What? Paula went insane? "What are you talking about? Are you Ok?" He propped her up and she groaned from the pain. "She has your eyes." Paula said. She began to cry. "Paula, were you shot? Who are you talking about? Who has my eyes?" Twenty felt liquid coming from her back.

He raised his hand. Blood covered it. "Your daughter." Paula told him. Twenty wasn't listening. He was shocked from the blood on his hand. He thought he heard Paula say his daughter. "Paula, I need to get you some help!" He said frantically. "Twenty." Paula said. "Janet is your daughter." Twenty stared her in the eyes. "What?" He said softly. "Janet," Paula said. "She's your daughter." He thought from the first time he ever met the little girl. She looked exactly like him. That's what motivated him to push so hard. He felt some type of connection with her. This was the connection. She's his daughter. "How?" "The month you went in. I was pregnant." She said. "I hooked up with Jeff a month later to hide it. You had life. I couldn't let her grow up without a father." "Jeff." Twenty said. "Did he know?" "No," she coughed up blood. "I never… I never told him." She began to slip. "I got to get you help." Twenty began to move. He picked Paula up and carried her to her car. He opened the passenger door and he gently placed her in the seat. Paula grabbed his hand. "There's… no time. You have… to save her." She whispered. "I love… you." Her head slumped to the side and she passed away. "Paula," Twenty cried. He patted her cheek and shook her shoulders. "Paula!" She was gone. The only woman he had ever loved was dead. Tears streamed from his eyes as he closed hers with two fingers. "Paula." He whispered. "I will save her." He kissed Paula on the lips and closed the door. He took on a final look through the window and felt that agony that let him know how much he loved her. He ran to the restaurant door. All he could think about was killing everybody inside. Rather, they had something to do with Paula's death or not. A beast was on the loose and… it was hunting. He kicked the restaurant door open. He aimed his 9 in every direction. He couldn't believe what he saw. El' Nino and the massive Nacho stood behind a woman tied down to a chair. Twenty focused on the innocent woman. "Rosa." He muttered. That Mexican they called El' Nino smiled. "What took you so long, my friend? I thought you said fuck that Mexican they call El' Nino and left me with the girl." Twenty held his chrome 9 on El' Nino. Nacho had his pistol aimed at Rosa. "I'm going to kill you." he said through clenched teeth. "Are you threatening that Mexican they call El' Nino my friend!" El' Nino roared. "I hate threats!" "Don't worry." Twenty said harshly. "After today. You won't have to worry about any more threats." El' Nino laughed. "You see, my wife. After years of marriage. She betrays me. My feelings for her are gone. She tried to rescue the girl. For that, she will die today my friend. I knew she cared about you by the way she looked at you at the Ball. I knew something was going on. I felt it so I kept a close eye on her." El' Nino kissed his crying wife on the cheek. He walked to his office door. "Nacho, when you're finished taking care of them. Order me three tacos and a large fruit punch." El' Nino went into his office and closed the door. Nacho pressed his pistol against Rosa head.

*Chapter 70*

# THE BEAST

Twenty took the first shot. He had to react and fast. Rosa was going to die. Nacho pulled the trigger. The shot fired at the ground missing Rosa by a half inch. Nacho grabbed his arm. "Ah!" He groaned like a massive bear in agony. He aimed at Twenty and fired while he dodged the assault. Twenty fired at Nacho but the monster ducked behind a flipped table. He couldn't take the risk of hitting Rosa. "I'm going to kill you like I killed your girlfriend!" Nacho roared. He held his arm behind the table. He made sure his clip was full. Twenty knew the big Mexican was trying to get his head. He had to remain calm and not let Nacho catch him off guard. He hid behind the host desk in the front. He peeked from cover… Rosa was still alive in the center of the room. Nacho fired and nearly took his head off. Twenty returned fire while he ran closer to Rosa. He flipped a nearby table. "After I kill you!" Nacho yelled. "I'm going to rape and kill the girl!" Nacho came from cover and fired at the table. "You know what!" He aimed at Rosa. "You can't protect her and hide!" "Shit!" Twenty came out from cover. Nacho was going to free pick Rosa to lure him out. It was either come out or Rosa is dead. He immediately kicked the side of the chair. Rosa fell over still strapped to it. Nacho smiled. He aimed at Twenty and pulled the trigger. "Ah!" Twenty groaned. His gun flew from his hand. Nacho shot him directly in his arm. Nacho came emerged from cover. He kept his gun on Twenty. "Now we both have been shot in the arm." The 7-foot beast came closer and stopped two yards away. "But it is I who have the weapon." Twenty held his arm. This is how it was going to end. He wasn't afraid to die and would've been more than ready. He wished he could've had the chance to see what it would've been like to raise Janet. Nacho pulled the trigger. "Click, click." He looked at his weapon. When he raised his attention to Twenty. He saw nothing but a twelve shoe flying at him. Twenty connected with a flying kick to Nacho's face. The big man stumbled back. He hit him again with a straight kick. Nacho caught his foot and slung him to the ground. The massive Nacho grabbed a table and threw it at him. Twenty rolled out of the way. He ran up to Nacho and stuck him with a jab. Nacho head turned sideways.

Nacho slowly brought his attention back on Twenty with a big grin on his face. No effect. Nacho grabbed him by the neck and lifted him off of his feet. He was ten times stronger than Twenty. Twenty held on for his life. He was going to choke to death. He took his thumbs and dug them into Nacho's eyes. Nacho growled and tossed him on the ground. His vision became blurry. Twenty fell on his back. Something he landed on caused pain to his spine. He turned over to get up. The pistol. He landed on his chrome 9. He picked his gun up and turned back to Nacho. The Mexican stormed his way. He ripped three in his chest and the big man stopped. Nacho grabbed his chest and then looked back at Twenty. This is for Paula. Nacho rushed and Twenty fired. The bullet hit Nacho in the center of his head. The big man fell to his knees and hit the floor, dead. Twenty untied Rosa. "You ok?" "Yes." Rosa said. "I know where he has her." "Where?" He asked. "The Limo." Rosa said. "She's in the trunk." "Ok." Twenty had her fully untied. "You get her and go to the police. I'm going to deal with El' Nino." Rosa stood. "No! He'll kill you. Let's just go and get the girl together!" She cried. "Trust me." Twenty said. Rosa grabbed his face and kissed him passionately. "I love you." She then went to rescue Janet. Twenty exhaled. He walked to El' Nino's door. He was ready to face the beast.

*Chapter 71*

# EL' NINO'S SECRET

Twenty slowly opened the door to El' Nino's office. He let his 9 guide the way. He was shocked to see El' Nino sitting behind his desk. "I see you're ready to die." El' Nino puffed on his cigar. He wasn't paying Twenty any attention. He kept his back turned to him watching the wonderful view through his enormous office window. "You made it this far." He puffed a ring of smoke. "Did you care for her?" "I loved her and you took her away from me." Twenty answered through clenched teeth. "Not her." El' Nino said. "My wife. Do you care for her?" "Does it matter?" Twenty slowly walked closer. "Before you kill me." El' Nino puffed on his cigar. "I have something to tell you." "I already know." Twenty said. "She's in the trunk." El' Nino smiled. He remained watching the scene. "Not that. It's worse than that." "Make it quick." Twenty said. "You got a bullet to catch." "You want to know who set you up 10 years ago?" El' Nino puffed. "You want to know who told me about the great car thief? Who told me to free you, who I had watching you? Who's on my payroll and… who told me about Janet?" Twenty held his 9 firm. Could El' Nino possibly know? He remained silent. "The Spokesman." El' Nino said. "You may know him as your best friend Jeff." "You're fuckin' lying!" He said harshly. "Check the pictures on my desk." El' Nino continued facing out the window. "That Mexican they call El' Nino don't lie." Twenty had noticed the pictures on El' Nino's desk, but he didn't bother to look. He came closer to the desk. "Go head." El' Nino taunted. "I won't bite." Twenty picked the first picture up. It was breathtaking. It was a picture of Jeff in El' Nino's office snorting coke. He picked up the next one. Jeff was talking with another woman and El' Nino. Other one showed Jeff banging another woman in the restaurant with Nacho. He couldn't believe his eyes. His best friend was in every single picture with El' Nino. All he could ask himself was why? They had been friends forever. He considered him family. He loved Jeff more than his drug addicted mother. They have always been there for each other. Now this? How could he? "That's pain." El' Nino spoke turning around. "That's something my mother showed and made me learn to avoid. Never care, never love. Now you know your friend secret." He produced a weapon of his own. Twenty was in shock to notice. He looked at El' Nino. He saw the gun aimed at him. He didn't seem to care anymore. This new discovery was compared to Paula's death. He let his weapon slip from his hand to the ground. Janet was free. Rosa saved her. He did what he came to do. Why continue the fight? El' Nino could tell he damaged his soul. Twenty eyes were vacant. He stripped away what he cherished most. His friendship with Jeff. "Now you will die!" Twenty stared into the barrel of El' Nino gun. El' Nino knew he wasn't afraid of death by the way he stood there motionless. He lowered his gun and let it fall to the floor. He jumped on his desk with a bunny hop. "You will face me!" He roared. El' Nino ripped off his button up shirt. There was a tattoo of his mother on his chest covering most of the center. She was a beautiful woman and the tattoo showed every detail. Twenty looked up at El' Nino. He noticed the beautiful tattoo of the woman on his center chest. He also noticed that El' Nino was huge under the suits he wore. All of his muscles were bulging and he was cut. He wasn't bigger than the massive Nacho but El' Nino looked like he was a skilled fighter or he was doing a good job of acting like he was. "I'm done." "You will face me Twenty!" El' Nino front flipped off of the desk and heel kick him in the dead center of his forehead.

*Chapter 72*

# MY LAST STAND

Twenty stumbled back and dropped to one knee. The shot made him dizzy. Was this what Rosa was talking about when she said El' Nino would kill me? El' Nino is some type of fighter. He has to be, he thought. He just front flipped off the desk and heel kicked me. Twenty shook it off and came to a full stand. El' Nino stood in front of him in a fighting stance. His next move proved to him that he was a very skilled fighter. "You die!" El' Nino kicked low, mid and then finished with a high kick to Twenty's head. All three kicks were faster than lightning. Twenty spent sideways and fell to the ground. He was already spitting up blood. Damn, he thought. I didn't see that coming. He picked himself up off the ground. He faced El' Nino. The Mexican was in a different fighting stance. El' Nino smirked. "Nice." He swiftly kicked low three times, then mid, high and finished with an unexpected spin kick to his chest. Twenty fell back and crashed into the wall. He slid down the wall to the ground. "Fuck." He muttered. This was going to take everything he had. El' Nino was very skilled with kicks. He hasn't thrown one punch and had him against the wall, spitting blood from his brutal kicks. El' Nino kicks were lethal. He held his chest slowly picking himself up from the ground. He took a stance. This time he would strike first. He jabbed with a quick left and then a right. El' Nino block both blows. Twenty went for a chest kick and El' Nino caught his foot. He tripped him to the ground and stomped on his chest. "Ah!" Twenty groaned. He felt like his heart skipped a beat. What the hell am I going to do? He's faster than me and more skilled. This was going to take everything John Kim taught him. All ten years of it. He picked himself up. He ripped off his shirt before taking his stance. El' Nino smiled. "Love the tattoos. They're intimidating. Brings out your eyes." He joked. "You ready to fight me now?" El' Nino didn't wait for an answer. He swept kick across the ground and Twenty jumped over it. He spent off his back and hopped to his feet with a back kick. Twenty blocked it and grabbed him from behind. He slammed him to the ground with an armbar. He locked it in the position John Kim showed him. He pulled with everything he had and broke El' Nino's arm. El' Nino groaned. "Ah!" Twenty then swiftly rotated while still on the ground. "Ah!" Twenty broke his leg, he broke the other and finally his other arm. Every limb on El' Nino was broken except for one thing. Twenty lifted him up with a headlock. "This is for all of the evil you've ever done." He snapped his neck. He let his body fall to the ground slowly. "Twenty!" He looked up. "You ok man?" Jeff asked. Twenty met him with a cold stare. "What's wrong?" He asked concerned. He noticed the pictures. "Why?" Twenty asked. Jeff held him at gunpoint now. He found out about his secret. "Because I always loved her." He whispered. The anger hit his tone. "But there was you! She always wanted you! So I got rid of you by setting you up ten years ago! My gambling and snorting problem made me go into debt. I had to make more money. El' Nino needed a car thief, so I gave him you! That way I could make some money and send you back!" "Janet?" "What about the little bitch!" He said. "She's your daughter! Paula tried to hide it, but there's something call blood test! I only pretended for her! I always knew Janet was your daughter and I hated it! I hate that she fuckin' looks like you!" Jeff was extremely pissed. "Die!" Twenty closed his eyes. His best friend was going to kill him.

# MY FINAL GOODBYE

Twenty opened his eyes. He wasn't dead. He stared at Jeff. He was still holding his gun at him. What was going on? Where had the gunfire come from? It sounded close enough to be in the room. He wasn't shot and Jeff still had the gun on him. Suddenly, blood spilled down the side of Jeff›s mouth. Twenty eyes grew wide. Jeff dropped his weapon and grabbed the back of his head with a confused face. He fell to his knees and smiled at Twenty. He fell over dead. Twenty attention was caught by the person holding the smoking gun in the doorway. "Janet." He said softly. Janet lowered the gun and ran over to her father. She heard everything Jeff had said. She knew the truth. She knew this man her mother always told her stories about is her father. Janet cried after she found out her mother was dead. She resisted going to the police with Rosa. She wanted to kill El' Nino for her mother's death. "He killed my mother." She cried in Twenty's arms. Twenty couldn't respond. He had to let her grieve. He lifted her up with his good arm. He didn't care how old she was. He wanted to carry his daughter from this dreadful place. Rosa showed up in the doorway. She saw that it was over. Twenty had won and Janet was safe. In her heart, she was free too. "Twenty." She whispered. Tears ran down her face. He carried Janet over to her. "C'mon." He said softly. "Let's get out of here." They walked through the restaurant. It was finally over. Twenty didn't know exactly how to feel. Out of this entire situation. He lose the only woman he has ever loved, and whom he called a best friend, and brother. The good thing about this is he did what he promised Paula. He was walking her daughter, his daughter, to safety. Rosa opened the door for them, Twenty stepped out with Janet. Just when things were starting to shape up. It all comes crashing down. "Freeze!" Daverson yelled with a large team of police and FBI agents. "You're under arrest! Put the girl down and put your hands up!" "Daddy!" Janet cried. This was the first man she ever called dad and now he was going to be taken away. "No!" Twenty exhaled. He sat Janet down. He wiped the tears from her eyes. "It's going to be ok. I need you to go with Rosa." "I don't wanna!" She cried. "I wanna stay with you! They can't take you!" "Janet." Twenty got teary eyed. "You have too. I have to go with these men. We'll be back together." He hugged her. He wished he could've promised that, but that was something he couldn't do. "I love you." "I love you too." She whispered. Twenty finally released his daughter. He was emotional because there was a chance he won't get to know her. She went to Rosa and cried. He stood to face the officers. Daverson walked up. "I told you son." He cuffed him with a smile on his face.

*Chapter 74*

# WHAT A WOMAN THREE MONTHS LATER

Twenty was on trial again for only ten of the vehicles. News cameras followed Twenty the entire trial. He was on the stand now. The prosecutor stood. "Explain the twenty dollar bill left at the scene of the crimes. The CLS63 AMG, Dodge Viper, Porsche 911, Camaro HP-ZL1, Gallardo, Aston Martin V-12 Vantage, Bentley Mulsanne, Mosler Photon and the Ferrari FF. Everyone knows that's your trademark. So why is it after ten years? You get out, the GTA goes up and the bills start showing? Not to mention, you were caught with the Land Rover. Your prints were all over the vehicle." Twenty didn't know what to say. Jeff had done him again. Jeff had been setting him up the entire time. All of the cars he was getting charged with were the cars Jeff lifted. Even though he had saved a kidnapped girl. The prosecutors still wanted his head. If he was convicted. He would be serving life in prison, again. El' Nino couldn't save him this time. He looked over at his family. There was his daughter Janet, his friend Tech. There were his brochunski's Bobby and Jimmy Neutron. Finally, there was his lover, Rosa. They all were there to support him through this. This wasn't how he wanted it to end. If he would've known it was going to go down like this. He wouldn't have prayed every night in prison to be free. At least Paula would've still been alive. Janet would've still had her mother. Even if he never found out about her being his daughter. Paula's life was more important to him. "Do you have anything to say?" The prosecutor asked. Twenty was silent. "He's guilty your Honor!" The judge adjusted his glasses. After five minutes of going over charges and evidence against Twenty. He made his decision. "I have no other choice but to sentence you to lif-" The courtroom door flew open and interrupted the judge. Everyone in the room turned around. No one couldn't believe who they saw. Mouths dropped all over the room. The First Lady entered the courtroom with guards and the President's personal lawyers. "This man will be relieved of all charges brought against him." The First Lady spoke and the crowd awed. "What's the meaning of this?" asked the judge. "The President, my husband is grateful for his services for our country. He has written a pardon relieving everything brought against him for putting an end to terrorist acts, risking his life for the President and the First Lady, saving the First Lady, putting an end to a notorious Mexican cartel, and saving a kidnapped girl all in one day. My people will provide you with the necessary paperwork." The lawyers went to the judge. One handed him a document signed and dated by the President. The judge sighed reading the documents over. He is to be relieved of all charges and released immediately. The judge exhaled. He had no choice. He raised his mallet. "Not guilty!" He banged his hammer. Twenty jumped to his feet. The entire courtroom erupted. Twenty hopped over the stand and hurried over to his family. Janet was the first to greet him with a big hug. Everyone hugged him. Rosa gave him a passionate kiss. Twenty noticed the First Lady. He walked over to her holding Janet's hand. "How did you know?" "I watch the news. I am the First Lady of America." She said with a sarcastic smile. "This is the little one?" "This is her." Twenty said. "She's Beautiful." The First Lady said. "Enjoy being a father." She hugged him. "Thank you for saving my life." She whispered. "Thank you for saving mines." He whispered back. Everyone made their way outside. The news was all around. "Twenty." Tech noticed Daverson yelling through the phone. He pointed in his direction. "I have a surprise for you." Twenty watched Daverson. "What do you mean your car was stolen!" He asked his mother frantically. "Fuck!" He slammed the phone down and stepped on it repeatedly. He then noticed Twenty and Tech smiling at him. He gritted his teeth and stormed off. They laughed. A Ferrari Replacement 599 pulled up and two girls called to Tech. "Tech you didn't keep the-" Tech cut him off. "Geek swag, two girls." Popped his collar and went to the car. Twenty smiled. A Fox 5 newswoman held a mic to him. "What are you going to do now you're free?" Twenty looked at his daughter Janet. "I'm taking my family to Disney World." Lifted Eight Years Later "Honey get the phone!" Rosa called from the kitchen. Little Twenty ran to the phone. "It's for dad!" He took Twenty the phone. Twenty took the phone. "Thanks son." He answered. "Hello." "Twenty." Matt spoke. "I need your help." "Matt I told you, I'm done." "I know, but this is serious." He said. "Someone is using your trademark." "And?" Twenty asked. "Three hundred cars vanished last month." "Nothing to do with me Matt. I'm done." "I know Twenty. That's why I need your help. This person is better than you. We caught a picture of the suspect. It's... your daughter, Janet......

The End

# ABOUT
# THE AUTHOR

New York Times & International Best Selling Author Billie Dureyea Shell was born in Compton California and now lives in Ladera Heights with his wife and kids who he loves to spend time with. He is the Owner of several properties in the Los Angeles area and gives back to his community by providing low income housing to those who need it. He stated "It doesn't matter where you at or where you from it's what you do with your time. There's nothing you can't do if you put your mind to it".

www.ingramcontent.com/pod-product-compliance
Lightning Source LLC
Chambersburg PA
CBHW061056210726
48294CB00001B/175